Kismet 2:

Some Things You Will Never Understand

Kismet 2:

Some Things You Will Never Understand

Raynesha Pittman

www.urbanbooks.net

Urban Books, LLC
300 Farmingdale Road, NY-Route 109
Farmingdale, NY 11735

Kismet 2: Some Things You Will Never Understand

ISBN 13: 978-1-60162-128-3
ISBN 10: 1-60162-128-0

First Trade Paperback Printing April 2019
Printed in the United States of America

10 9 8 7 6 5 4 3 2 1

Distributed by Kensington Publishing Corp.
Submit Orders to:
Customer Service
400 Hahn Road
Westminster, MD 21157-4627
Phone: 1-800-733-3000
Fax: 1-800-659-2436

Kismet 2:

Some Things You Will Never Understand

by

Raynesha Pittman

Prologue

I broke my ass to get a job at that depressing hospital to tend to Savannah's crazy ass, and the only words she let come out of her mouth were, "So, what made you decide to bring your ass back, Mama?" She didn't waste her facial muscles on a fake smile. Nah, that would have been too generous of her, and I quickly learned generosity was missing from her character. It wouldn't have killed her to have given me a weak embrace, or even a "Thank you, Mama, for rushing back to be by my side during my time of need." Or a peck on my cheek, but I guess that would have been expecting too much from her.

Her attitude and that raggedy-ass mouth confirmed that little heffa was my daughter without a doubt. That sass was a gift she had inherited from me, and she knew how to use it well without my help. I can't lie; it was sort of funny to hear her talk shit seeing that she could barely say Mama when I left, and truthfully, I would have been in her ass too if the shoe were on the other foot. Knowing me, I probably would have punched her in the face and then called the police, saying she hit me.

I convinced myself to believe that everything would work out in my favor, and she'd welcome me back with open arms, but that's not what happened. Savannah didn't have a problem with bringing me back to the reality that I wasn't shit for leaving, and I couldn't blame her. It's not like I was returning from deployment or had awakened from a coma and finally remembered who I was after twenty-nine years. I wasn't expecting a hero's welcoming with flowers and a welcome home sign. Why would I when my grown ass decided to walk out on her and her brother, Memphis, almost thirty years ago? I left because I wanted to and made sure not to take any of the baggage I accumulated from playing wife and mommy without looking back. I was so fucked up back then that I didn't even think to send a "Thinking of you" card or add them to my Christmas card mailing list. Yeah, that was cold-blooded.

Some might read this and call me foolish for ranting about my daughter's reaction, but I am not a damn fool. I wasn't looking for a happy reunion. I only hoped for a little respect, that's all, and she didn't have any to give.

Savannah doesn't know where I've been or what I've been through while she's been singing the songs of a motherless child while tormenting others, and, if she did, she wouldn't have understood it anyway. You see, she thought the little shit that happened between her, Dre, the baby, and them other fools in California was something. Ha! That was prekindergarten playtime compared to the shit I've been through over the years, and if she'd let me in, I'd share some of my big-girl stories with her.

When I tell you I've been through some shit and am still standing to tell it, that's only the surface of it. I'm a letterman jacket-wearing member of the high school graduating class of 1974, baby, and dick got me that jacket, not playing sports. I fucked to get who I wanted and what I wanted and didn't feel any shame about it because I was numb to everything around me. I was in high school during the good weed-smoking and cocaine-experimenting years. You know, before weed had 420 chemicals and cocaine was cut with other shit to make it stretch. I smoked a joint or two with a little taste of cocaine in it, but everyone in those days did, and if they tell you they didn't, you can tell them that Peaches said they're a motherfucking liar, or pay me to keep them secrets to myself. It was the '70s, baby, and we would party all night and get high.

This generation is the same way, but willing to experiment with more methods of getting high than we were. Instead of doing enough to get high, these fools are running around doing anything to get higher. Sniffing paint, taking anxiety medications. I even hear they found a way to get high from letting parasites suck on their bodies. It's some crazy motherfuckas being born these days. Don't get me wrong; we were crazy too but only crazy enough to experiment with the shit the government had already given us to use. However, that's another story that I don't have enough proof to tell, and I enjoy my freedom.

The point I'm trying to make is life was taken seriously back then. I became a woman during the sink-or-swim days, and drowning wasn't an option. I've had to do a lot of shit that I'm not proud of just to ensure I'd still be here today. Even though my decisions broke my mother's heart and disgraced my father's name, I'm still here standing strong.

I didn't return after all this time because loneliness or old age was kicking in like I'm sure one of them ignorant assholes is thinking. Being alone is the way I liked it. That meant no baggage or emotional ties holding me back. I came back for one reason alone, and that was because Dre asked me to. I don't know his background story, but that man is a true bloodhound. How he tracked my scent, I'll never know, but he was so sure that I was what Savannah needed for her rehabilitation. I heard him out, and I agreed to give it a try for reasons I don't wish to share, but I can assure you, there isn't one good feeling attached to it after spending time with her.

Being honest, I never thought Savannah's witty ass would discover who I was without me sharing that information first. I asked Dre to allow me time to get to know my daughter before revealing my identity. He agreed; however, Savannah's ass is smart. I won't discredit her college education, but what I'm yearning to know is how good is she when it comes to detecting bullshit? That's what I want to know because bullshit is my native tongue. Bullshit-ology is the subject I studied after high school, and I'm proud to say that I've obtained a doctorate in it.

It kills me to say this, but you win, Savannah, my beautiful, cutthroat daughter. I'm ready to answer your question. You asked me why I decided to come back. Well, here's my answer. Take this as my cover letter that's attached to my résumé that goes along with the application I'm putting in for the position of being your mama and a grandmother to your beautiful baby girl, Sade. I'm going to give you a glance at my mental diary, an inside peek at my shit, and it does stink! There will be no candy-coating or making shit sound better than what it really is or what it really was. I just hope the new, reformed you can handle the information you asked for, 'cause, damn it, you are going to get it!

If, after you get the answers you've been waiting for two point nine decades and decide not to let me back into your life, remember, there is a price to pay for every decision we make, and I'm the loan shark that's coming to collect. In other words, don't let your mouth write a check that your ass can't cash because I'll enjoy levying everything you got.

Please don't forget, it's *my* blood flowing through your veins. With that being said, know that what makes us happy can also make us sad. The same things we pride ourselves on may be the same things that cause our failure. You will learn soon, baby girl, that the apple didn't fall far from the tree, and there isn't a way to change from who we are, not even for a good man. You might as well tell Dre that I apologize because the puppy he's fallen in love with is bred from a true bitch, and if I don't get my way, I'm going to sink my teeth into your life and tear some shit up. Call it tough love!

Chapter One

Miss Me with It

Ain't that about a bitch—the ho that donated her egg only to abandon me thinks I'm supposed to care that she has hurt sweltering in the bottom of her eyelids and etched across her sorry ass. This estranged mother of mine was back from who knows where, after all these years, and acts like I'm supposed to give God the glory for finally having her by my side. Bitch, why? Can someone please tell me when, what, who, why, and where in the hell people are doing that at because I didn't get that notice, nor do I want it!

Hell nah, I wasn't going to jump for joy that she was in my face and not under a missing person ad on the back of a milk carton—not after twenty-nine years of her being a missing-in-action mother, I wasn't. She could miss me with that shit. Even if she felt moved to cry until bags of water formed under her eyes, she could drown in them for all I cared. I wouldn't play lifeguard.

I told myself if she were ever to come back, no matter what her reason was for her leaving, I'd ball up my fist and knock the spit out of her mouth as she tried to explain. You know, get in a sucker punch when she least expected it that would rock her world. Now that she's sitting in my face, within arm's reach, I don't feel the need to because the clown-ass bitch was pathetic.

For years I spent my nights dreaming of the day we'd meet, and those dreams had finally come true. I won't play saint. I did get the urge to ball my fist when she introduced herself and knock her ass out cold before she could complete the sentence. After wanting to for so long, it was mandatory that I caused her some type of physical pain to match my feelings of growing up motherless, but those feelings must have temporarily been put on hold because of the kindness she showed me and my daughter, Sade. Her kindness not only bought her time to talk with me, but it also caused me short-term amnesia. When she asked me what my plans were after beating cancer, I couldn't wait to tell her. I was under the impression that I was chitchatting with a cool-ass nurse that's dealt with some shit.

"I'm going to raise my daughter and my future stepson and give this family thing a real shot. It's never been in me to be somebody's wife or someone's mother. I lived for me, and that didn't work. So, I'm going to try something new and live for them."

I was feeling like every woman, whatever that meant, and that my words were truly a lioness's roar. I saw something strange when I looked into her pathetic eyes. It was weakness and, since I disliked weak people, it forced me to pay attention to the weak shit I knew she was about to say.

"That's right, baby, take care of your family. It won't work if the woman is weak and selfish. You got to put what you want to the side and get what is best for you all. You're young, so it's not too late to get back in them babies' lives the way you should be. Once you leave them, a lot of times, you don't get to come back, even when you beg to."

And I finally saw the truth.

It was like a light switch being turned on the way my amnesia went away, and the truth shined bright. Everything around me began to get clearer than it had been before. Hurt and anger from everything that happened in my life that I had decided to let go came speeding back. And, at first, I still didn't know why, but, the longer I sat there staring at her, the clearer it became. I could see her dimples, the same dimples my daughter had, for the first time out of all her visits, and she said her name was Peaches because of her love for peach cobbler. Something about the way she said my favorite dessert made my stomach growl, and that's what gave her ass away. I couldn't believe that I was face-to-face with the sorry, two-legged dog that birthed me, and she had the nerve to give me a pep talk that she thought was good advice that included a lie about her begging to come back.

The bitch never begged me to come back, I thought, and Memphis had never mentioned anything to me about meeting her, so I had to ask, "What made you decide to bring your ass back, Mama?"

I've asked her that same question twice in the last ten minutes and haven't received a response yet. She just grinned with those deep dimples of hers and stared at the ceiling like it would reveal the answer. There had to be something else wrong with me that the CAT scan didn't find because I don't know why the doctors aren't removing my foot from her ass, but what I do know is she isn't leaving this hospital room without telling me what made her decide to come back now!

"I still don't hear shit, and I know your mouth works. You run that motherfucka well. That's how I knew who you were. Answer me!"

Until now, she didn't have a problem with running off at the damn mouth. I couldn't pay her ass to shut up, but all of a sudden, she decided to turn mute. I don't know who she thought she was dealing with, and I didn't care. She had another ten seconds to answer my question before I jumped out of this hospital bed and gave her a reason to wish that she hadn't returned. I don't give a damn about her egg donation.

"Trisha, Peaches, whichever you go by, I asked you a question. Or do I have to wait another three decades for the fucking answer? I didn't ask or beg for you to come back, so what in the hell are you doing here, and most importantly, why?"

I was still weak from the combination of medicines they had me on and sore from the waist down from surgery. It didn't take a degree in pharmacology to know cancer medications and pain medicine didn't mix, no matter what those doctors and their research said. However, even in my weakest moment, she had me feeling tough, and if she didn't answer to my liking, I'd show her just how tough I was. The fucked-up part about it is that I knew her response would confirm, without a doubt, she was my mother. I had a feeling it would sound like something I would say with a lot more heat and wisdom behind it. That woman, or lack thereof, standing in front of me, returned the eye contact as her mouth opened.

"Who in the fuck do you think you talking to, Savannah? You must be smelling your own shit and think you can say whatever it is you want to me; is that it? Let me tell you something, little girl, I'm going to answer your smart-ass question, but for me to do so, I'm going to need a teaspoon worth of respect from you. Not as your mother; that will come with time, I'm sure of it."

That woman was going straight to hell. Her devilish smile was nothing more than a boarding pass for her one-way trip. If I were spiritual, I would have prayed before she continued.

"And only my close friends and makeshift family call me Peaches; you can call me Trisha since we don't know each other. You don't have to ask me again, smart-ass. I see you're not ready to treat me like I'm your mother."

I smacked my lips as loud as I could and mumbled, "Bitch, please!" at her words, but that didn't stop her. She picked up right where she left off.

"I will repeat that just in case you didn't hear me over that stank-ass ego of yours! We don't know each other, so we need to respect each other like we are two strangers meeting for the first time in the streets. Am I overstood? Because understanding ain't never been good enough for me."

I liked her style already. Straight to the point and demanding, but she seemed to have forgotten she was on *my* time now.

"Yes, we have an understanding, Trisha, only if you remember my name is Savannah, *not* little girl, and surely not *your* little girl. I don't have, want, or need any mothers in my life, stranger. This little make-your-wrongs-right session you have going on will work at my pace, so, don't get comfortable with running the show. *I'm* the star in this drama, and having a costar ain't never been good enough for me!"

We rolled our eyes at each other simultaneously, as if we planned it. Daytime soap operas' hospital scenes didn't have shit on what we were acting out in this room. If I weren't a star in all of this, I'd love to be a nosy-ass fly on the wall to witness it.

Trisha leaned back in her gray, run-down hospital chair, turned her stare up to the ceiling where there was nothing besides the track lights that ran parallel in their dirty, off-white casting, and shook her head. I hated to have to admit, but she was beautiful. Everything on her face was proportioned to perfection, from the deep curves of her lips, the depth of her dimples, to the Asian-like slants of her dark brown eyes. My father was in his sixties; there was no way I was going to believe she shared his age. She didn't look a day older than forty, especially not with her long, jet-black hair pushed back into a ponytail. Neither wrinkles nor stress lines had yet to touch her light brown face. Her skin tone resembled slightly darkened caramel shined with a bronze glow that reminded me of that first week of summer tint most women received from the sun. The scent that radiated from her skin was welcoming and relaxing. It wasn't harsh on the nose like older women's perfumes tended to be. There was something about her smell that reminded me of freshly baked sugar cookies, hot out of the oven. The alluring scent filled my body with warmth and comfort, causing my mouth to shut, and allowing my nose to do all my breathing.

To sum Trisha up, she looked like a childless woman with no cares in the world. Even her Coke-bottle shape that seeped through her white and pink scrubs gave me more reason to protest her age. Her small, ringless hands and average-sized feet gave the impression that she had never worked a day of manual labor in her life. Checking out the flawless woman who sat in front of me pissed me off even more.

"Any day now," I said, so she could snap out of whatever it was she was thinking about. The sooner she answered my question meant the sooner she could get out of my face. If my imperfection caused her to leave me as a child, why would she allow it to be the reason she came back? I needed to know.

"Savannah, I'm sure Dwight has given you his side of the story. All I ask is that you listen to mine. I wanted to come back and tried many times, but your father, he just wouldn't let me, honey."

Oh no, she didn't, I thought. If she thought she was going to put any blame on my daddy in that fake-ass, loving mother voice she was trying to use, she had another think coming. I sat up as tall as I could for a woman who just had a hysterectomy earlier that day and said, "You need to tell your story without shifting any blame on my daddy, or you can get your shit and leave like you normally do. I want to hear your side, without your fingers pointing at anyone because, at the end of the day, *you're* the one who did all the wrong, so cut the shit, Trisha. I speak and comprehend bullshit fluently. Now, am *I* overstood?"

She had the nerve to give me a crooked smile before she said, "I had to see who I was dealing with. Forgive me."

"Trisha, I'm not that bitch, nor is this the time you'd want to test me. You can go ahead and answer the question or get the fuck out. How's *that* for showing you some respect? Talk or walk!"

She began laughing like the shit was funny. "Oowee, if looks could kill, I'd be cremated. You're more like me than I thought. I guess I was wrong, and you can handle the truth given to you straight. After hearing about all the

crazy shit you did in California, you just might understand it too." Her laugh, which had gradually changed
into a smile, turned into a shame-on-you type of head
nod. She eased back into her chair to get comfortable
once again.

This was a game to her. I wanted to call her a bitch
badly and tell her to get the fuck out of my face for
attempting to lie to me after all these years, but I bit my
tongue to show respect to the mother I didn't know. I
couldn't believe she nodded her head in shame at me
without hearing my side of what happened in California,
and why did I care that she had? Who was she in the first
place to judge me for my act of revenge on my childhood
enemies anyway? In a way, the drama that unfolded in
California was all her fault, if you think about it. I was
made fun of for being boyish and had to move away from
California after high school to get away from hearing my
name in a sentence with the words "dyke" or "lesbian." I
smoked two ounces of weed a week, some weeks, even
more, to help deal with the torment I went through
growing up motherless.

My father and uncles tried their best to make me as
ladylike as possible, but a man can't teach a girl how to
become a woman. That's what a mother is there for, but
I wasn't lucky enough to have guidance from my mother.
She ran out on the one responsibility she owed me, and
it shows in everything I do. Just look at me, now engaged
to a college-educated drug dealer named Andre, who I
only knew for a week before he went to jail. I'm sure if
I had a mama around, she would have taught me better
than to settle for this shit.

Dre, as he preferred to be called, was a one-night stand
that went all the way wrong. I don't do serious relation-

ships, but I fucked up and got pregnant by him after that one-night stand turned into five days of amazing, backbreaking, leg-shaking, and knee-knocking sex.

I do have to give Dre his props; that man knows his way around a woman's body with no map or GPS needed. I have never been one of those women who instantly fall in love with a man just because I've slept with him and the dick was superb. Sex was nothing more to me than a way to release built-up energy like exercise. If it took more than one machine to exercise my entire body at the gym, it would take more than one man to release my built-up stress completely; or, that was my thinking before meeting him.

No, love wasn't in my vocabulary, but there was something about Dre that made me leave Nashville, Tennessee, headed back to Atlanta, Georgia, with my heart on my sleeve and the pink slip to my pussy signed over to him.

At first, I thought it was because of the dick and tried to shake the feelings Dre left me with. Then, I found out I was pregnant, and, even worse, it was too late to terminate the pregnancy. I quickly decided to correct my mistakes by giving our daughter away to foster care two days after her birth. I didn't want a child in the first damn place, and if I had known I was pregnant sooner, she would have been aborted like all the other pregnancies that came before her. I know it sounds fucked up, but sometimes the truth *is* fucked up.

After that drama, I packed up and moved to the other side of the country so my steps couldn't be traced, but Dre played detective and tracked me down just like a bounty hunter all the way to the West Coast. I did all of that to free myself from this man. However, everything I did quickly became a waste of time once I saw his face again. That was the moment I knew I had fallen in love with him during those five days of paradise. I'm sure Dre will expect me to break my agreement with the Jeffersons to get our daughter back, and then he'll go snatch up his son to play house, which is a game I have no interest in, and it's all her damn fault!

In truth, no one held a gun to my head and forced me to agree to this lifestyle change. But the only reason I agreed to this shit in the first place is that I felt guilty about doing my daughter the way Trisha did me and leaving Dre the way she had left my father.

Whether or not she realized it, her absence affected so many people's lives. That slut, Keisha, one of the hoes who tormented me as a child that I had my revenge on, wouldn't be fighting for her freedom behind bars or fighting HIV for her life if Trisha would have faced her responsibilities as my mother.

I will admit that I did take getting revenge a little too far, and now I must live with the fact that I passed out potential death sentences, but I don't feel bad about it. I didn't make any of them decide not to use protection with strangers. That was a death sentence that they brought upon themselves. Honestly, I didn't know the prostitutes I selected were infected with the virus until after my plot was done, and honestly, I didn't care enough to question it. I'm not trying to make excuses for what I did, just trying to kiss Karma's ass a little more before she comes to visit me. I know she's on her way.

The point is, my life is fucked up because of Trisha's decision to leave, which was something I had no control over; otherwise, I would have forced her to stay, made her be a mother to me mandatory and not a choice, and then she would have known there was an obligation to love me. I still can't believe she dared to come back when I got sick with cancer to play a mommy. Where was she when I started my period? Or decided to fuck girls because I was scared to get dick? Huh? Where the fuck was she then? Now I'm supposed to smile and be thankful that she's here for me like she never left? Fuck that!

I'm angry and can't let go of the anger, no matter how hard I try, and I don't feel like I have to. I was going to let my past go after I avenged my childhood, but it was like fate stepped in and brought this entity called a mother back into my life so that I wouldn't change the person I've been for the past fifteen years. Fuck it, then; that's fine with me because I'm comfortable in my own skin. Always have been even if it brings hell to others. I've already dealt with Karma for some of the shit I've done before today. I got a little wiggle room on my slate to start my life over with, and I'll try to keep it clean the best that I can.

I started my journey to greatness as a certified public accountant but being licensed to provide accounting services to the public wasn't good enough. I needed to be the most recognized and world renowned in the field, and to become that, I worked my ass off in school to ensure that CPA was changed into a chartered financial analyst. Corporate financial analyzing and portfolio managing is what I do on a daily basis, and now that I'm a partner at Williams and Williamson, I'm also managing the accountants on our payroll. If I could block out the drama in my past to focus on being the best in school, I'm sure I could do it now. But first, I must know the truth.

During my rage, I missed the first five minutes or so of Trisha answering my question. When I tuned in, she was already at her pregnancy with my older brother, Memphis.

"I couldn't believe I was pregnant! I thought about leaving and getting an abortion, but I knew it was too late, and if I left, who would pay your father's bills? Dwight didn't like the fact that I was flying back and forth from California to the South to sleep with different doctors, but that was my side hustle before I met him. After his drunk driving caused those people to die, he quit his job and didn't have a dime to his name, so he wasn't going to stop me from—"

I had to cut her lying ass off before she could finish her sentence. "What do you mean, his drunk driving? My daddy doesn't drink and furthermore—"

She returned the favor by cutting me off. "He doesn't drink *anymore!* After the accident, he picked up smoking cigarettes to ease his nerves. I'm surprised you ended up fighting cancer before him." She had a look of victory on her face as she continued. "Oh, I see the saint didn't air his dirty laundry. Well, let me tell you about your superhero father. He used to drive 18-wheelers back then, and from what I could tell, he loved it. The night we met, he was involved in a bad accident. He and the other two accident victims, a young high school-aged couple on their way to prom, were rushed to my hospital. Your father was banged up badly, but not as bad as the young couple. The girl had to be airlifted from the scene, and it took the Jaws of Life to cut the young man out of the overturned vehicle, which didn't matter because he arrived with internal bleeding that no one would have been able to stop. Dwight had a few broken bones, but he would live. Your father was pissy drunk; the smell of alcohol was fuming through his skin like a loud aftershave."

She waved her hand in a fanning motion across her face and squished her eyes as if she could still smell it.

"I was assigned to him for intake and a mandatory drug test required by the Highway Patrol and his job. When I went into your father's room, he had completely lost his mind. He saw the couple after the accident before help had arrived, and from that point, he was ready to take his own life because he knew they weren't going to make it. He kept saying he had too much on his plate, he needed to be a better man than his father, and he would rather kill himself than spend life in prison like his dad. He said he didn't want to break his mother's heart again and asked for the Lord to kill him without her every finding out. Girl, his words brought me to tears, so I used my own urine and blood to pass the test for him."

She lowered her head, then shook it. I could see the regret written all over her face. She took a deep breath that caused her chest to rise. When she exhaled, the shaking of her head had stopped; yet, she refused to let her eyes meet mine as the next words came out of her mouth.

"I sedated him with morphine, Savannah, so he wouldn't be able to answer any questions that night. Good thing for him the teenagers were rushed to the hospital without being questioned before they died, or your father would have had the ugliest vehicular homicide charge Los Angeles County had ever seen. When he woke up and was sober enough to comprehend the previous night's events, I told him what I had done and that he needed to say the young couple ran the light."

Finally, she gave me eye contact. I'm not a mind reader, but the look in her eyes and body language said she wasn't done with her confession. Her eyes began to plead for understanding. I decided to wait for her to continue on her own instead of urging her to continue like I was interested, but the suspense in her silence was killing me.

"Well?" I heard myself ask.

She repeated with a hint of anger in her voice, "Well, I gave him the lies he needed to tell to clear his name. The lies the police would pass on to the parents and families of the deceased teenagers. The lies that the newspapers would share, and the lies that made the entire hospital staff find more sympathy in the hurt he felt than they had for the 'reckless' teenagers that didn't take life seriously. Instead of their legacy stating their lives were snatched away at the hands of a drunk driver, the county used the two careless teenagers' deaths as an example, and new laws surrounding teenage drivers were put in place instead, all because of the lies."

I know my father, and lying is something he can't stand. Trisha must have known that would be argued because she quickly continued.

"He didn't want to lie and planned to confess his wrongdoings, but I told him I would lose my license for what I had done and face jail time right along with him. I gave him a guilt trip that would cause a sane man to label himself crazy. Finally, your father agreed. I felt horrible about lying, but once I got to know your father, I was glad I had saved his life. His charm soon swept me off my feet, and I knew I wanted to be Mrs. James."

I was in shock. She continued to talk with a smile on her face, but my ears turned completely off to the sound of her voice. She had to be lying, I kept telling myself. She *had* to be lying! My father wasn't an alcoholic, nor was he a murderer who never confessed to the crime. He wouldn't lie about something that serious because he didn't want my mother to get in trouble.

Or would he?

The more I replayed Trisha's story in my head, the more I was starting to feel like I didn't know my father at all. He never mentioned his relationship with his father; I assumed he never knew him. That wasn't the case if Trisha was really telling the truth. My grandfather was sentenced to life in prison or lost his life in prison. I'm not sure because it happened before I was born, and he was never talked about, as though his name or situation were taboo.

Trisha's words forced me to reflect on my daddy's relationship with his mother. Now that she had mentioned it, it was sickening and almost obsessive. My daddy never left my granny's side, even with both of his brothers living with us, like he was born to be her slave. My granny always seemed to be his sole responsibility, and she only called on him. I thought he might have felt responsible for her since he was the oldest child, but there was more to it than that. They had too tight of a bond; yet their relationship never seemed authentic. There was a deeper love missing. The love you'd see a mother give her son was replaced by an awkward friendship that both felt strongly dedicated to, like a soldier fighting for his country while fighting hard not to miss his wife and kids during his absence. What secrets hid in my father's past with his parents? It wasn't any of my business, so I wouldn't ask, even if I'm now dying to know.

This was confusing. I knew I didn't know my mother, but how could I not know my father either? What if this was Trisha's plan from the beginning, to tell my father's dirt to get a fair playing field with me? I didn't trust her; she was shady, and I didn't know how much of her story I should believe. I decided not to comment on anything she said and to monitor my facial expressions. I couldn't let her know the thoughts that were forming in my mind.

When my hearing kicked back in, Trisha had just given birth to me in her story. She said, "Two kids! I knew it was time to get our own house, but your father wouldn't budge. He didn't want to leave your grandmother, so, out of frustration of wanting more, I left and got you, your brother, and I our own place. As I said earlier, one of the doctors I used to work for owned land in the South. He invited me down to help clear my head and make some extra money between him and his friends, so I took you all back to your father before I left. I stayed with him in Mississippi for about three months. When I came to see you and Memphis, I realized how much I missed you. I told your father I wouldn't leave again if he went out and found work. I missed your father and was tired of sleeping with different men to provide for our family. Sex had become meaningless, and only your father knew how to bring the meaning back. I wanted our marriage to work.

"Months passed, and your father still didn't have a job, and from what your uncles were saying, he hadn't tried to get one. He just lay around moping over the loss of the kids, and to make himself feel better, he volunteered to be your grandmother's slave, best friend, and his father's replacement in her life. He was still living with your grandmother while you, Memphis, and I had our own little place, and I still had the only income for both houses. I couldn't take it anymore; I wanted more than what your father could give. I went back South to get what I was missing from your father. This time, I stayed longer than my last few trips. I left all of you for four years."

"Four years? Who in the fuck leaves their children for four fucking years?" I yelled at her. She jumped at my words. My yelling must have caught her off guard; I couldn't wait to hear her excuses.

"I called all the time to check in on y'all, Savannah, and sent money, but I couldn't come back to California until

I had enough money saved up for us to live good, in our own place, and still be able to take care of your grandmother and your lazy-ass uncles. In my head, I knew I had your father wrapped around my finger. I knew without a doubt he would take me back, and he would have if the doctor I had been sleeping with for two of the four years I was gone hadn't called your father requesting him to give up his rights over y'all so we could get married and raise y'all together in the South. I had no idea he even knew how to contact your father."

Damn, not only did my daddy fall in love with a well-paid ho, he even took disrespect from her johns, I thought. Trisha spoke of her prostituting like it was an everyday act, like washing your face and brushing your teeth. She wasn't ashamed to sit here in my face and tell me that selling her ass was more important than my brother and me, or her marriage to my daddy. So, I wasn't ashamed to ask the only question she had yet to answer, and that was, "Did my daddy pimp-slap your ass for letting your john call him with that foolishness?"

I followed that immature question with a hopeful, childlike laugh to let her know I was praying he did. I was hurting inside but made sure it wasn't visible on the outside until she looked at me with the most painful expression of truth.

"No, he didn't hit me, Savannah. He punished me even worse. Your father swore on his mother's life that if I ever attempted to contact or see you and your brother, he would turn himself into the police for those teenagers' deaths, and bring me down with him by telling how I forged the test results, drugged him up without a doctor's consent, and gave him the story he needed to tell the police. He also had information on me sleeping with different married doctors that he promised to share with their wives and ruin their careers."

She moved her chair closer to my bed and said, "It wasn't you that I begged to let me come back, to let me have another chance to make it right. It was your father. There's a lot about me that you'll never understand, but I need you to try to understand that it was the hardest decision I ever had to make. In the end, and with a lot of nights crying into my pillow, I knew it was for the best. I felt like your father gave me a new start, so I officially moved to New Orleans and started my life over, without prostitution and any family.

"Hurricane Katrina moved me back to California after all these years. In the process of finding you, just to steal a peek at you as a successful adult, Dre discovered me or so that's how he made it look. It seems we both decided to walk through your condo by the beach on the same day, at the same time, to do the same thing, which was to lie to you. He was setting up pizza boxes, and I was going to pretend to be an interested buyer."

"What?" I heard myself say, but I didn't remember opening my mouth to talk, which meant my emotions were about to take over. I couldn't take any more of this shit tonight! The last five years of my life have been filled with so much drama. I did bring a lot of it on myself, but that didn't change the fact that it was there like a permanent fixture in my life that I had no control of.

I needed time to stomach what she had said, and since I was on the verge of tears, she needed to leave now. I demanded that she leave and quickly. I didn't want to give her the pleasure of seeing me cry. The tears had started falling out of my eyes without my permission, and my voice started breaking up.

"Go now; please, go!"

She stood up, dug in her purse, and placed something down on my nightstand on her way to the door.

"Savannah, I will leave and give you some time to think things over, but I need to know if you're going to accept me back into your life. I have a life that I need to get back to."

I screamed, "Get out!"

She nodded her head at me in understanding.

Once she was out of my room, I turned out all the lights, then the television, and cried myself to sleep in the crucial company of silence.

Chapter Two

The Wrong Reflection

Silently, I rode home from the hospital to give my thoughts their just due. Today was the first day of my new life with Dre, and I've never wanted anything as much as I want him. Some don't get do overs, and here I am with a second chance to prove it. No more games, lies, and no more dishing out the hurt I've stored in my heart since childhood. That was the old me, and if the newspaper failed to print the fate of my past in the obituary section, I'd let the world know that heffa died of cancer, and like a phoenix born in her cremation, a new me was birthed. From today forth, my only desire is to mend these broken relationships I'm in and strengthen the foundation of the ones I'm building. Memphis needed his sister, Sade needed her mother, Dre needed his wife, and Trisha needed the forgiveness of her daughter she was banished from. Everyone makes mistakes and doing what's right is the best way to give and receive forgiveness. I can do it. There's no way that making the right decisions in life could be hard.

"Welcome home, baby," Dre announced as he swung open our living room door. You would have thought that he made a wrong turn into a daisy field by the way he had them covering the room. "That's a lot of daisies, right? I went up the street to the expensive-ass flower shop and asked what flower means get-well-soon, and the old lady said daisies were the ideal flower. Do you like them?"

I wanted to lie and pretend to be thrilled by the beautiful white daisies covering the room identical to snow after a heavy fall. Instead, down came the rain as tears filled my eyes.

"They are beautiful, Dre, and I know your heart was in the right place but—"

"But what, baby? Why do you look like you're about to cry?" he asked, rushing over to me and pulling me into his arms.

"Daisies symbolize childbirth and motherhood. I can't have—"

"Aw, shit, baby, I'm sorry. Here, come sit on the couch while I throw these out."

"No, it's okay. You didn't know, and they're beautiful. Leave them."

"Honestly, they fuck with my allergies. I was trying to be romantic, but once the delivery people started covering the house in them, I felt trapped in a flower child's evil lair. They can go." He kissed me on my cheek. "Allergy meds don't mix well with weed," he chuckled.

For what seemed like hours I sat on the couch propped up on every pillow we owned and watched Dre fill trash bag after trash bag with daisies. He wasn't exaggerating when he said they covered the house as I watched him remove bags from each room, even the kitchen countertop was covered from what I could see. I hated seeing his money go down the drain, but I knew there wasn't going to be any convincing him to keep them. It was irony's first gut punch visit, and I was certain there would be more because irony always followed behind Karma and walked hand in hand with Kismet.

"How are feeling? Is it time to take another dose of your meds?" he asked once he had all the flowers gone and joined me on the couch.

"No, not for an hour. Dre . . ." my head said shut up, but my heart yelled, *Run your mouth, fool,* and I decided to listen to love, "I know we talked about us being together before my surgery, and you've told me how you feel about us. I just want you to know that I love you, and I want us. If you want to get your son from Tennessee, and we raise him together, I'm all for it." I took a deep breath before saying my next words. "And I can break my agreement with the Jeffersons and bring Sade home with us."

Dre was holding his index finger over his lips. I didn't know how long he had been trying to silence me. The patterns on the pillowcases won my eye contact. The choice was staring at the pillows or him. I chose the former of the two.

"I love you too, baby, but let's be real. This isn't a fantasy we're living, and we aren't characters in a romance book or movie. I'm ex-drug-dealing Dre, and you're ex-high-class-ho Savannah."

"Excuse me?" I snapped, but he kept going as if he didn't hear me.

"We have real shit to focus on. Not saying the kids aren't real, but we can't just pack them up from stability and move them in our—"

Yesss, because I'm not ready for them to come or to break the Jeffersons' hearts, I thought as he continued.

"—bullshit off the strength that some fucked-up shit happened to you, and you've vowed to switch up your evil ways."

"Are you saying you don't think I can change for you, that I can't change for love?" I questioned.

"I didn't say that, which means I need to get to the point. If you want this with me, I need to see it. Hell yeah, I want my kids under the same roof with me, but that roof doesn't have to cover us, Savannah. I don't want to keep bringing it up. You know the shit you did and pulled better than I could ever throw it back in your face. I'm saying that everything happens in time. Let's get to really know each other while that pussy is on a leave of absence, and let's grow our love." He smiled and then pinched my chin. "I love you. You're it for me, but I'll be single, rocking a fuck-whoever-I-want-card before I spend my life doing that shit again. Kiss me, baby."

Kiss me, baby? How about I kick you in your mouth? I thought. Dre was speaking in truth, but the way he served it always hurt. *More irony to go on top of this humble pie,* I thought, reaching in to kiss him.

His lips were like the entrance to a safe haven, and he used his tongue to lure me in to the protection of his love. His strength radiated over me in the same manner sunlight covered a tanning body. There was no denying the power Dre had over me, but where was the physical proof of it? His kiss always made the whiskers on my cat stand from the static electricity, and my kitty's tongue tingle; however, there was nothing. The Sahara Desert had more movement and water than the feline that lived in my panties. I pulled away from the kiss and quickly came up with a diversion for doing so.

"When is everyone coming over? I'm sure they've been bugging you to find out if I made it home," I asked, forcing on a smile. I didn't want him to see me sad anymore today.

"They aren't coming over. I set up a phone and your laptop by the bed. They can call, text, or email. The doctor said the surgery and chemotherapy affected your immune system, and it can take weeks to get it back up. I don't want nobody to breathe germs on you, not even me. You're taking the room, and I'll either be right here on this couch or in Sade's room."

"Dre—"

"Dre, nothing. I need you to heal quickly. It's been years since I've been inside my pussy. I need to remind you of a few things," he laughed.

"Well, can we watch a movie together before I go into my jail cell?" I moaned, hoping he'd change his mind.

"Let me go get your face mask, and then you can lie on me while we watch it."

"Face mask? Don't you think you're taking this too far?"

"Per your nurse, Ms. Peaches, no. She came by late last night with a lot of hospital goodies for you and asked me to give you her number so you could call her when you felt up to it. She seems like a real nice lady, and she's genuinely concerned about you."

Trisha. I hadn't forgotten her. She was on my list, just not the next in line. I wonder how she knew where I lived. She must have gotten that out of my chart.

"Well, there's no need to go through all of that because these meds don't let me stay awake more than an hour at a time. I guess I'll go get in bed and call my nurse until I fall asleep."

"Okay, baby, but try to stay up for at least another forty minutes to take your medicine. I don't want you to miss your dose."

We relocated me to my new jail cell that I'd be locked in for the next few months, and with all the flowers gone and the hospital equipment, the room felt like I was housed in a room for the criminally insane. My crimes against Dre were many, and if I had to chalk them up to anything, it would be to insanity.

"Hello, may I speak to Trisha, please?"

The voice didn't sound like the one I'd spoken to while in the hospital. There was a hint of a Caribbean accent to.

"May I ask who's calling?"

"Um, her daughter. You can tell her it's her daughter, Savannah, calling." I whispered, not wanting Dre to hear me. He knew that Trisha was my mother and hadn't said a word to me about it. I didn't know why he'd chosen not to tell me, but I was up for playing his game. Until he had proof that I knew she was my mother, I'd keep pretending that she's my caring nurse.

There was a silence, and if I wasn't mistaken, it sounded like the phone had fallen, and the noise from the television in the background ceased as she confirmed it was her.

"It's me, Savannah. I couldn't pick up on your voice. I thought you were another bill collector trying to take the little I have left. What did you decide to do with me?"

"I haven't decided, and I don't know why I called you. I guess a part of me misses the nurse who sat with me every night. If it's okay with you, I'd only like to speak with her." I tried to sound nonchalant, but the tears made that hard for me to pull off.

"Well, baby girl, I want you to know that I don't want you to forgive me. That would be asking too much of anybody. I missed my opportunity to be called Mama and don't deserve the right for you to call yourself my daughter. Trisha is fine, and you can call me a friend of the family, but will you please do me one favor? Can you talk to your brother away from your father and let him know I'm back? Dwight doesn't need to know I'm back. I don't know if his threat holds until he's dead and gone, and I don't want to go to jail to find out. See if Memphis would be willing to hear me out, and then, maybe I'd get to be a mother to at least one of my children."

The thought of sneaking behind my daddy's back to set her up with Memphis felt wrong. He's always been forgiving. It made me wonder if he would forgive her. Lord knows it would break my father's heart if she got to Memphis on her own with me knowing she had returned, and I hadn't told him. If there were a statute of limitations on murder in any degree, I'd risk setting up a meeting with all four of us to make this reunion public. That way, everyone would know the outcome together.

"I believe I can do that. So, what made you become a nurse?"

In two hours, I learned more about my mother than I would have ever imagined. She told me these wild stories, and I couldn't help it. I was sort of envious of her life as a single woman. She had traveled to 80 percent of the places scribbled on my bucket list at least twice. When Dre entered to bring me my meds, I placed the phone on the nightstand until I took them, then our talk commenced again. She was becoming my hero as I began to hate her more for abandoning me.

"Savannah, I enjoyed talking to you tonight, but I have to get off this phone now. I met a very nice fisherman from Alaska who promised me a free dinner tonight. He's uglier than a hyena mauled by a bull, but he smells good, dresses nice, and he's treating," she joked.

"How are you getting by, on Social Security like my daddy?" the question shouldn't have left my mouth. I had gotten comfortable and shot off.

"Huh? I wish," she sighed. "There isn't a pension or retirement fund set up for you when you retire from prostituting. I'm getting by with every hyena I can make my pet."

"I'm sorry. I didn't think before I asked. If you ever need anything, Trisha, I'm in a position to help."

"I don't want your money, baby. I'll get by the way I get by and don't you be apologizing for being who you are and speaking your mind. Being sorry isn't in your blood, I made sure of it," she giggled. "Oh, before I go, how is that big ape of yours? Did Dre tell you about our little 'encounter' yet?"

"No, he hasn't. Funny thing is, he's still calling you my nurse and pretending he doesn't know who you are."

"Now, that's strange. Why wouldn't he tell you that he met your long lost mama . . . I mean, family friend?"

"I don't know. I was trying to figure it out before I called you."

Trisha cleared her voice. "I'm going to tell you something and keep it under your hat. He asked me when we met to try to build a relationship with you because it might help you be a better mother to Sade."

"Is that why you're doing this?" I hollered.

"Hell no. You of all people should know that our kind is as stubborn as an old mule. I don't take orders, and I damn sure don't trust any man that sneaks behind his woman's back for personal gain. I saw it like he wanted to control you, and the last time I checked, you weren't birthed with a battery pack in your back. You won't be his or anybody else's robot."

"Damn right!" I agreed. Here I am ready to give him my all, and then I found out he did this. You never involve outsiders in your insider business. If we have a problem, it takes us to fix it. There's no "them" in the word "marriage" or in "couple."

"I can't give you any advice, and if I could, I wouldn't because that's your bed, your man, and your dick, but I can tell you what your grandmother told me. If he has one secret, there's a baker's dozen more. What he's baking and how much of it is he selling is the *real* question. I'll check in with you tomorrow if that's okay."

"I'd like that."

It's been forty-five days since the talk with Trisha at the hospital, and it still had its effect on me as if it happened less than an hour ago. I hadn't quite decided what to do with the information she had given me, but I knew I didn't want to see my father or brother until I did.

What I did decide was that Trisha had to be telling at least 75 percent truth. I just hadn't determined what made up the 25 percent lie yet. I was sure some of it was true because she knew all it would take to verify the information she had given me was a talk with my father or confront Dre about their little meeting. She didn't discourage me from doing either. Although my father more than likely wouldn't have told the story the same way she did, he'd give enough information for me to conclude the truth.

The picture she left on my nightstand of her holding me while Memphis sat on my father's lap was the very first baby picture I had ever seen of myself or Memphis. My father had always said my mother took all our baby pictures with her. Guess that part was true. In the picture, Trisha looked like a happy woman and proud mother, but the camera lied because the woman in that picture was a professional streetwalker who walked out on her family and never mothered those children. I wanted to forgive her for leaving us, but when we talked, she never seemed interested in apologizing for it. Truthfully, she acts as if it never happened and didn't even mention the picture.

I didn't know what her true purpose of leaving the picture was, and I could ask her reasoning, but it just felt better to guess. Maybe she was hoping it would open me up emotionally, and I'd gain a soft spot for her like I have, or maybe it was a keepsake to show proof that we were all together happy once. I was confused by Trisha's actions again, and I thought about voicing my concerns; yet, every time I heard her voice, I decided to wait for a better time. I was hurting myself by trying to hold on to the hurt and trying to convince myself at the same time that I was over it. I felt like I was in a guessing game when it came to what her true intentions were but to share these moments with her, I didn't mind being torn.

"Savannah, listen to yourself!" I whimpered as more tears slid down my face. I hadn't done this much crying in my life, and some days, the tears felt good. They gave me a release, and that helped me stay focused on my change. There are too many maybes and nothing concrete when it comes to her. Is that how Sade looks at me? How in the hell could I even consider allowing my mother to walk back into my life without a stable, new beginning with my own daughter? But is that what we were building during our daily talks? I had gone thirty years without knowing a mother's love, and I'm sure I could go another thirty years without it, but if that was true, why were thoughts of her always on my mind, and when we talked, why did I always feel sad when she said she had to go? Now, I can honestly say that I know *exactly* how my daughter feels.

I reached for my purse that lay on Dre's unslept side of our bed to review the picture taken so many years back. As of late, he's been trying to invite company over, mainly my father and Memphis; however, I declined their visits. I didn't know what to say to either of them without bringing up Trisha, and I wasn't ready to spend time with Sade because looking at her grow up without her mother would be a reminder of myself. I hadn't talked to Dre about any of this. He was still pretending like Trisha, or should I say, Ms. Peaches, was my nurse, and the longer he did, the more I began to despise him.

Dre walked in with a dry expression etched on his face.

"Damn, Dre, can't you knock before entering?" I said, making sure he saw me rolling my eyes at him as I tucked the picture away. The attitude I was giving him was a small dose of what he had been giving me for not wanting company and for asking him for a little space. I understand that he's a man and that he wouldn't understand what it feels like to have your woman parts taken away from you, but I was moody as hell. Some days I did want him to lie in bed with me so that we could cuddle, and other days, the hot flashes made me want to scream when he came close. I tried to explain to him what I was going through, and he acted as if he understood, but some days, he chose to let me have it.

"Yeah, I could, but why would I knock on my own damn bedroom door? I see you are in your usual fucked-up mood today. Still mad at the world, Savannah, and want to take the shit out on me?"

He stood in the doorway awaiting my response. I hadn't confronted him yet about his plans to have Trisha come back in my life to "rehabilitate" me. Come to think about it, I hadn't had a conversation that lasted over a minute with him since last week when I declined movie night with him and Sade and didn't plan on having one now. I turned my back to him.

"I already told you that I can't control the mood swings, and that's what those little blue pills are for. I love you, but what do you want, Dre?" I said it in the nastiest voice I could muster. Trisha was right. Dre wasn't acting like a man in love. He complained about everything I did, which, for the last forty-five days, was nothing.

"Well, Savannah, since we're stuck on dropping names like we need clarification on who we're talking to, I know Your Royal Highness said you didn't want anyone seeing you until your hair had fully grown back, but I couldn't get Will to jump back on a plane and go back to California. So, what does your royal ass want me to do with him?"

At that moment, Will pushed past Dre, rolling his eyes like a diva being offered fake jewelry, and stormed in my bedroom.

"Best friend, you need to tell your security guard *I'm* the only exception to the damn rules, now get your fake, sick-acting ass out of bed and give me some hugs."

I couldn't hide the feeling of joy from Will's surprise visit, and Dre made sure to comment on it as he walked out the door saying, "Damn, that's the first time I've seen her smile in about a week."

We hugged for what felt like five long minutes in silence before Will pushed me away to start part two of his fussing.

"Why in the hell are you in this dark-ass room with the blinds shut and the mirrors taped up? I hope you ain't in here feeling sorry for yourself now, not after all the foul shit you did. Bitch, pleeease. If you don't get your ass out of your head on them evil-ass shoulders . . .!"

Will snatched the string from the blinds pulling down, forcing them to rise all the way up and permit sunlight in. The unwelcomed light immediately attacked my eyes and caused me to wince. When my eyes adjusted, I peeked out of the window. It was a beautiful day outside. From what I could tell, there wasn't a gray cloud in sight, which surprised me because the mood in my bedroom before Will came gave me the feeling that it had been storming out.

Next, Will attacked the newspapers that covered the mirrors. He talked shit while he did it, but I paid his rant no attention. I was floating from his salty words because they were exactly what I needed.

"This bitch took down an entire village back in Cali without sweating her fucking makeup off and then turned into a fucking vampire when Karma bit her. You can't hide from Karma, ho. She has your pretty-ass face on the most wanted poster, and she's coming to slay you. I knew I should have gotten out here sooner. I hope the sunlight melts your evil ass. Come here."

When the newspapers were down, he demanded that I stand in front of the mirror with him to view my reflection. I refused.

"Vampires can't see their reflections, remember? I don't do mirrors!"

"I'm not Dre. That smart-ass mouth of yours doesn't scare me at all. Bitch, I bite too, and I will if you don't come to look at this pretty bitch a little I'm staring at through the mirror."

"Pretty, yeah, right," I laughed halfheartedly.

"Yes, pretty please. Don't make me pick your ass up and bring you to this mirror. I'm not in the mood to have to whoop you and your buff-ass bodyguard's ass. I brought my pistol!" he said, lifting the side of his shirt to reveal his piece.

I hadn't seen myself in over five months, but I could tell that I gained weight by the way all my pajamas fit. I thought I would have lost weight being sick, but I guess with all the steroids and lack of exercise, I blew up instead. An occasional rub of my head informed me that I had a little over an inch of hair on my head, which meant it had grown some and gave me a visual of myself, which was that I looked horrible. I didn't need to look in a mirror to figure that out.

When I was released from the hospital, Dre helped me to get in our bed. We passed the mirror in the hall-way, and I saw something hideous staring back me. I demanded that all the mirrors in our room and bathroom be covered that very second. Who would want to look at themselves in their worst possible state continuously?

The only reason I made it to the mirror today was by Will pulling me by my arm with force. I made sure to only look at my body; I didn't want to see my face. Will must have been watching my eyes because he said, "Yes, my love, you put on some pounds, but they look good on you. Look at all that ass. Make that big ole thang bounce!"

He grabbed me by the shoulders and turned me side-ways in the mirror.

"Um, shake it, um, shake that big ole' thang. Shake that big ole' thang." He rapped to his own rhythm as he slapped and knocked on the dresser to create a beat.

My butt was huge; it looked like I had a dent in my back, and my cheeks were hanging out the bottom of my shorts. A quick glance down my hips, past my thighs to my thick-ass legs led me to see the bullet wound for the first time. I had forgotten Keisha shot me. My entire hospital stay was focused on cancer once I had awakened from the coma I was in. The bullet was nothing compared to that. I felt myself getting angry again as I touched the wound, but Will's words quickly terminated it.

"That bitch is locked up for attempted murder, and she has HIV. You got your revenge. That bullet don't mean shit! So, fix your face with yo' evil ass. That ain't shit but a scar from Karma."

"But, look at—" I started to say in a pout.

"Look at what? Demon seed? The bullet could have gone into your brain, or if the simpleminded bitch had an aim, it could have gone into your heart, Ms. Vampire. Stop worrying about the little shit and be thankful that you are still here, and that I'm here to cuss you out. Damn, bitch, I see I'm going to have to hit the reset button. You must have lost your wit while you were in that coma!"

What would I do without Will? was the only thought that came to mind. He was the first person to know about Sade and all the scandalous shit I did; yet, he loved me like I did nothing wrong. I turned to face him to tell him about the visit from my long lost mother at the hospital, but he still had his hands on my shoulders and turned me back face-to-face with the mirror. He lifted his left hand off my shoulder and snatched my scarf off my head, revealing my uncombed hair.

"Now, look at yourself, Savannah. You're as beautiful as the day you came back to California. That hair doesn't control your beauty. Hell, I think you look better without it. You know I got a thing for that boy look. You might finally get this dick if you're willing to let me hit from the back, and you put some bass in your moans, but you can't tell anyone. Don't want folks knowing I hit a baddy and start assuming I'm straight. Yuck!"

"You don't have no type of filter on your mouth!" I screamed while trying to speak out the words through my laughter.

"A filter for what? What do I need one of those for?"

Shaking my head, I continued to evaluate myself in the mirror. I knew I was looking at myself in the mirror, but I felt like an outsider staring at a stranger. The woman in the full-length mirror was beautiful, but she wasn't whole. She was missing so much mentally, emotionally, and physically. I pitied this bitch that was standing before me. She could never have children again. So, what if she never wanted kids in the first place? At least she had the satisfaction of knowing she could make them if she wanted to. Now, she had no choice but to adopt. It was like having the right to be a woman snatched away from you, leaving you to feel like another. This bitch in the mirror didn't have enough qualifications to be a man, yet she was still short from everything that makes a woman a woman. I wanted to help her become whole again, but where do I start?

I've always heard outer appearances didn't matter; it's who you are within that really counts. I was determined to fix the inner me, but not yet. My outer appearance meant more to me after being shot and winning my fight with cancer. I wanted to feel beautiful, and I needed to hear it from everyone, not just family and friends. I would deal with my inside baggage later. That shit wasn't too heavy for me to carry yet, and when it got to that point, I'd hire a therapist to act as my bellhop. It's going to take at least two therapists, a priest, a village of monks, and a week of charm school to fix the issues I have. I know I'm not ready to face that shit yet.

"So, bitch, what do you think? And I love your bed. Is it a Cali king?"

I almost forgot Will was standing here with me. He walked over to my bed, lay on it, and started making invisible snow angels, moving his arms up and down while opening and closing his legs like a pair of scissors. I had to laugh and then said, "I think it's time to get a weave and hit the gym to tighten this shit up! You're right; I still got it."

"Yes, sexy, you still got it."

Will got up, and we gave each other a high five. After a few more minutes of playing catch up and some useless chitchat, we headed out of the bedroom. Dre was in the living room doing push-ups when we entered. He had his shirt off, and his dreads were pushed back into a ponytail that ended in the middle of his back. I hadn't seen him this close to naked in almost five years, and I loved what I saw. Jail had gotten him swollen. He was as wide as the refrigerator now, and it was all muscle.

The sweat that covered his back looked like it would have a toffee flavoring to it if I went and licked it, and, boy, I *really* wanted to lick it. I watched him go up and down in his push-ups and pretended to be under him until my stares made him stand on two feet and face me. I was surprised to see "Savannah" tattooed across his chest. Each letter must have been three inches long and two inches wide, in all capital letters that stretched from one side of his chest to the other.

I've always thought getting someone's name permanently inked into your skin was the dumbest thing a person could do but looking at my name on his chest caused me to blush, which Dre also noticed.

"I got that done after I read the 'fuck you' letter you sent me while I was in jail. Sounds crazy, but I fell deeper in love with you by the more bullshit I read. I knew when I was done reading it for the third time, I was coming to get you when I got out, and that I'd make you mine. If you had somebody else, I'd end that," he smirked and then said, "Good thing it all worked out for me, huh?"

I couldn't help it. I smiled and nodded my head. He was confident I would be his if he had my name tattooed, and he was right. I'd never felt this way about anyone, even if I do doubt our relationship has what it takes to withstand the test of time. Staring at my name almost made me wish I had been nicer to him earlier about knocking on the door.

Damn, Dre was fine; it was that tattoo under his left eye with those full, black lips turned up in the corners to form a sexy smile, with perfectly straight, white teeth that got me going every time. I still didn't understand how he kept his teeth pearly white considering all the weed he smoked. Looking at him made my mind start drifting into dirty thoughts that included me, Dre, some hot oil, and a lot of biting, scratching, and slamming. I felt myself getting wet from a place that was missing its inner parts. Depression would have kicked back in, but the words of the doctor who released me came to mind. "We recommend you wait six to eight weeks before you have intercourse, but ultimately, your body will let you know when it's ready. It will start functioning like normal, minus the occasional hot flashes you might have."

I hadn't been wet or in the mood until now. I made Dre sleep in Sade's room instead of his choice of sleeping on the couch and kept him out of my face as much as possible. He was still a stranger to me, and I wasn't ready to get to know him, which forced sex out of the picture. There wasn't anything sexy about me to turn myself on, so masturbating to make sure my plumbing worked never happened either, but I'm glad my water was now back flowing like it used to.

"Stop drooling over him and wipe your nasty little mouth, tramp. Please don't forget what your little hot ass came in here to tell him." Will stared at me as he waited for me to tell Dre whatever it was he felt I was supposed to be saying, but I couldn't remember. My mind flashed back to the last time Dre was inside of me, and I was stuck there.

"Hello? Don't you have something to say? Ugh, get up out of my face!" Will rolled his eyes at me and then looked at Dre. "Umm, Security, we're about to leave to go hook your Mrs. back up, then dinner, and then she'll be on her way back home, apparently to drool on something attached to you." He shot his eyes back at me and said, "You're still standing there staring at that man like you want to lick him or something. Dam, slut, show some restraint!"

"No, I was not!"

I should have known Will would catch on to what I was doing. He was probably looking at Dre's body thinking the same thing I had been thinking. The truth didn't matter because Dre was already smiling when he tossed me his keys and said, "I'm having your Cadillac looked at today since it's been sitting so long. Y'all can take my truck."

I went to the bathroom to freshen up before we left. There was too much moisture down there for a feminine wipe to clean up the wetness, and I needed to change my panties.

"Can I holler at you for a minute? I know you're about to leave." Dre was standing in the bathroom door, and I don't know for how long, but the smirk on his face said he'd been there long enough.

"Yeah, baby, and before you say whatever it is you're about to say, I want to apologize. It's not okay that I flip from hot to cold with you as if you're supposed to put up with my shit. I do love you, Dre; just all of this is hard."

"And it's hard on me too. I'm trying to understand the no company, taped up mirrors, hold me and then don't touch me stuff, but it's like being engaged to two people. Yo' ass flew to your feet when Will walked in, but I can't even get you to sit on the couch with me, but that's not what I stopped you for." Dre walked over to the toilet and took a seat on the lid.

"The doctor gave you six weeks of bed rest. I wanted you to have the first month to yourself—nah, I'm lying. I wanted you to have them with me, and the first three weeks were amazing, and then it's like something happened. I didn't do shit, so it leaves me to think, is someone putting something in your head about me or us?"

"Like who? The only people I talk to are Sandy way in France and my nurse. I haven't spoken to any of the family or extended family. Sandy only knows good things about you, and the nurse doesn't know either one of us."

I looked into his eyes waiting for a sign that showed he knew her, but his facial expression didn't crack.

"Then why are you dodging getting closer to the best part of me?"

"I'm not. I thought we've gotten a lot closer since I've been on bed rest. I love the way we are now. Well, not this last week but before then. We've made a lot of progress in becoming one."

"I'm not talking about me; I'm talking about Sade. Are you avoiding her? Is that why you're milking this bed rest thing out?"

I didn't know what to say because, in all honesty, the answer was yes. That's the exact reason I was milking it, but it wasn't only to avoid Sade. My father and Memphis made that list too. Sade irritated my soul with all of her damn questions whenever she was around me, and that probably makes me a bad mother to say it, but it was the truth. However, I prepared myself for it and actually was looking forward to spending time with her, just not right now. I needed to get my feelings in order with my mother before I could step in my role as a mother, and I knew this long before Trisha returned. I think Dre must have forgotten, but that's why she's living with the Jeffersons now. I gave her up to focus on my own shit.

"Have the Jeffersons bring her over. That's the only way I'm going to answer that. I'll see you when I get back." I kissed him and walked out.

I met Will outside at Dre's truck. I'm lying. It wasn't a truck. It was an army tank built for war. Dre was pushing a yellow and black Hummer on huge tires, and it was packed with TVs. I had to use the step rail to climb into the vehicle and pull myself into the passenger's seat. There was no way I was going to try to drive.

Once the engine was cranked, the Hummer was filled with so much base that the seats shook, and the windows vibrated.

"Turn that shit down. Is Dre deaf? Who listens to music that loud anyway?" Will shouted, and he was right. I couldn't even tell who the artist was because the base was louder than the lyrics. As I tried to find the right button to lower the volume, his TV screens came on, but it wasn't a movie we were watching. It was more like video surveillance of our surroundings. The television built into the dashboard had a four-way picture-in-picture mechanism. The top left picture was the front of the vehicle, the top right view was of the right passenger side, the bottom right was the rear view, and the bottom left was the driver's side of the Hummer. I watched the screens, wondering where each camera was located on the Hummer as Will lowered the music by a button on the steering wheel.

Once the music was all the way off, Will looked at me and said, "I bet those cameras can record more than the circumference of this damn truck. Are you sure you're not marrying a Fed or CIA agent, girl? He got more than just a master's degree in Criminal Justice. Somebody has trained Dre!"

"Yes, he has," I said, in between laughs. "Dre was trained by the drug dealers' mistakes that got them caught for slanging dope out of their cars. He's been to jail and not trying to get caught again. I understand the need for the cameras."

Will gave me the side eye with disgust on his face. His look said more than words, but that never stopped him from saying it. "You need to take this shit more seriously, Savannah. Sometimes, I wonder how you managed to graduate college and land that good-ass job. It must've required a whole lot of swallowing and knee burns because you got to be the dumbest rich bitch I know."

"Fuck you!" I said, holding up my middle finger.

"You're supposed to be all book smarts and no street smarts, but you do remember that we grew up in the same hood, right? Bitch, you ate sugar toast with butter and called it French toast like the rest of us." Will was now the one laughing, and I wore the look of disgust. "I'm just saying, Dre is too damn mysterious and too perfect to be a real felon. To say he spent all that time in jail, he hasn't checked me out once. With all this ass and lip action I'm throwing around, he should have at least taken a quick look." Will was damn near the point of tears, laughing. It took him a few minutes to regain his composure to finish. "But seriously, while you were sick, I had plenty of conversations with him about you and his vocabulary, sentence structure, and pronunciation don't match his street credibility. Blame it on the movies, but I think he's a double agent or working undercover and fucked around and fell in love with you. I think when you put that pussy on him, you blew his case, and they had to sit him down!"

I didn't respond because I didn't know what to say, so I continued holding my finger up until he focused on driving. Will was a sheriff for the Los Angeles Sheriff's Department, so his guess on what Dre did in the past would be better than mine. The only thing Dre told me was that he had an interest in criminals and that he made more money being a criminal than studying them. It sounded like he was speaking from firsthand experience and instead of probing him for more information, I left it at that. I'm sure the cameras were put in his truck when he was still selling drugs to check his surroundings. Dre was too smart to be caught slipping . . . but how smart was he? Maybe I should start to get to know him. I mean, we do live together, after all. I was snapped out of my thoughts by Will hitting the brakes.

"What's wrong?"

"Bitch!" he screamed with a look of horror.

"What, Will, what happened?"

"Did you really walk out of the damn house with those ashy-ass lips? I caught a glimpse of those dust buckets from the side and almost swerved off the road. You will *not* go anywhere with me with your mouth looking like you've been sucking ghost dick." He dug in his pocket and handed me his balm. "You keep it. I can see that you need it more than me." He started back driving while I tried to stop laughing so I could apply it.

Fifteen minutes of driving and laughing, and then we made a quick stop at the bank. Not wanting to be seen, we went through the drive-thru teller and then headed to the mall. I couldn't believe that I had to buy size 14 pants just to get my butt and thighs in them. My waist was a size 10, but I couldn't pull a size 10 past my thighs, and the size 12 I managed to squeeze in looked painted on, or like I was going to bust out of them if I sat down.

After grabbing a few outfits, I bought a pair of workout sneakers and clothes and then headed to find some sexy sleepwear. I ended up buying a few little naughty pieces and prayed to God to wear one of them tonight for Dre. I wanted to trace my name on his chest with my tongue as he lay in between my legs towering over me like a dread-headed African god.

Daydreaming of freaky encounters with Dre as we were walking out of the lingerie store made me almost not notice that Will had stopped this beautiful, bright-skinned young lady in some bad stilettos to ask rudely, "Who does your hair? Your weave looks really good, almost like you grew it naturally, but I can see your edges have bid you adieu."

"Excuse me?" the now-offended young woman asked, but not with the tone of being offended. She was too mesmerized by Will's sexiness. Her cheeks turned rosy red on her light brown face as she twisted the corner of her mouth to reveal a gaped-tooth smile. I'd love to watch him hurt her feelings by saying he was gay.

"Please don't pay him any attention. I'm sorry I let him come out in public," I quickly apologized. "I'm new to Washington and am looking for a hairstylist. You are rocking the hell out of that look, and I was too shy to ask you, so that was his attempt at it."

She gave an understanding smile, then turned her attention back to Will. "Jackie does the best hair here. Period. She's expensive, but you will get your money's worth. Here's her card. She works by appointments only."

I had to snatch the card from her to prevent her from handing it to Will. She looked at Will for an explanation of my behavior, but all she got in return from him was, "Thank you, balding eagle." Before I could tease Will about his effect on women, he was dialing the number on the card. I had never had hair weaved into my hair before, but it sounds like Will knew what to ask for. He even explained that I was a cancer survivor and only had about an inch and a half to work with. Will didn't look like the type to date drag queens to know about weaves, nor did he look gay, for that matter. He quickly jotted down the address and informed the person on the other end of the phone we were on our way.

"Your hair is going to be 450, but I'm paying for it. I'm also picking out the style, so don't get in here and start talking shit about the length or I'm going to embarrass you. That's your only warning, smart mouth."

I nervously agreed with Will's threat while he punched the address into the GPS. When we arrived, I was seated in the shampoo chair and immediately serviced. The salon had a jazz club feel to it and had John Coltrane playing softly under the dim lights. I had never before been to a hair salon so relaxing and quiet. Conversations went on, but each booth was a distance from the next, so all you could hear were whispers. I could see Will up front in the beauty supply portion of the salon, looking over hair and explaining what he wanted Jackie to do while rolling his eyes at me as he talked. I had no complaints about any of this, just one request, and that was for my styling chair not to face the mirror until she was done.

For thirty minutes, the hairstylist braided my hair, and then I watched as a needle was threaded. Bright lights were now turned on in my booth, indicating the show was about to begin. Then came an hour and twenty minutes of sewing, followed by fifteen minutes of cutting, with an additional thirty minutes of curling, and I was done.

When I finally faced the mirror, my jaw dropped. It was beautiful. It had the same natural look like the woman's in the mall, but it was more fitting on me. I had a very long, layered cut that was flipped out in the middle of my face, then wrapped inward toward the bottom. The hair went about an inch past my breasts, which I wasn't too sure about, but I wasn't going to dare complain in front of Will. Jackie said I could treat it like it was mine. I could pull it back into a ponytail, go swimming with it, wash it, and she recommended conditioning the hair with a light conditioner so it wouldn't look dry. I advised her I would be back for all of that. There was no way I was managing this hair by myself. I thanked her a million times as we headed out the door.

I was looking good and feeling even better by now. Will took me back to his hotel, so I could shower and dress for an early dinner. I threw on a pair of denim, straight-legged jeans with a white camisole and a burnt-orange blazer. Then I put on my new burnt-orange pumps and threw on matching accessories. I was looking and feeling like me again, thanks to eighteen inches of human hair and clothes that complemented my weight gain.

"Now *that's* the Savannah I know! You're looking good, beautiful," Will said while stepping into the room, looking dapper in his cream sports jacket, tight-fitted black V-neck, dark blue jeans, and cream loafers. Will's looks were breathtaking and panty-wetting, if I may say so. He was five foot ten with about 180 pounds of muscle on his perfectly sculpted frame. His head sat on his body in a perfect circle, but it wasn't big. The low haircut with waves, neatly trimmed sideburns leading to his beard gave him a sharp, clean look. If it wasn't for his wide nose and puffy, dark brown eyes, Will's race could be questioned due to his reddish-brown hair and beige skin tone. But I knew him since we were kids. I was two years older than he, so I knew both of his parents are black. His parents must have dug deep into their gene pool when creating Will because none of his ugly-ass brothers came close to looking that good. If Will weren't gay, I would have attacked him like a wild beast looking to feed its hunger. I don't know if gay men picked their lovers like we women did, but if they do, Will had to be one hot commodity.

We ate at a Japanese restaurant near his hotel that had a hibachi grill at every table, and the chef cooked and served you everything from the grill except drinks. They were brought to the table by the waiter.

The half-moon-shaped table seated eight customers at a time. We were seated in between three black, business-suit-wearing men on our left and three young, white college students, two females and one male who proudly wore shirts with their school's name written across them on our right.

Once the chef came, he put on a show for us as he cooked the food we previously ordered with the waiter. High flames shot up almost to the ceiling causing me to jump back in my seat. Will fell out laughing, but the suited gentleman, whose shoulder I had the pleasure of leaning on, assured me he wouldn't let anything happen to me.

"I gotcha, baby," he said while placing his arm more securely next to mine. He reached in his pocket and handed me a card, and then extended his hand for a shake.

"Royce Reed, and you are?"

I glanced at his card which read *"Royce Reed, Attorney at Law."* I quickly dug in my purse, removed one of my business cards, handed it to him, and said, "Savannah James."

He read my card over thoroughly, as only a lawyer would, and then said, "Miss Boss Lady, in other words," referencing my card and giving a seductive smile.

Royce must have been in his mid- to late-thirties; about six foot and two, but it was hard to tell his height since he was sitting. He was multiracial, but his African American heritage was dominant. He had a normal, Caesar haircut with an edge up, light brown skin, thin lips, with freckles across his nose and cheeks, and a pair of invisible frame prescription glasses over his eyes. He was cute, not my type, but I was going to enjoy his flirting anyway.

"I didn't mean to jump all over you. The flames caught me off guard," I said, blushing, still feeling a little embarrassed.

The private conversation that I thought I was sharing with Royce wasn't private at all. One of the other suited men seated with him joined in by saying, "Royce hasn't had a woman jump all over him in months; you just made his day." Then, he nudged Royce in his side and chuckled.

I watched Royce's freckles and cheeks go from light brown with dark brown spots to red with the dark brown spots; obviously, he was embarrassed. He took a sip of his wine, wiped the corners of his mouth with his cloth napkin, and said, "What my colleague, Edward, here, meant, is that I am recently divorced and haven't started dating or meeting anyone yet."

Edward had no problem with being the third wheel in our conversation and proved it.

"Six months isn't recent at all, especially when his ex-wife is remarried and expecting a child by one of his college buddies."

"Oh wow," the words flew out of my mouth. I guess they didn't believe in personal space. That was a lot of information to give a stranger, but in Royce's defense, I said, "I can completely understand that he is choosing to wait before getting his feet wet again. Divorces are hard, and who wants to jump back into the dating scene after losing the person that they assumed was their soul mate? Take your time, Royce; trust me, you aren't missing anything."

That was Edward's cue, who, might I add, was so unattractive that after my first glance at him, I refused to look his way again, to get out of our conversation but not before he mumbled, "Yes, he is; he's missing pussy."

I pretended not to hear him but was dying laughing on the inside. He was right; that's six months of pleasing yourself, and it must be torture.

"Savannah, are you divorced also? You seem to understand my exact feelings on why I haven't moved on." Royce had a curious look on his face, but I immediately fed his curiosity with facts.

"Oh no, marriage is not for me, but if I ever were to jump the broom and then my marriage was terminated, that would be my reasoning for not diving back into the dating scene. I'm single, a status that I am very comfortable with."

Will choked on his food at the sound of me saying I was single and hurriedly took a sip of his wine to get the food to go down. Once he placed his glass down, I could feel him staring at me. It was like he had daggers in his eyes with the way his look was stabbing the side of my face. I didn't dare continue my conversation with Royce in fear that Will would join in and speak his piece.

Royce and I ate in silence. The food smelled and tasted delicious. I wasn't going to ruin it with meaningless flirting or the embarrassment Will's truths would have brought me. Royce and his colleagues stood up to leave after they finished their meals. That's when Royce told me he would be calling me soon if it was all right with me.

"I'll be waiting," I said, with a smile, and Royce's friends cheered him on. Will didn't let them reach the exiting doors before he started in on me.

"Bitch, are you stupid? Why did you tell that man you were single when you know your ass is a courthouse trip away from being married to Dre? Stop playing with fucking fire, Savannah, before your ass ends up burnt! Not just burnt but *cremated* with your ashes in an urn because Dre's ghetto spy ass went to work on you! That motherfucka you had a baby by ain't no joke, and you should know that by now. Bitch, you must have left that hospital more retarded and slow than before you went into it. You need to request a checkup on your brain, 'cause your mind isn't functioning the way it's supposed to, or else yo' ass is possessed."

Will looked at me like I wasn't shit as he ate his stir-fried jumbo shrimp. The remaining customers at our table and the chef seemed to be listening in, awaiting my response. I didn't want to seem like the fool Will was making me into, so I snapped back.

"I'm a single woman until I'm married, and that's *only* if that secret agent can get me to say I do. After the shit Dre pulled to invite my mama back into my life without giving a fuck about how it would make me feel, he better hope I don't pack up, say fuck him and our daughter, and get back to the old me. He has a baker's dozen of secrets, and I don't know what he's baking and how much of it he's selling, but he's had plenty of time to come clean. Sick and dead ain't the same thing, and I'm no longer worried either. Who gets a second chance to live to spend it caged in a box?"

Will looked completely confused, and I could see the anger leaving his eyes the longer confusion set in. That's exactly what I wanted. Now it was time to calm him all the way back down. "Can we please go back to your hotel room and talk? There's some shit I need to tell you, but I don't need all of the state of Washington in my fucking business like you have allowed them to be thus far." I pointed my finger at the chef and the college students who had stopped what they were doing to eavesdrop, without shame openly.

Will stood up without saying anything to me and turned to face the people I had just pointed out and said, "Get some fucking business." As he paid for our food, I headed to Dre's truck. Once we pulled off, I started talking, and Will turned the music up sky high to drown me out. We made it to the hotel in less than five minutes. When we arrived at the hotel's entrance, Will grabbed my hand and said, "I don't trust Dre. That's why I didn't let you start the conversation in the car. It might have been recorded."

Will was my best friend, and it showed as we passed the elevators and headed straight to the bar. As usual, we got drunk, and Will spilled his guts first.

"I didn't want to call and upset you while you were getting ready to leave the hospital, but I caught Alvin cheating a month ago."

"Shut up! I don't believe you. He was crazy about your extra-buff ass."

"That's what I thought too. I've been trying hard to deal with it and forgive him, but after finding out who it was with, I had to move on." He swallowed his drink down in one fast swig and then said, "He got a thing for softies, and I can never be that. Don't get me wrong. I love my flowers and soft scents, but I love my look and size too. I'm one of the sexiest men on this fucked-up soil, and I don't need to dress up like a woman to be gay. Honestly, I like when women break they necks to look at me. I get a thrill telling them that their jaws aren't strong enough to suck this big ole dick."

The male bartender who pretended he was drying and storing away glasses dropped his tray, and the glasses shattered on the floor at Will's words. I knew Will's mouth was coming next at the obvious eavesdropping, but I wasn't ready for how far he'd let his mouth go.

"Yes, handsome, I'm talking about the jaws of man. Come here for a second; let me get a good look at yours."

"Will!" I yelled in shock.

"Will what? If he weren't in my mouth, I wouldn't be trying to put my meat in his." He shrugged innocently, and the bartender dashed to the other side of the bar.

Two female waitresses were left to clean up his mess and take our orders for the rest of night from a booth sitting way in the back. At the hotel manager's request, we left our seats at the bar.

When it was my turn, I told Will how Trisha was my candy striper at the hospital and everything she said to me, even the part about Dre asking her to be a part of my life to help with my "rehabilitation," like I was a mental health patient. I told him everything except that we talked daily. At that moment, I decided that would stop too. I needed to give myself some space from her until I knew what I wanted for me.

"I'm selling your life story to one of them soap opera channels, girl! What the hell are you going to do?" Will asked, then killed another shot and flagged our waitress down to order another.

"I don't know."

A soap opera was exactly what my life had been since before my birth if you leave it up to Trisha. I didn't have any answers yet and didn't want to come up with any now. I just stared into the mirror behind Will's head that had some crazy-named beer company's logo on it and thought, *Damn, I really like how good I look.* Look at how easy it was for me to pull successful men like Royce Reed. I wasn't trying to do anything but eat, and that alone was enough to get his number. Stress, drama, and heartbreak were on a never-ending cycle in my life, and it would never stop. Soap operas stayed on for years, and the watchers grew old with the actors; however, I wasn't going to grow old with mine. That was it. It was a good run, and I've had enough. Maybe it was the liquor giving me the boldness, but why should I care about the cause? Fuck it; I was going to have fun in Washington. Kick my feet up and maybe even spread my legs a few times. I didn't have the details right then, but I'd come up with my game plan later. Not even Will was going to get me to deal with the shit within. Life is too short, and I'm going to live mine however I want, but what did I really want to do about Dre?

Chapter Three

Ready or Not

I was too drunk to head back home last night, so I crashed with Will. After breakfast, we said our goodbyes until later in the day. When I pulled into the driveway back at my house, it didn't surprise me to see Dre outside sitting on the trunk of my car looking pissed off. I had forgotten to call and tell him I wouldn't be coming home. The truth was, I didn't feel the need to. It did cross my mind to call as Will and I headed up to his room, but like I said before, the liquor made me bold, and I said, "Fuck it." I have never checked in with anyone but my daddy. Why start checking in now?

I parked, got out of the truck, handed Dre his keys, and walked into the house without saying a word to him. I was pissing him off, and he wanted me to know it by the way he was following me heavy-footed down the hallway to our bedroom.

"I know I can't be invisible because you handed me my keys. Your first day out of bed and your disrespectful ass leaves the house overnight and didn't think to pick up a phone to notify your man you wouldn't be coming home? Is that how you do it, Savannah?"

I wasn't in the mood to argue with him, so I started unpacking my bags with the clothes I had purchased the day before and putting them in their rightful spots.

Dre didn't like being ignored. I watched him out of the corner of my eye fold and unfold his arms, and then he took a seat on the edge of the bed and fumbled with his keys. I could tell he had an inner fight with his thoughts and that his thoughts had won because he stood to his feet and said, "From now on, you pick up a motherfucking phone and let me know you're safe. I don't give a fuck about who you're with; ain't nobody gon' protect you like me!" he said, and he stormed out the door making sure he slammed it. I'm glad he did leave the room, or he would have caught me smiling at his words.

It felt good to know he saw himself as my protector, but what did he feel he was protecting me from? Everybody I had revenge on was in jail except for Big Ant, and he may as well have been considered dead after shooting himself in the head. Alive, but living as a vegetable. How much harm could he cause me in that state?

I gave Dre a little over an hour to cool off before I made my way to join him on the couch. I didn't feel like talking with him; however, putting it off meant it would never get done. I was feeling uneasy about the can of worms I was opening, and it didn't help that Dre was sitting there in a muscle shirt and jeans looking sexier than ever. My pussy would convince my mind to work things out for some dick. It was going to be hard not to want to have sex, or so I thought.

"Look, Dre, I'm going to stay as calm as I can, but there are a few things that I don't like that we need to talk about." He lowered the volume on the television and faced me. I took that as the okay for me to continue. "I don't know where to start, how much you have been told, or already know but—"

He cut in and said, "Why don't you start from your reasoning behind giving up Sade, then fast-forward to why you felt the need to fuck all those niggas to get revenge?

Putting miles on my pussy like I was done with it. Yeah, all that shit you kicked up in Cali still bothers me like a bad dream. In the back of my mind, I feel like I'm chasing down a ho, and I've been trying to fight this feeling for the past two years now."

This nigga might need some therapy, I thought; yet, contrary to my belief, I didn't interrupt his couch session.

"Then you go and do that disrespectful shit last night."

"What disrespectful shit? I don't think our definition of the word is the same. Disrespectful would be hanging out with a straight man that I didn't know. I was with my best friend the entire night who you know is gay," I snapped.

"I don't know shit, and even your definition sounds like it came out of the D-section of Sluts-R-Us. When you're in a relationship, not calling or coming home is as disrespectful as it gets. How about you help me to understand your thought process because I'm going to tell you right now, that ho shit you used to do has to stop."

Who in the fuck does he think he's talking to like that? I thought. I knew he was mad about last night, but to go there with it after I was going to be as nice as I could be was low. Fuck it; I forgot Dre's mouth was just as deadly as mine. My mistake for trying to ease up.

"Damn, you are throwing punches below the belt? Why didn't you ask my mama why I did all the shit you want answers for since you went behind my back without asking me how I felt and invited her to come back into my life? You're so focused on trying to figure out if you're chasing down a ho when you need to be focusing on if and when I'm putting your ass outta my house, criminal. You have gotten too comfortable with thinking we will have a happily-ever-after when ain't shit in our relationship been happy except for your dick and my pussy. That love shit has you blind, Dre, but not me. It was five years ago when I felt you were my type; you ain't done shit to prove you still are my type yet. You feel more like a stalker to me than my man anyways, and you can kiss my ho-ish ass because I don't owe you shit—not even this conversation."

I tried to get up from the couch to get the hell out of the room before the shit got worse, but Dre pulled me back down. At first, I thought he was going to hit me from the look in his eyes, but then he opened his mouth to talk.

"Sit your ass back down, Savannah; you ain't getting off that easy! Talk shit and run, that's what you do best. You really good at using your mouth. It's way better than that pussy you keep passing out. You said you wanted to talk, and that's what the fuck we're going to do. Who do you think slept at the hospital in California with you every night after that bitch beat you into a coma, and you didn't even get a fingerprint on the ho? Huh? Who do you think had your ass transferred to one of the best cancer centers in the United States when we found out you had cervical cancer and probably got it from passing out all that midgrade dust between those chafing-ass thighs? That was me! The same nigga you had a baby by and threw our child away like yesterday's trash. I still don't understand how I missed the opportunity of being an honorable pallbearer at your funeral after I knocked you off for the way you did my daughter, but look at you. Alive, well, and breathing.

"Yeah, I did ask your mother to come back, thinking if you had a mama, maybe my daughter would have a mama in you. Guess I was wrong." He scooted a little closer to me and looked over his right shoulder as if something had temporarily caught his attention, and then continued to talk. "You said I ain't proved what we shared in a week is still worth sitting here by your side? I ain't proved I'm still your type yet? Are you serious? Your *stalker*? Ain't that some shit? Why is it so hard for you to accept that we're in love? I've had to accept the shit. I realized who my heart selected for me to love is out of my hands, and I'm trying to make the most of it. It's like you don't understand the shit, as if I'm speaking in a foreign language to your ass, but I think I know how to get you to comprehend. I got to treat you like a ho."

At that moment, Dre grabbed me by the hair on the back of my head and pulled me into him for a forced kiss. I dug my nails into his hand to try to get him to let go, but it wasn't working. Instead, he pulled my head back to extend my neck and started kissing me all over it. With his free hand, he groped my breasts and twisted my nipples until they stood erect.

"Sex is the way you like getting your points across, ain't it, baby? That's why you had to fuck them niggas in Cali so their baby mamas could understand you, right? Well, fuck me and make me understand you, but peep this shit here. I'm going to make love to you so that you can understand *me*."

He continued to kiss on my neck as he kept talking shit and tugging harder away on my hair. It was obvious Dre was high, and a quick glance at the coffee table proved I was right. There was a fourth of a weed-stuffed blunt in the ashtray with a lighter next to it.

"I bet this is the first time in your life that you've turned down some dick, huh? You see, baby, I'm breaking the ho in you already."

I started pounding on his chest with my fist to get him to move and screamed, "No, Dre, please stop!" But, it didn't seem to be bothering him at all.

Dre pushed his body in between my legs and pinned both of my arms to my sides with his hands, then said, "Stop fighting me and just feel it; you can't feel that, Savannah?"

I didn't dare say it out loud, but I was thinking *Feel what?* The only thing I could feel was Dre about 60 seconds away from raping me, and that was a feeling I had never felt before. Unlike the majority of women I knew or have met, I was lucky enough to say I had never been violated that way, but that was about to change. Dre had the upper half of my body pinned to the couch, and he was too big for me to free myself from his grasp, so I did as I was told and hoped it would be over soon. I sat there in silence and didn't fight back. I just stared Dre in his eyes like he was doing me and held back my tears. If I was going to be raped by my child's father, I wasn't going to give him the satisfaction of seeing me completely weak and helpless.

I couldn't believe he was about to force me into having sex with him, but why wouldn't he? I didn't know Dre. We shared an unbelievable week of great sex and conversations that matched, which caused us to fall in love. Sleeping with him didn't make me know him, and our conversations weren't personal enough to judge his character.

Dre made me feel safe and protected that week the same way a child predator does to lure in their victim. They get you to feel comfortable with them before they strike. What if Dre was a convicted rapist, or, even worse, a rapist who had never been caught and punished for his crimes against women? *What in hell have I gotten myself into now?* I thought, and the more I let my thoughts flow, the harder I searched Dre's eyes for the answer. I went deeper on the quest to find the answer, and instead of completing the journey, comfort found me. My breathing slowed down, and so did his. It was like we started breathing on the same rhythm, and that's when I felt what Dre was talking about.

I don't have a name for what I was feeling, but it was something. It was the same thick feeling that you get when you walk in a room full of tension; yet, it had a more positive and electrical vibe. I began craving his kiss, touch, and protection from the world. I was staring love in the eyes, and I knew it when I could see myself in his eyes. It wasn't my reflection bouncing off his pupils. It was a peek into his soul, and there I stood, broken, hurt, lost, and confused. I wanted him inside of me now, making love to me and fucking my wrongs away.

He brushed his nose from the cleavage my shirt revealed up to my mouth and slightly kissed my lips.

I puckered up and kissed him back.

In a soft tone, almost a whisper, he said, "Now, you feel it. I don't know what to call it, but if that isn't love, I don't know what is."

I didn't want to kill the mood, but I knew I needed to correct Dre. "It's not love, Dre. We lust for each other. Our bodies and minds lust to feel each other." I was lying and felt it, so I knew Dre would pick up on it too.

He kissed my lips again, then shook his head and said, "My dick lusts, and so does my mind about doing all types of shit to you in every position I can do it to you in, but not my heart nor my soul. If I were to give you this dick right now out of lust, I wouldn't be satisfied with the nut I caught because my heart and soul wouldn't be in it. I want you to have it all when I'm inside you, and I want you to give the same back. You really don't feel the same way? This feeling right here is stronger than lust."

I nodded yes. I knew exactly what he meant. I was in love with Dre, and in the hospital, I did admit it to him and my family. But that doesn't change the fact that I'm not ready to be a wife and a mother or to only have sex with one person for the rest of my life. I wouldn't allow myself to live in a fantasy. This is the real world, and you don't just map out a future with a stranger. I needed to get to know more about Dre and would try to do so, but I wasn't about to put my life on pause to give us a full try. I was just given a second chance to live and wasn't going to waste it trying to make us work. I'm going to make the most of it and live my life to the fullest. I refused to let love stand in the way.

Dre's grip loosened, and he started moving away from me like he read my mind. I was in the mood to have sex; my negative thoughts regarding our future hadn't changed the fact that I was sexually attracted to him.

"What are you doing, Dre? I want it, daddy."

He leaned back down and looked me in my eyes, then said, "Not like this, baby, and we have company." Then, the doorbell rang. How in the hell did he know the doorbell was about to ring? On his way to answer it, he turned around and said, "Grab that weed off the table and put it in our room on my side of the bed because I will be sleeping on it from now on. And, by the way, I love your new look, baby. When our company leaves, I'd love to fuck those curls up and put a little bit of this conditioner I'm shooting out in your hair and face."

I smiled to myself and did exactly as I was told.

There was more than company at the door; it was a reunion—one guest at a time. Mr. and Mrs. Jefferson, my daughter's foster parents, arrived first with my daughter, Sade. After two minutes of quick hugs and kisses, they went to the kitchen to get the food started, and Dre went to light the grill.

Sade followed me around like a shadow, asking question after question. My daughter was beautiful and very intelligent for a 4-year-old, but all the damn questions started getting on my nerves.

"But how did you get sick, Mama?"

"I don't know. You'd have to ask my doctor."

"Did you forget to wear a jacket when it was raining outside because Mrs. Jefferson said if I don't put on my raincoat, I'm going to get sick. Do you have a raincoat, Mama?"

"Yes, I have a raincoat, and I always wear it in the rain. The sickness I had isn't the same as a cold," I answered, trying not to let my irritation leak in the tone of my voice.

"What makes your sickness different than a cold?"

"My nose didn't run."

"Then where was the cold?"

I wanted to say in my pussy, so she'd get scared and run off. Instead, I said, "My ovaries were sick, and before you ask me what ovaries are, I want you to know that I don't know how to answer that question. You'll have to ask someone else, okay?"

"Okay. Can I ask you a different question?"

"No, you've already asked more than enough today. Save some for your next visit, okay?"

"Okay, Mama, but—"

"No buts. I said no!"

I wasn't trying to be mean, but it was time for her to help her other mother, Mrs. Jefferson, for a while. When the Jeffersons sent the letter saying that they decided to tell Sade they were not her parents but her godparents, and they wanted her to know she had a mother and father out there who loved her and still took care of her, but they were just too far away to see her, they set me up for moments like this. Answering the door was my excuse to get away.

Our next guest was Will, loud ass and all, and he came in talking shit.

"Did you get some yet? I don't know if I can spend another day with your evil ass until you get some. Your hormones are all over the place."

"If you're not going to give me some, then don't worry about if I got it yet." I said it loud enough to gain Dre's attention because I knew Will's response wouldn't melt away any doubt or questions Dre had about his sexuality.

"Give you what? Bitch, please, let's get something straight quick, and I'm not talking about my sexuality. If you want to take a ride on this train, you're going to have to undergo more than a hysterectomy and grow you a set of dangles. As a matter of fact, change the subject before you kill my appetite with thoughts of that soggy fish taco you've been feeding Dre. Ugh!"

"Fuck you!"

"No, thank you!" he said with a bow, and I saw the smirk on Dre's face that confirmed he heard what he needed never to question Will's sexuality again.

One of the cooks from the Jeffersons' restaurant that I didn't know came in, followed by my secretary and friend, Stephanie, who wouldn't shut up about how thick I had gotten and how good I looked with a weave.

"The hair and style fit your face. If I didn't know you, I'd think it was naturally yours. And look at that butt. It's swollen. You grew a donkey in your absence!" she chuckled. I'd give her an hour before she hints that she wants me to sleep with her again. If she does, I might take her up on her offer. I hadn't slept with her in over a year, and I can't lie and say I didn't miss it.

The last guests to arrive turned my stomach. It was my daddy and brother, Memphis. As soon as I opened the door, the entire conversation I had with Trisha came to mind. I could even smell her scent, which was a mix of lavender and peppermints.

"Hey, y'all."

I greeted them both with a fake hug and kiss and rushed back to Sade. I'd take her thousands of questions over talking to my daddy any day.

I didn't mean to take it out on Memphis; he was innocent, like me, in this, but I didn't want to slip and tell him she came back yet. I planned on telling him once I heard my father's side of the story.

I must have answered a few dozens of Sade's questions before I could no longer take it again, and then shipped her to her godfather, Will, outside by the pool, as I headed to talk to Dre at the grill.

"So, you invited Will and everybody over here for a welcome home barbecue for me, I see. You think you're slick, huh?"

Dre flipped the meat and said, "I *am* slick, just like I sent for Will to get you out of that bed and take you to go look good for daddy. I set that up and gave him the money to do it. I was tired of seeing my baby lying in that bed depressed. You're too fine to be ducking and dodging mirrors."

"Well, if I'm that fine when everyone leaves, can we pick up where you left off, Dre?" I tried to say it in my bedroom voice.

"Aww, baby, I told Sade she could stay the night with us tonight. I'm sorry."

I snapped before Dre could finish his thought. "That little girl asks too many questions. She can't stay here tonight, Dre. My nerves are too bad. She has been irritating the shit out of me since she got here. I'll go tell her she can't stay."

Before I could turn on my heels, Dre grabbed me by my arm and pulled me close to him. So, close I could smell the mouthwash he used.

"Aye, you need to watch your mouth! That little girl is our daughter, Savannah. I know this mothering thing is new to you, but you gon' have to learn to bite your tongue. Sade is staying tonight, and the three of us are going to watch a movie as a family, and when she falls asleep, I'm going to bring you outside and smoke a blunt with you by the pool. Then, I'll give you this dick, but you better be the best fucking mother you can be tonight. My daughter came here with a smile; she better leave tomorrow with one too!"

"Yes, sir! How could I object to that? Weed and some dick. I might make it through Sade's visit after all." I kissed Dre on the cheek and then headed back in the house to see if Mrs. Jefferson brought a peach cobbler with her, and, of course, she did.

"I made two, one for the guests and a smaller portion for you. I didn't think you'd want to share."

"I'm not sharing. I'm going to put this one up for later and help eat this other one," I said as I took them both out of her hand. I put mine in the refrigerator and grabbed the French vanilla ice cream to go with the other.

Call it greed or gluttony, but I cut myself a piece that almost covered the plate, scooped about a cup's worth of ice cream on top of it, and dug in. It was the best peach cobbler I had ever eaten, and, seeing that it was the only dessert I liked, I've had my share of not-so-good ones to be able to judge. Mrs. Jefferson made her peach cobbler from fresh peaches, not canned, like most places. That clumpy jelly taste that always sent those imposter peach cobblers heading to the trash wasn't a worry of mine when eating hers. She took her time and put love into it, and you could taste the love in each bite, even in her homemade crust.

"Look at all that peach cobbler you have on that plate. That's a damn shame," my daddy said with a chuckle. "It's funny that you've never really been around her, but you love peach cobbler just as much as your mama did. She could eat a whole one by herself in one sitting."

I had always hated when my daddy compared me to my mother, but this time, it ticked me off since her recent visit left me with a wide-open wound to my pride.

"Daddy, please don't compare me to her. Hell, I don't want you to ever bring her up in front of me again. She left us, Daddy. Why do you keep acting like she was this wonderful woman?"

"What in the hell is wrong with you? I say a few words about peach cobbler and your mama, and you say all *that?*" he asked, puzzled.

"I'm just saying, stop bringing her up like she's relevant or is a part of our lives. She left you and abandoned us. Her ass should be dead to you; yet, you talk like she's gone on deployment. Fuck her!"

My voice seemed to travel through the house and out the back door because Will came flying through the house, trying to get me to come outside with him. He knew any talk of my mother would send me into questioning my father's real past relationship with her.

"Savannah, I think your security-turned-chef is out there burning the meat. Help me help him so that we can help you. Now ain't the time for this, best friend."

"I'll be out there when I'm done handling this."

"It will be crispy black by then, and you know how—"

I hushed Will with my hand because I could tell my father wanted to respond to my question, and I couldn't wait to get this confrontation started.

"Do you have something you want to say, Daddy?"

"I just don't understand how can you hate your mother more than me, and you have never even met her. You don't know anything about the woman, but since she wasn't around, you made it okay for her to be the first name at the top of your people-to-hate list. That's my wife, and she's wrong for what she did to all of us, but there are a lot of things you do that remind me of her, including giving up Sade to live the life that's best for you and pushing that man outside away. I see you still have a lot of growing up to do, little girl, if you don't see yourself as the fruit that fell from that tree."

My daddy had the nerve to have anger in his voice when I asked him not to bring my mama back up in my presence.

"The fruit that fell from the tree? Is *that* how you see me?" I snickered before heading to the trash can to throw away my half-eaten peach cobbler, and Will ran straight out the back door to Dre knowing that it had reached the point where I was about to show all my ass. I watched Dre give the spatula to Memphis and tell Sade to stay with Stephanie, and then he and Will came into the house. Dre made sure to lock the door behind him, and that's when I went ahead and snapped.

"Your *wife?* Why don't you tell us all how you and your wife met or about the last conversation you had with your wife since we're talking about her? How about taking us step-by-step through this beautiful, long-distance marriage y'all have. Hell, I didn't realize you still considered yourself married to her after all these years of not seeing or hearing from her. How about telling us how this out of sight, out of mind nuptials works? I'm all ears!" I took a step closer to my father.

That's when Dre said, "This is a conversation you two should have in private, Savannah. Why don't y'all go talk in our bedroom about it? The rest of us don't need the entertainment."

I hesitated for a moment, thought about checking the shit out of Dre for crossing boundaries once again when it came to me and my parents, but he was right. If I had confronted him right then and there, our voices would have escalated, and Memphis would have gotten involved, so I led the way to my room. Once we got in there, my father started telling the same story he always told, which I know is a lie.

"I told you I was in a car accident and broke my arm. Your mother nursed me back to health. That's how we met, and you know I don't believe that I'm still married to your mama. I was talking fast like I always do. Why are you putting weight on my words, like they are causing you a burden, and asking questions you already know the answer to?"

Trying hard not to curse, I said, "Because you don't know how to answer the question honestly. I asked you how you met my mama, and you give me this fairy-tale shit that you've convinced me to believe, but the shit wasn't a fairy tale, was it? The truth is that you were drunk driving and caused an accident which killed two people. Two young kids at that, and my mama, I mean, Trisha, covered for you so you wouldn't spend life in prison like your father. Another secret you didn't bother telling us. Guess knowing that our granddaddy had been sitting on death row or died there wasn't any of our business either. I can understand your choice not to speak about your parents, so let's get back to my missing parent. So, Trisha saved you from jail, y'all fell in love, and then you found out she was a ho. A paid one at that. You got fed up with her and her johns' shit and banned her from seeing us ever again with a threat to turn yourself in for the murders and take her down with you. The fairy-tale part is missing in the truth, but I guess you added it to keep me from knowing that both of my parents ain't shit."

He turned around and backhanded me so fast I didn't get the chance to tell him how I knew. I lost my footing at the power in his hit but didn't fall. Fear sent me to take a seat on my bed, holding my face, and I was too scared to say anything else.

"Respect will get you far. You better learn that quickly. That's why everything around you crumbles. You don't respect nothing or nobody. Savannah made it out of the hood, got her education, and filled up the bank, so she thinks she can say whatever she wants to whoever she wants. I'll kill you before I let you think your money will allow you to disrespect me." He reached in his pocket, grabbed a cigarette, and lit it.

If he weren't so upset, I would have protested him smoking in my house, but I knew this was one of those times where I needed to keep my mouth closed.

Inhaling once, then exhaling, he reached under my vanity and grabbed the bench. He sat down with his body facing mine. "You said all of that and disrespected me to make yourself feel better about your fucked-up life. Did it work? Do you feel better about yourself, Savannah?"

I didn't respond.

He took another puff while saying, "So, Trisha is back and in Washington."

I didn't know if he was asking a question or making a statement, but I answered, "Yes."

"Isn't that some funny shit!" He smoked the whole cigarette, then lit another and shook his head.

Staring at my daddy like I had never done before made me realize that stress had overtaken his handsomeness. Don't get me wrong, my father is a very handsome man with looks that would make you think he was Billy D. Williams's twin brother, but there was hurt, pain, and a lot of stress in his features. His once hazel eyes were now trimmed in a yellowish-white cataract film and sank into his skull with dark rings and bags around them protruding. I knew raising two kids and taking care of his mother caused a lot of the aged look on his face, but I wouldn't say Trisha and cigarette smoking hadn't played their parts too. My daddy's back now curved into a perfect "C" from all the weight he carried on his shoulders over the years. He was once six foot tall, but with his curved spine, I'd say he was now five foot ten. It was hard to stomach looking at the physical effects of stress on his body; yet, if Trisha hadn't told me his story, I wouldn't have noticed it.

"Savannah, do you know why I like and respect Dre the way I do?"

I shook my head.

"It's because he reminds me of me; in love with a woman who will never love him as much as she loves herself. No matter what Dre does or how much he shows you he loves you, it will never be enough. I stand by what I said to you in the other room. You're just like your mother, regardless of whether you like it. You're greedy, got to have your cake and eat it too, with us like ice cream on the side, melting away, and y'all don't give a damn. Couldn't pay you to care, and you and your mama both love money. Y'all find power in it instead of seeing the power in the love of a real man."

He took another puff on his cigarette, then looked at it like it wasn't strong enough. Yet, he puffed on it again before saying, "I sat there like a fool and let your mother walk over me like a throw rug. She would get out of the bed with me at night to hop in bed with another man. Not because he could make love to her better than I could, but because he had more money than I could give her. I would follow her to her destination, stay out there the entire night just staring at and debating if I should kick in the door, whoop on the man, and take my wife back home with me. I always decided against it because I didn't want to piss her off in fear she'd decide to leave me for good. I'd question her about her whereabouts the next day and listen to her lie with the prettiest smile on her face. I'd swallow my pride and anger to meet her smile with one of my own as another piece of my heart broke. Everybody she slept with wasn't a customer of hers, but I pretended to believe they all were. It made it easier for me to handle if I looked at her infidelity as work-related incidents." He took a break to smoke without his words interrupting the peace he found in the cigarette.

Now I knew why he smoked. Tobacco had become his only friend to get through the shit he was going through with Trisha. I didn't say a word, nor did I make a move while waiting for him to continue.

"My wife came home all the time with other men's scents on her after she claimed to have been at work the whole day. I would just close my nose to it and treat her like my queen. If that's what my wife wanted, I wouldn't stand in the way, even if it meant killing a part of me."

My father had always seemed to be a strong man, but now I know he is weak when it comes to women, or, should I say, when it comes to Trisha. Maybe that's why he was so hard on me. He was in fear of me controlling him like his mother and wife had done.

"If Trisha was free to do whatever she wanted, as you just confessed to me, why was she not given another chance? It doesn't sound like she could do anything worse than what she had been doing." It took everything in me to ask him that question. I even managed to mumble it out in a sweet and innocent voice.

His response was, "Your mother didn't have any more chances. I took a little bit of everything from her, but one thing I wasn't going to let her do was neglect you and your brother. That I wouldn't stand for. The day I knew it was time to get her out of y'all's lives was when she left the two of you alone for a few hours to go on a date. We fell out badly, but she promised never to do it again, so I let it go and told myself to keep a closer eye on her. I should have never given her that second chance because, less than 24 hours later, I watched her jump in a cab and leave y'all alone again. I broke into the house and took y'all back to my mother's house. When we got there, your uncle Steve told me she had called and said for someone to go pick y'all up, and the key to the door was in the mailbox. She had something very important come up and had to leave town again."

As he told the story, I watched the mixed emotions flash across his face. They went from anger to hurt, and then, for a brief second, I could see love in his eyes, but it quickly faded back into anger as he continued. "Your mother didn't pick up a telephone for four years, and, when she did, she was asking for a divorce and full custody of you and Memphis so she could start her life all over with a real man who had a backbone and could buy her the mountains if she wanted them. That's when I made my threat to turn us both in to the police if she didn't get out of y'all's life. She never sent divorce papers, and I was sure she would, so we never divorced. The sad part about it all is I still love your mother after all she has done. When the divorce papers never came in the mail, I thought she had changed her mind and would come back to all of us. Even as I sat there watching you get your master's degree, I was sure she was sitting somewhere in the crowd waiting to approach us when it was over to say she was back and that she was proud of you." He shook his head, and I got a view of the tears he was holding back as he said, "The effect she has on me, I can't explain, and you have that same effect on Dre."

I didn't realize I had been crying until the salty taste of my tears had gotten to me. Now I know why my daddy never remarried or dated. After all that Trisha had done to him, he was still in love and devoted to her. This was touching . . . yet completely stupid of him in my eyes. Why in the hell would he stop living his life knowing that she had moved on and was living her life?

"I know you don't understand my choices or feelings, and this is one of those things you aren't meant to. I just pray you change your ways, not just for Dre's sake, but so you won't grow old like your mother without knowing how to give love back. I don't know if you plan on having a relationship with her, but let me warn you from my experience. Your mother is far from a fool, and nothing comes first in her life but money, which you have a lot of. I'm not bragging, but if she came back because she wanted love, she would have reached out to me first. I'm broke, the same way I was when she left, and if she's done her research, then she knows everything I have was inherited or given to me. That house went up in flames, and that insurance check I got was because you paid for me to have it. I haven't spent a dime of that money and only cashed the check because it was timed and dated. That money is in a suitcase I don't think about because my successful daughter gives me more than I need. If she knows, like I'm sure she does, that you have money, she's coming to get some of it, and she doesn't care what she must do to get it, either. I'm actually shocked that she was bold enough to confess to you who she was without you having to pay her for the information first."

"She didn't make me pay for it, but I could tell she wanted to." I spilled my guts to him about our first encounter, starting with Trisha being the nurse who sat with me every night while I was in the hospital and the purchaser of Sade's cake. I told him about Hurricane Katrina moving her back to California and how she met up with Dre at the condo. "I have no intention on rekindling shit with her. She's always been dead to me, and that's how she's always going to be to me."

I wanted my father to know that I meant it. There wasn't a need for him to warn me about her. We would never get that close for me to give her a dime. She ruined my life in ways that can never be fixed; her return wasn't welcomed at all.

"I know, baby girl, I know!"

We hugged, and he apologized for slapping me. He asked me not to mention her return to Memphis because he was sure Memphis would welcome her back with open arms.

"Your brother," my daddy said, in a loving, parental voice, "isn't the sharpest knife in the drawer and is influenced easily. If she gets into his head, he will turn on all of us." My daddy made sure to say one more thing before we walked out of my bedroom door and that was, "Be careful, Savannah. I don't trust her at all. She came back for more than reuniting with her kids; I'm sure of it!"

"*She* needs to be careful, Daddy, not me," I countered. "The only money passing between her and me is the back child support she owes me from not being there."

We joined the rest of the group like everything was perfectly fine, and no one, not even Will, questioned our conversation.

"Memphis, can I ask you something?" I waited for hours to catch him by himself. With the mess that happened earlier, I was sure my father would have found it strange that I requested for Memphis to step away with me. The house was occupied with a loud, rowdy spade game, and I went to relax from the day in the Jacuzzi. About ten minutes later, he joined me.

"As long as it doesn't require me to get out of this hot tub made in heaven, you can ask me whatever you want," he chuckled and then closed his eyes and lay his head back.

"Do you remember anything about Mama? I know you were young and all—"

"Aw, shit, what's up, sis? You've never asked me anything about her before, so don't lie and say you were 'just wondering.'"

I needed to make up a lie. Never in a million years did I think he'd catch on that fast. I was used to thinking he was slow. He must have grown out of some of it during the years we didn't talk.

"You better not laugh at me, or I'll come over there and beat you."

"Man, you ain't beating nothing but cancer, sis. Go ahead. I'll try not to laugh."

"I have these dreams. I know they aren't real, though, sometimes, I wish they were. It's you, me, and Mama sitting in the food court in the mall eating and laughing. I can never hear our conversation, but I know we're having a good time. The way I see her in my dreams is an older version of myself with a body I would pay for at her age. No one looks hurt, and then Daddy walks up, and we get up and leave her sitting there alone."

"Damn, you should write movies. Nah, I don't remember nothing about her, and for Daddy's sake, you might not want to tell him about your dreams. You don't want to come off unappreciative."

"So you believe him. You think whatever happened between him and Mama is her fault?" I prayed he'd say yeah, and then we could be done with it.

"Of course not. Daddy's a square. I don't have dreams, but I have a vision of Mama. She looks like you, and she's a combination of both of our cool. She comes back and gives me some lame-ass ex-party girl reason for leaving—"

"And do you believe? Do you forgive her?"

"Hell yeah, I do. She's our mama, and we only get one. Good or bad, that's how the cookie crumbles, and if she asked to be forgiven, I would. I prayed she'd come home for years, and stopped believing in God when she didn't. If she rolled up on me, I'd get baptized and be the first nigga in church every Sunday."

"What about the way she abandoned us and the way she did Daddy? She broke his heart. He's probably a square because of what he went through with her," I snapped.

"Isn't that the same shit you're doing to Dre and Sade? If she came back, I'd think you'd be the first to forgive her, seeing that you're her mini-me. Sade is visiting you. I would have loved to have been able to visit Mama. I'm sure if I had her in my life, everything would be the way it should. Don't let anger blind you. There ain't shit like a mama's love, sis."

"Yeah, if that's true, then I'll pass on it."

"Why are you getting mad? Did Mama reach out to you?"

Memphis was on my side of the Jacuzzi faster than I could blink.

"No, boy. I just thought if there were anybody I could talk to about my dreams, it would be you. I thought you would have felt the same hurt like me."

"Sorry, little sis, but I don't."

I didn't say another word. I'm glad to see that my father knows his son.

Chapter Four

In the Wrong Company

"Why are you sitting there staring at the wall like you just lost your best friend?" Dre asked as he grabbed his pajamas out of the drawer.

"Why does it matter? Even if I did lose my best friend, you wouldn't care."

"Shit, depending on which one of your best friends it was, that might be the truth," he joked. "But seriously, baby, what's wrong?" he asked, taking a seat on the edge of the bed.

"Still no dick, that's what's wrong." Dre stood up faster than a courtroom full of people when the judge walked in and started making his way to the door. "I'm staring at the wall trying to figure out if you still like pussy, or if you decided to take a vow of celibacy."

"Stop playing with me," he laughed. "You know I want some of my pussy, but baby girl is here, and you know how she loves being up under me. I got you when she leaves tomorrow night. Can't have you questioning if I love that pussy or not."

Dre was smooth but must have thought I was one of these clueless chicks out here that he could play games with and not see the toying. I'm guessing he thought that I hadn't noticed how he went out of his way to avoid having sex with me. He has allowed Sade to spend the night with us every weekend since the cookout, and that was over a month ago. He conveniently allows her to sleep in the bed with us or went and joined her in her bed because she is "scared to sleep in her room by herself," which he quotes all the damn time.

That "sleep in the bed with your parents" shit might work for her at the Jeffersons' house because they're old and probably ain't fucked in years, but it wasn't going to work here. Besides, why couldn't we have sex while she was here anyway? I know how to be quiet or to bite the pillow when I need to. I waited until I was sure he was in the shower to call her in our room.

"Sade, come here, baby."

I sang my request which is something I saw on a television show. From what I could tell, the method worked on kids by making them excited before letting them down.

"Yes, Mama."

"I got you something today. It's big, pink, and has a trunk. What do you think it is?"

I assumed the child would answer incorrectly once, maybe twice, but her imagination had taken over, and after naming every car, animal, and food she knew, I gave her the answer.

"No, it's Miss Elephant, and she wants to be your friend. Here."

I handed the oversized stuffed animal to her, and she hugged and kissed it while thanking me a hundred times.

"Mama, is her name Miss Elephant because I think her name should be Sparkle? When I hug her tight, her eyes sparkle bright, and Miss Elephant could be any girl elephant name. She's too special to be called that."

"Baby, you can name her whatever you like, and that's not all her eyes can do. Look." I flipped the switch on the elephant's stomach, and her eyes lit up. "Sparkle's eyes light up when you hug her, but if you turn that switch on, her eyes become a nightlight that doesn't turn off unless you cut the switch off or her batteries die. Do you know what a nightlight is for?"

"Yes, it's for reading bedtime stories in the dark while my Pop-pop is asleep. When I sleep in the middle, we have to use it so we won't wake him up reading our books."

"Don't you think that you're getting too big to sleep in the bed with them? I mean, damn, you're almost half their height, and you have your own room to sleep in."

"Ooh, Mama, you said a no-no word," she said, shaking her head at me.

"Damn isn't a no-no word, but sleeping in bed with your parents is a no-no. You don't want to keep doing a no-no, do you?"

She lowered her head like she had the conversation of sleeping alone before which I was hoping she had. I loved the Jeffersons, but their old asses needed to stop babying her and let her nerve-wracking little ass grow up some.

"No, ma'am, but there's scary things that live in the dark. I saw them on TV, movies, and some books talk about them."

"That's why Sparkle's eyes won't let it get dark in your room. Now, go tell your daddy you have a new friend when he gets out of the shower and that you want to sleep by yourself tonight."

"But I don't want to sleep by myself. I want to sleep in bed with you and Daddy. Sparkle can sleep in bed with us too."

"Why do you want to sleep in bed with us now that you have Sparkle?" I snapped.

"Because I love you."

That's when that mother instinct is supposed to kick in and make you feel warm and cozy inside, but the only thing that wanted to feel warm and cozy rested between my thighs.

"That's nice, baby, but if you want to show me that you really love me, you will go tell your daddy you don't want to sleep with us tonight and give Sparkle a true chance. I need some alone time with Daddy tonight to talk about Mommy and Daddy stuff. You said that you love me, right?"

She lowered her head until I could see her crown.

"Yes, Mama, I love you, and I'm going to tell Daddy that I'm a big girl and want to sleep by myself so that you can have a Mama and Daddy talk tonight."

"Good, but don't tell Daddy that you know about the Mama and Daddy talk. Kids aren't supposed to know about it, okay?"

"Okay, Mama. I love you."

"I love you too, baby, and Sparkle."

Sade left the room with a smile on her face, and one grew on mine. To say everyone thought I didn't have what it took to be a good mother, I was able to break my daughter's fear of the dark with a stuffed animal and a few words. Feeling great, I grabbed my black teddy out of the drawer and headed to the bathroom in our bedroom. Before my panties could hit the floor, Dre was busting through the door.

"What did you say to my daughter, Savannah?"

"You mean *our* daughter!"

"Cut the fucking semantics and answer the question!"

Dre was pissed, and I guess his use of the word semantics was supposed to make me tuck my tail between my legs, but I couldn't, because my tail was in his pants, and he was refusing to give me any of it.

"I got our daughter a stuffed animal, so she can beat her fear of the dark, unlike the rest of these enablers that keep telling her it's okay, and letting her crawl in the bed with them."

"I didn't ask you what you bought her or why. I asked about the words you used. Fuck you say to her?"

"It seems like you already know what I said to her, Daddy of the Year. How about you just skip the semantics and get to the point. Go ahead and tell me what I can and can't say to my child."

I cut off the shower and stood there with my panties around my ankles, completely naked. We were seconds away from an argument, but my body didn't care. My nipples hardened from wanting attention from his mean ass. He smelled like soap and deodorant, and that was enough to make me crave him. My nipples were hard, pointed, and screaming "hi." They were tired of me trying to tell him better than they could show him that we both missed his touch, but he ignored them the same way he had done me.

"You know what? Don't worry about it. Just don't say shit to my daughter without clearing it through me first. Fuck what you can and can't say. As of this moment right here, don't say shit until I give you that privilege back." He reached out and grabbed my nipple and squeezed it. "How is my dick supposed to get and stay hard when you show no love to what I love the most? I'm horny as fuck too. I should snatch this motherfucking nipple off and take it with me to give me something to suck on while I beat my dick in the middle of the night to one of those whack-ass flicks you got. That's why your ass is cut off. You keep doing my princess foul!" He slammed the door and left me there horny and mad.

Dre claimed that was the reason he cut me off, but it was just a lie he used as his excuse because Monday through Friday weren't any better. Before Sade started coming over frequently, he had already cut me off. During the week, he wakes up and leaves the house before I think about opening my eyes to start the day,

and comes home in the middle of the night from working at the restaurant with Mr. and Mrs. Jefferson, which
doesn't close till 11:00 p.m. Plus, he works an additional
two or three hours cleaning and performing next-day
preparations. When he gets home, he crashes on the
couch not to wake me up . . . or so that's what he tells
me his reason for not getting in the bed is. Now that I'm
back at work, our schedules are opposite, which helps
his little plan of cutting me off without him putting any
effort into it. If he were smarter, he'd know that a good
dick session would make me treat our daughter better.

Whatever the true reason was for him cutting me off, I
don't know, but I do know one thing, and that is, I'm fed
up with masturbating. I can't even make myself orgasm
knowing I have a man in the house. While he's in there
getting it in with his hand, my fingers are in the room getting carpet burn. I've tried to have a few sips of wine, puffs
on my herbs to put myself in the mood with my new vibra-
tor I named Howard, but the shit never works. I start off
pretending I'm having sex with anyone but Dre; then my
imaginary lover seems to fade away, and there I go, fucking myself and screaming for Dre to go in deeper. What
the hell is wrong with my imagination? I can't even control
who I'm fucking in my mind.

Dre put that Mandingo, African warrior, send-you-
home-walking-funny stroke on me, and that's what is
making it hard for me to want anything else. He leaves
me feeling as if I have Parkinson's disease, shaking
uncontrollably for hours after he's been doing his business in me.

If Dre thought he could cut me off from his lovemaking
to get me to do as he said, he was dead wrong. It was just
the opposite for me; good dick will make me do as I'm
told, and cutting me off is what sent me to rebel. I knew
it was going to be hard to find a lover on Dre's level, and

that was fine; all that meant was that I needed to lower my expectations. I wasn't going to settle for just any ole thing either. My pussy wouldn't allow that, but a "B" was still a passing grade in my book. I'll just have to settle for Mr. Second Place, AKA some good runner-up dick. The only problem I faced was how I would get some dick on the side without Dre's detective-playing ass finding out, or these love feelings messing it up.

Every time I developed a good plan, that ugly feeling called love would scratch it out of mind. Love was the ugliest feeling I've ever had to deal with. It presented itself like it was the most beautiful thing you could find in this world, and once you did, it showed you all the ugly shit that came with it, like being concerned with feelings and restricting you to be faithful. Some people think that's the beauty of love, but I'm not one of them. Love left me feeling out of control, and for a control freak like me, it was detrimental for any plans I wanted to put into motion. I fell in love with Dre, not what the normal definition of love is considered, but still, that version of love was standing in the way and blocking my judgment. However, it hadn't blinded me yet, and I wasn't going to let it.

I meant what I said to myself at the bar with Will. I'm going to live my life to the fullest, and that included protectively sleeping with whomever it was I wanted to sleep with, whenever I wanted to. I wasn't going to stop until Dre found a way to convince me to marry him, or he gave up on us and moved on.

I decided that when I clock out of work, I'm going back to Jackie's to get my hair done. Then, day one of my manhunt will begin. It was Monday; I promised myself to have a potential sex partner by Thursday, at the latest.

I wasn't going to keep begging Dre for shit. He would get tired of pleasuring himself and come back to me begging. He had too many morals to cheat, so I knew that I wasn't going to have to worry about him. He did lie to his son's mother to spend time with me, but that was completely different. She was setting him up with the police so that he could be arrested. Who would be faithful to a tramp like that? Plus, I'm sure she didn't have anything on me. Dre saw this full package and couldn't help himself; I completely understand.

I only had one thing to do, and that is to keep my shit tight. One sloppy move or not enough planning, and Dre would be all over me like a K9 that picked up a scent. Just to make sure it was well planned out, I took out a pen and paper from my desk to map out my plan. I wasn't going to keep my notes as a keepsake, especially after getting shot, because of the diary my secretary kept of my dirt. I just wanted to jot them down to get a visual.

- *Don't have sex with anyone more than once. Even if the sex is awesome, there is no doubling back.*
- *Linger around places near the airport in hopes to find men who are in town only for business or a convention and who reside elsewhere; anywhere but the state of Washington.*
- *Don't be greedy with it. Only step out on Dre when needed. That goes for giving up the tail and receiving head. Either form is a great release.*
- *No matter what, no one can ever know. Dre is a lot smarter than the people around me. Slippery lips will be the end of me.*

I read over my list and had to laugh at myself. This nigga had me so paranoid I felt the need to come up with a game plan just to cheat. If he were doing his job in the first place, I wouldn't have had to take it to this extreme. It was simple . . . What one man won't fuck, there's always a nigga around that will.

"Take care of the house or home, and you won't have to worry about your woman," or something along those lines. I never knew what the exact lyrics were, nor can I think of the artist's name who sang the song, but I used to hear it all the time on the radio. It was like he was preaching to the brothers. I'll have to look into it so I can play it at the house as a hint to Dre to handle his business. I snatched the list from my desk and put it in the shredder as Stephanie entered my office without knocking.

"Need me to do anything before I go to lunch?" she asked like she didn't just barge in.

I should have checked her about just walking into my office without knocking, but I let it go. "Yes, I do, as a matter of fact. It shouldn't take you more than ten minutes."

I had Stephanie call the hotel where Will stayed while he was in town to see if they had any conference rooms available for rental this week. Of course, I didn't tell her nosy ass why I needed the information. I was still pissed off at her for keeping a journal with my whole plot of revenge in it and then leaving it out in the open where it could be read, which is exactly what happened. If Keisha's sister, Ericka, wouldn't have read that damn journal, my plot wouldn't have been exposed, and I wouldn't have gotten shot by the main bitch I went after revenge on. I know I agreed that it was just a part of Karma's plan to get back at me, but fuck Stephanie. I lost everything, and she didn't lose shit. If she wasn't the best at this job and I had time to train another, she'd be gone. Writing shit down was worse than running your mouth. Nobody would dedicate all that time into tracking lies in a book. If I were Ericka, I would have believed the shit I had read too.

"Wait, I don't get it. What's wrong with the conference rooms we have here? Why pay a hotel money when we have our own, free of charge? That's why you and I chose this location, to set up shop. The senior conference room is huge and even has a door that allows entrance to the breakroom. Are we having guests and require additional space or something?"

She asked question after question and never knew when to shut the fuck up. She gave me the lie to use right back on her.

"Exactly; I was thinking of having an open house and inviting a few potential clients that have emailed us regarding our services. I'm typing up a potential explanation of events that will go along with the invitation I send out. No hotel, no event, no invitation, and no need to waste my time creating this. Do you see the importance of what I asked of you, or do you have more unnecessary questions to ask?"

She shook her head and seemed satisfied with the lie. She returned in thirty minutes with the bad news that all the hotel's conference rooms were booked. As usual, she went above the call of duty and found an available space at one in the same area. I thanked her, took that information, and ran with it. I was going to walk the halls in that hotel, post up at the bar, and depending on what the subject matter of conferences was, I might even attend a few. Somebody was going to be single in that building, and, even better, they weren't going to live in Washington. I could bet on it.

After my hair was finished, I went and sat at the steak house. It was dry as hell. I got a few looks, but no one approached, and I wasn't desperate enough yet to make the first move. The same thing happened when I went back Tuesday night. On Wednesday, I decided to be bold and sit at the bar in the hotel's lobby and watch the game.

The bar was packed, and besides the waitresses, I was the only woman there. I kept looking at the maroon-cushioned, silver-legged bar stool that was empty next to me and hoped that "Mr. One-Night Stand" would be the only person to occupy it.

I was somewhere around being done with my second drink and half a drink away from being tipsy when I saw the bar stool being pulled out. I was nowhere near happy by its new occupant. It was Trisha, dressed up, with makeup on, smelling like a million bucks, and looking like an older version of me.

"I wasn't sure if that was you sitting here alone or not, so I came for a closer look. I should have known it was you. Who else looks as good as me in the boring-ass state of Washington?" She laughed longer than anyone should laugh at their joke and sat down as if we had planned to meet here for drinks. She held up her index finger and asked the bartender for another round for us both.

"Look, Trisha, I'm meeting someone here, and I'm not in the mood for another fucked-up trip down memory lane, so, if you don't mind moving, I'd appreciate it."

Her smile didn't crack. She wore it like it had been drawn on her face. If there was anyone around us watching our every move, she didn't want them to think foul of our union.

"Savannah, let's have a drink, only one, in honor of you beating cancer and being a successful woman that doesn't need or take shit from anyone. Treat me like I'm just someone from the old neighborhood you haven't seen in years. I'm done trying with you. When our daily calls stopped, I washed my hands of it." She leaned in a little closer as if her next words were a secret password that she didn't want to be revealed, and then said, "This is real Versace I'm wearing, by the way. I got it while visiting Milan, and I chose tonight to wear it because I'm in a great mood. I don't want that depressing shit from our past ruining my night, if you know what I mean." She waved at two men across the room who had their eyes locked on us.

"Wow, I didn't know prostitution was legal in Italy. How do you say 'ho' in Italian or 'trifling-ass bitch'? I'm in the mood to learn something new," I asked as I smiled at the men and joined her in waving at them.

"I don't know how to say it, beautiful, but the next time you decide to sleep with all your friends' baby daddies, you should look into it. Wait, never mind. They were all broke and raggedy. You'd have to come out of your pocket to get them to Italy to sleep with them. Guess you'll have to continue to enjoy prostituting in the United States for free. From what I've heard, you don't mind slanging your pussy around for free."

Trisha's smile didn't fade. It actually grew. She enjoyed our word fights, and secretly, I did too.

"Yes, let's have another round on her, bartender. She's world-renowned," I said loud enough for everyone to hear me, including the men, and then I whispered to her, "or, at least her pussy is. I guess there isn't anything wrong with having one drink, as long as the past isn't the topic of conversation. I'm in the presence of an international pussy bestseller."

"How could the past be the topic of conversation when we don't have one? I made sure of that," she declared in a voice that held more joy than my liking.

"Yes, you did, and I can't thank you enough for removing all the weak and slutty women out of my life. I'm sure if my daddy were here, he'd thank you for doing the same for him."

"I doubt it," she laughed. "If your father were here, he'd be paying for our drinks and still going home by himself."

"Watch what you say about my daddy, bitch."

"Bitch, that wasn't even scrapping the surface to what I could say about him."

We finished our drinks and quickly began saying our fake goodbyes when the waitress handed us two more.

"That's from those two guys sitting over there; they said if you're free, they would like the two of you to join them, and, ladies, they been tipping good all night. I did my recon work, and they're entertainment agents here all week for a conference from New York. I'm sure y'all know tricks when you see 'em."

I immediately glanced over my shoulder. There were three tables between us, and the lights in the room were dimmed to give off a relaxing feel, but if I had to sum them up, they met my criteria. Both were in their forties, which was fine with me, and the fact they were from out of town put the sprinkles on my sundae. The only thing left to find out is which of them would bring me the nuts? I thanked the waitress for the information and excused myself from Trisha, explaining that I was going to take them up on their offer.

"I believe we were both invited, Savannah, and you have a man waiting on you at home; I'll tell them you had to run or something," Trisha said, facing me with a sinister smile, awaiting my response, and I knew I was going to make her day with it.

"Then I guess we are going over there together, Trisha."

"As two single women? I'm only asking for clarification. Wouldn't want to slip and say the wrong thing."

I held my hand out in front of me and then answered, "Do you see a ring on either one of our fingers, and you're the only one of us who is legally married."

She stared at me with an investigative look and then we stood up and made our way to the table. Both men stood to greet us with a hand shake and a name exchange.

I noticed they both had on wedding bands, which meant they were only looking for fun, which was right up my alley. I didn't pay attention to names and didn't want to know them. It was another rule I live by. If you go into knowing it's nothing, then make sure you leave the way you came . . . with nothing. I don't need to know your name, your occupation, or what you do for fun. Save it for girlfriend or wife trivia night. I don't want to know your name, so if I'm ever questioned about knowing Mike, Jack, John, or James, I can honestly say, in my own defense, I don't know them and wouldn't be lying at all. Yes, sometimes the truth is the biggest lie you can tell. Sorry, insecure ladies with strong reasons to be insecure, but I've never been an informant. If you don't know if your man is cheating on you, it's not my place to tell you. Mike who? Jack, from where? John, I don't know any, and, James, never heard of him.

I don't team up with women to play "Get that nigga." You know, the game where the wife/girlfriend tries to get their men's/husbands' lover to help catch him in a lie? Where the women act like best friends to make him sweat, knowing that they both are wondering who he really enjoyed fucking the most? Did she suck him better? Is she freakier than me, and they always want to know who looks better? That's what little girls do, and that kiddie shit isn't for me. Give him something that will make him keep his ass at home or end up watching him roam like a stray dog, fucking every bitch in heat that comes his way. If he's a dog that likes roaming anyway, there isn't a thing you can do to stop him except willingly hand him over to a new owner.

I normally would feel right at home in the presence of male company, but with Trisha sitting there, I couldn't get in my groove. However, Trisha had no problem getting into hers.

"What brings you two handsome men to Washington?" she asked, sparking the conversation first.

Exactly as the waitress informed us, the men were in town until the morning for a three-day conference they had been attending. They both confessed to being married at the opening of our union and in need of some company from a Northwestern woman. The four of us started out in a group conversation, but it didn't last long. We went into individual conversations with the man that was sitting closest to us.

I tried to tune out Trisha's conversation, but the lies she was telling kept pulling me into it. I overheard her telling her new friend we were sisters.

"Yes, that's my little sister, and she is very spoiled. Of course, it was my parents' fault, but I wouldn't lie and say I didn't play a huge part in it. I just wanted her to have the world and know she deserved it, but I kind of think it backfired. We can't get her married off because her expectations are very high. I take the blame for them too, seeing I've never made it to the altar."

She told her new friend lie after lie. I was now the 30-year-old baby out of all her siblings who were too many to keep up with. Then she lied and said she was 45 years old and in town celebrating my new promotion with me. The lies flowed out of her mouth like water flowed downstream after a rainfall. She was good at it; nothing about her demeanor gave the impression that she wasn't honest, and that made me uncomfortable.

I hoped she wasn't paying my conversation any attention because when I was asked if I was single by the man entertaining me, I said, "Yes, and I'm not looking." There wasn't a need for me to lie since he had confessed to being married, but I didn't lie intentionally. That was just an automatic answer I was used to giving. I could have told him I had someone waiting for me at home, but who was he to know my business?

Trisha and her friend had another round of drinks with no sign of calling it a night, and the time was now eight o'clock. It was getting late, and if I was going to get some dick tonight, I had to get away from Trisha. I stood and said, "I really should be heading home now; it was a pleasure meeting you both."

Trisha looked shocked that I was excusing myself to head home. She even asked, "Why so soon?" I explained that I had a company to run in the morning and needed the rest. The gentleman I had been conversing with said he would walk me to my car. When we got under the lights near the elevator, I got an opportunity to get a good look at him. He was on the short side, about five foot eight, 180 pounds, a solidly built frame, with some sexy-ass lips. His face wasn't all that, and, if it wasn't for his lips, he probably wouldn't get any action. The two cell phones he had clipped to his waistband and $1,000 shoes on his feet are what caught my attention. I could tell his shoes were authentic because they were hand sewn; I like a man who has class.

"I would really like to stay in your company longer, but I don't do the double-dating thing with my sister. I just can't let my hair down in her company, if you know what I mean. Hopefully, the next time you're in town, you will look me up." I bit my bottom lip and gave him a look that said, *I'm not ready to go.*

"If you don't mind coming up to my room, we can continue there. I can have a bottle sent up to us, and food, if you're hungry."

I agreed and dashed on to the elevator before Trisha or her new friend could see me. As soon as the bottle arrived at the room, I swallowed my first glass and pressed fast-forward on this sexcapade.

"So, tell me about yourself, Savannah; you never said what it was you do for a living."

I made my way from the table over to his bed and slid off my heels. I started unbuttoning my blouse as I answered his question.

"A lot of this and a little of that, but we both know you don't really care about what it is that I do. You have a wife waiting for you back in New York. You're looking for some fun, and I haven't been pleased by a man in over seven months. Let's cut the bullshit and get straight to it."

I intended to make him think I was drunk. Dog-ass niggas seemed to think that drunken pussy equaled easy pussy, and I was in the mood for some easy dick. I was nowhere near drunk, but if he thought I was, I was going to say whatever it was that I wished to say. Now that I had my blouse completely off, he could see my full double-D-sized breasts fighting with my bra to stay in it. I popped the snaps on the back and let my babies run free like dogs off their leash.

Whatever his name was just stood there, rubbing his dick through his pants and staring at my breasts like he was watching a stripper at a strip club. I played with my hardened nipples for a while and then asked, "Are you going to stay over there all night or come get what you really brought me up here for?"

He rushed me like he was sacking a quarterback for the first time on a televised game. I hit the bed with a thud, and my breasts bounced forward and brushed his face.

"I love when a woman is confident and not afraid to say what she wants," he said as he took my nipple into his mouth and started sucking on one, then the other.

"Umm, and I like when a man knows how to shut the fuck up and get him a treat without killing it with words. Stop sucking them like that and lick my nipples hard."

He responded to my demand by licking my nipples slow and hard to a rhythm that only he could hear. He ran his semirough hands over my stomach moving south.

Rubbing on the cat in between my legs, through my pants, I purred, and he showed he liked hearing me moan as he took a handful to pet while continuing to suck on my nipples. It felt good to be touched this way again. His licking and sucking my breasts made me come in the palm of his hand.

Feeling the moisture, he unbuttoned my pants and pulled them off me with a tug. That shit turned me off. I wasn't against being roughed around, but he had been gentle until then. The new roughness he was showing had caught me off guard. I understood it was going to be a fuck, but damn, show a little tenderness, why don't you?

"I was hoping I would get you out of those pants so you can try this dick on for size. Bring your pretty ass here!"

He then proceeded to drag me by my legs to the edge of the bed and got on his knees. He was one of those dudes that were into panties and left my thong to feed the freak inside of him. Slightly pushing it over to the right side, he spread my legs apart and licked my old come until new juices joined it.

Pretending to be drunk wasn't a good idea after all. He was too rough with me. He wasn't trying to pleasure me with the head he was giving me; he was only focused on making sure I was wet enough for his penetration, and when I heard him spit and spread it with his tongue around my back door, I had to show him I was sober.

"Damn, is this the best head you have to offer? I should go. You aren't as good in bed as I thought you would be."

I started scooting up on the bed toward the headboard to get away from him, hoping it would make him promise to do better and beg me to stay. My plan worked like a charm.

"Hold on, baby; I just got excited. I ain't had a woman as beautiful as you since high school. Let me give it to you the right way."

I sat there for a minute, pretending to be stuck in a debate, and then I made my way back down the bed slowly and opened my legs. I wanted him to see that my pussy was as pretty as my face, and he needed to treat her with care. I slid my thong to the side and traced my pussy from the clit, around the opening and back to where I started from with my index finger.

"She's pretty too, isn't she?" I purred my words.

"She's the prettiest I've ever seen, baby. That pussy right there is breathtaking."

Damn, did he say breathtaking? I thought while making a mental note to recalculate her value as he got closer and placed a finger on top of mine and traced my prettiness with me. After completing our finger travels twice, he pushed my thong aside and went to work the right way. He used a lot of pressure from his lips while licking and sucking my erect clit. The shit felt wonderful. This man knew what he was doing when he stuck his head between your thighs, and I was thankful that he forced his wife to share her experience with me.

"Now, *that's* how you treat this pussy, sir. That tongue on this pretty pussy is breathtaking." I was moaning loudly and licking my lips as if I could taste the same juices he tasted. There was a part of me that wished his wife was here to join in and dub it a threesome. I'd lick her clit right in appreciation for the head she allowed her husband to give me.

When I closed my eyes, my breathing changed, and my imagination shifted the encounter. It was Dre in between my legs giving me head, and there was no need for a third party to join in. The head I was receiving was still a little bit rougher than I remembered Dre's oral pleasure being; yet, it still satisfied me. I started rocking my hips back and forth to fucking his tongue until my juices dripped down his chin like Dre always urged me to do. I felt my blood boil and a chill shot up my spine at the same time. I was about to orgasm all over this man's face. I started rocking my hips faster, so my pearl could slap against his tongue and make that water collision sound I liked hearing. The sound caused my orgasm to be more electrifying and longer in time than the orgasms that went unheard. I wished that I could have squirted, just to get the illusion of coming all over his face, just like the male porno stars did their women costars as they attempted to catch it with their mouths. I wanted to paint his nasty little face in my warmth and watch him lick it clean. For kicks, I'd try to shoot a little in his eyes to ensure he knew I didn't give a shit about him. The freakier my thoughts grew, the more I could feel the explosion building up. I grabbed him by the back of his head and pushed his face as deep as I could in my pussy, hoping he'd suffocate in my come because I had reached the point where I could no longer hold it back.

To my disappointment, it was a regular orgasm. Nothing spectacular at all. No shaking, eyes rolling in the back of their sockets, or talking in tongues. He fucked that up trying to force me to preserve my nut. When I could no longer prevent releasing the pressure that I let build up, he stopped licking my spot and started kissing my inner thigh. I tried to grab his head to put his mouth back on my hot spot, but it was already too late.

"Why the fuck did you stop?" I cried out.

"I wasn't ready for you to come yet, baby."

"You weren't ready for me to come yet?" I asked, emphasizing the words *you* and *me*.

"Yeah, sexy. I had some other things I wanted to do to you first. I didn't know if you were one of those one-orgasm-and-quit kind of women. I'm sorry."

"Hell yeah, you're sorry."

That's how I was brought back to the reality that I wasn't with Dre. Dre would've sped his tongue motions up in an attempt to make me have multiple orgasms instead of just the one expected. He would have locked on to my thighs so that I couldn't run away from his tongue during those back-to-back orgasms. Dre wouldn't have given two fucks or a pocket full of care if I was a one-orgasm chick, and if I were, he would have made sure that I wasn't one after he was done with me. The orgasms Dre caused me to have with his tongue were far from regular, and I was greatly disappointed.

Once I had finished releasing that watered-down orgasm, I was done with this second-rate lover. He hadn't won the right to advance to penetration, but that didn't stop him from trying. He pulled down his pants and started waving his little chunky dick in my face, expecting me to return the favor. I immediately turned my head, so it wouldn't touch my lips and said, "I don't do all that."

"I can teach you," he countered.

"And I can bite you," I followed with a nonchalant shrug.

He seemed disappointed but grabbed my legs instead. Folding me in half with my knees just inches away from my shoulders, he positioned himself to go in me raw.

"What are you doing? You need to put a condom on."

He kept moving his body in closer as if my words went in one ear and out the other. He didn't take me seriously until I started pushing him away with my hands and pressing my feet into his stomach.

"Baby, I know when to pull out, and I'm faithful to my wife; this is my first time ever stepping out on her. Trust me; you can't catch nothing 'cause I don't have anything to give you."

How many times have I heard both of those tired-ass lines? My favorite lines were, "I know my shit, I know when to pull out" and "You're the only person I'm fucking. What do we need a condom for—unless you're fucking somebody else?" I even had one nigga tell me, "I just went to the doctor, and they told me I was grade-A, baby." I mean, damn, how stupid do I look? It was easy as hell to set Tyrone and his boys up in Cali to sleep with those prostitutes. They even decided on their own to sleep with them all night and unprotected. Everybody walked away with HIV and no telling what else.

I wasn't naive enough to sleep with anyone raw again. I wasn't worried about getting pregnant; I didn't have eggs to fertilize anymore. I was worried about Karma. What goes around comes back around. I helped HIV make its rounds, and like a boomerang, it was destined to try to make its way back to me. Yes, I do know that I can contract the virus from getting head from him too, but I'm relying on all the alcohol he drank killing any and everything he might have had floating around in his mouth and into my open womb.

"I don't have any condoms, and I'm not fucking you without one!" I kicked my legs out, which caused him to stumble backward. I had condoms in my purse, but after the lame shit he said to match the lame head he had given me, I wasn't going to give him the pleasure of using them. I had already decided after the head he had given me, we weren't going any further, and I meant it. I looked in his eyes and said, "Then, I guess we are done here."

I stood up before he could lay me back down. I walked to his restroom, wet a towel, and freshened up. When I returned to get my pants from the bedroom floor he was sitting on the edge of the bed, pants off, johnson in hand, which was chunky but wasn't that big, might I add. He was working with six inches maybe on a good day, but today, he was holding four and a half and stroking it like he was trying to save its life.

"If you can't suck it, at least put your spit on it and jack it for me, baby. I'll pay you."

I took one more look at his manhood and walked out of the door laughing. If I wasn't in a rush to get the hell away from him and his mini-me, I would have gone back and responded to the "bitch" he called me as I walked out of his room. Instead, I entered the elevator with a smile on my face.

As the elevator's doors were closing, the hotel room that was facing the elevator's doors flew open, and there stood Trisha in the doorway, looking at me with a smile. She winked her eye at me, waved like she was in a Miss America pageant, and then I disappeared behind the elevator's closing doors. *Damn,* I thought. I had been caught.

I ran to my car so I could pull off before she took the next elevator flight down. I jammed the keys in the ignition to crank up my car, and the starter wouldn't turn over. It was like everything in the car was dead. I must have tried ten times, and nothing happened. I sat in my car for fifteen minutes hoping not to see Trisha emerge from the hotel's entrance. I finally went back inside to see if someone could give me a jump. Every man in the building volunteered to give me a jump, but it took almost another fifteen minutes to find a willing body that owned jumper cables to do it.

I didn't want to call Dre for help for obvious reasons or use my roadside assistance because I didn't feel this was a big enough emergency, and I'd have to wait another hour or so for a tow truck. Before jumping my car, the gentleman I found sitting at the bar who said he had cables asked me to try to crank it so he could get an idea of what was going on with it. When I turned the key, my car cranked with no delays. I thanked him for his time and drove off. I was going to have to ask Dre to take it to be checked out again. That was weird.

It was only 10:30 p.m. Dre didn't get off until 11:00 and still wasn't expected to walk in until 1:00 or 2:00 a.m. This gave me time to shower and be in a deep sleep before he ever made it home, but not tonight. Dre's truck was parked, and he was sitting on the couch, smoking a blunt and watching the highlights from tonight's game. I headed straight to my bedroom to shower and get ready for bed, but Dre was in the mood to talk.

"Hey, baby, you must have had a long-ass day."

How would he know if I had a long day or not? He was never home when I got there anyway. I knew it would be easier just to agree.

"Yes, I didn't leave the office until six o'clock; then I went and had my hair retouched before grabbing me something to eat. I would have been home sooner, but my car wouldn't start. I had to get a jump, and that took hours. Can you take it back to the shop this weekend?"

I took a few more steps in the direction of the bedroom, but Dre wanted a full conversation.

"Hold on, baby, come here. I know you're tired. Just give me a few minutes. Yeah, I'll take your car to get looked at Saturday morning. Is everything else okay? You never break down your day for me like that; you gave me a timeline and all. What's up?"

Damn, I hate talking when I'm nervous. I always seem to snitch on myself. I sat on the couch not too far away from him; I didn't want it to seem like I was keeping my distance, but I could smell that guy's cologne on me. It wasn't a bad smell. I just didn't want to explain why I was wearing some man's cologne.

"Everything is fine; it's just been a long-ass day, Dre, and I'm ready to shower and get in bed so I can end it. I gave you the timeline to stop you from questioning me like Sade. She had to get that nosy shit from one of us."

"Is that right?" He handed me his blunt, and I took a hit. When I went to take another puff, Dre reached in between my legs with his hands, and I jumped and dropped the blunt on the living room's hard wood floor. We both reached for the blunt at the same time and almost bumped heads. "Calm down, baby; I was just hoping tonight would be that night. I ain't touched my pussy in years. I need some," he begged and then grabbed a handful of Miss Breathtaking. He adjusted his hand until he held most of her in his palm and then said, "And you already got it wet for me; I can feel it through your pants. What have you been thinking about? I hope this dick."

Dre was high as hell. His eyes were low, and I could barely tell they were open. I was glad he wanted some. It was my turn to say no and cut him off. I stood up, regained ownership of my pussy, handed him his blunt, and then headed to the room.

"Not tonight, Dre; I'm way too tired. I thought about your dick on the way here, but the thrill is gone now. I'm too tired to get my pussy wet again."

"Too tired? Come on, baby, you know you're never too tired to let me get it," he begged.

"That statement you made was based on the fling we had years ago, and I'm tired tonight Maybe this weekend or something." I snapped my fingers like a memory came to mind, "Oh, you'll have Sade again this weekend, I almost forgot. No fucking, licking, or sucking when the princess is in the building. Well, maybe the next time I'm not tired, and you're kid free."

He cut me off.

"You mean, the next time our daughter isn't here spending time with us."

"I thought that's what I said, but you seem to know what I meant. Yes, the next time our daughter isn't here, we'll finish what you started all those weeks ago. I just hope it's as good as we both remember it being. A lot can change in a few years, like what we think we like."

I giggled, and Dre mumbled something underneath his breath, but the words he truly wanted me to hear, he managed to say clearly.

"I'm sure whenever I give you this dick, it will be better than what you remember or have been getting, and nice cologne. I used to have a bottle of that cheap shit when I couldn't afford the real thing," he said, and then laughed hysterically. I closed my bedroom door and locked it. There was no way I was going to respond to that.

Chapter Five

Getting My Feet Wet

Dre had been acting funny since the night I came in smelling like cheap cologne. His daily routine had changed from me never seeing him to seeing him too much. He was working fewer hours at the restaurant, spending less time with Sade, and replacing it with working out and staying high as hell all the time at home. If this is what having a man living under your roof feels like, I don't need it.

It didn't bother me that he was wasn't working. From what I was told, Dre was volunteering at the restaurant. Mr. Jefferson had tried to pay him numerous times, but Dre always declined, saying it was the least he could do since they were helping raise his daughter.

I knew money wasn't an issue for Dre. He had confessed to me while I was in the hospital that he had grossed well over a million dollars in his three years of street hustling before he did his jail time. I don't believe jail rehabilitated him, so I'm sure he started or had a new hustle once he got out. I wasn't in his pockets and didn't care how much money he had stashed as long as he paid all of the bills on time. Nothing in life is free, that includes in-house pussy. As a matter of fact, in-house pussy deserves a larger payout than price-tag pussy in the streets. In-house pussy has more expectations to live up to like accepting when you know he hasn't washed his ass. In-house pussy should be paid for those nights he rolls over and slides his dick in you after he spent the day talking shit to you or when he isn't talking to you at all but still pulls his dick out for you to suck. There should be a bonus given for sucking dick when he's on his man period. Don't nobody have time for mood-swing dick. My rule is, any man who's been under my roof for over fifteen days has to be paying bills, taking out the trash, and fixing everything that comes up broken, and that isn't up for debate or negotiable. Hell, after fifteen days, you can't put their asses out without an eviction notice so, you might as well treat them like a tenant. The law does.

It didn't look right for me to be dressed in business suits every day headed to work with my man at home lying around the house, but I didn't care about the look. It didn't bother me that he wasn't doing shit while I was on the clock, nor the fact that Sade had been put on the back burner. What I did care about was Dre having three- and four-day workouts without showering and kept my living room with a musty onion-smelling odor. Sweaty balls, arms, and ass crack had replaced the clean linen scent the house once had. I paid $18,000 for my Eye Candy furniture and living room décor. That might have been on the low end for some, but I was trying to create the perfect Feng shui, not Funk-Kay!

Dre smelled like sweaty gym socks, mixed with corn chips and loud shit breath from all that smoking without brushing his teeth. The man's breath made me scared to talk to him and made me fear him wanting to talk to me. I was sure he had to smell it and taste the shit that filled his mouth by now. It wasn't newborn shit you'd find in a diaper swirling in his saliva. It was bum shit. It smelled like a bum took a shit in his mouth and wiped his ass with Dre's tongue.

I couldn't understand why he decided to let himself go. He always kept his hygiene up before now. Whatever was eating him up inside had him smelling and looking bad on the outside. His dreads needed retwisting. He had thick patches of facial hair growing in, and he stopped dressing. White wife beaters and gray sweatpants became his new uniform.

The new grunge look he decided to wear was a complete turnoff. If he ever thought about getting in between my legs again, he needed to take a bleach bath.

The worst part about it is that everyone knows you can smell yourself before anyone else can, which meant Dre just didn't give a fuck. I had seen and smelled enough of his new "I don't give a fuck" attitude to know my choice to creep around was a good decision. Dre's beautiful muscular build, although funky, made you feel protected when you lay in his arms, and ironically, he was weak. I wasn't going to spend forever with a weak-ass man, and I couldn't. I'm too strong of a woman for that shit. He needed to deal with his problems, and if that was too much for his sensitivity to handle, then he needed to pretend like he didn't have any.

He needed to get back to being the man he normally was and without a pep talk from me. I'm his woman, or in his eyes, his future wife, and it should embarrass him to regain his strength in his supposedly weaker half. Furthermore, I'm not trying to be my man's strength, and if being the strength for your husband when he's weak is a part of the marriage contract, then I might as well marry a woman. I'm not signing up to spend forever with a bitch born with a dick.

Maybe Dre would do best talking with a man about whatever it was he was going through. Before I head to the steak house tonight, I'll ask my daddy to stop by to try to talk some sense into him while I'm gone and to keep him occupied while I do me.

Dre wasn't about to kill my mood with all his moping around. I waited all week for tonight, and I knew it was going to be my night. I had gotten good with keeping up with the conventions coming in town and even signed up for email updates which gave a brief description of what each convention was about. The emails also gave information about what the groups holding them stood for. It was easy to pick and choose which ones had the best chances of having black men in attendance.

I decided to take my chances at a two-day seminar called "Be Your Own Boss." The company was known for uplifting and empowering the common man, at least that's what the description said.

My daddy agreed to come over and have a man-to-man with Dre. He didn't say much when I described Dre's behavior to him, but how deeply he pulled on his cigarette said enough. He'd already accused me of treating Dre similar to the way that Trisha treated him, which ultimately meant whatever Dre was going through was somehow my fault. I hurried up and thanked him for agreeing to the talk and got off the phone.

I went into the funk factory that used to be my living room. "Hey, baby, I was talking to Stephanie at work about us spending some time, and we came up with this whole girl's weekend idea. I'll be staying at Stephanie's until Sunday afternoon. It's going to be like going on a retreat," I laughed, and he just stared at me.

"Uh-huh."

"What does that mean?"

No matter what I had to say to Dre recently, I received no type of verbal response. Always strange looks or grunts. Dre had turned into a caveman right before my eyes, and only fire excited him because he lit his blunt. He didn't answer; he only stared.

"Why are you just sitting there staring at me like that?" I inquired, and he shrugged. "Then stop it. The shit is weird, and I don't like it."

Dre looked deeper into my eyes like the eye contact was supposed to do something to me, and once he saw it hadn't, he broke the contact and shrugged again. I couldn't wait for my daddy to pull up so I could get the hell away from his funky ass. I grabbed my purse and overnight bag and walked out of the house when I heard my daddy pull up. I tried to tell Dre bye, but again, all I got was a head nod and a look.

"Savannah, I think you should stay and talk with us. Maybe you should hear what's going on with Dre too," Dad said, voicing his opinion once he got out of his car. I badly wanted to look my daddy in his eyes and say, "Fuck Dre" in a coldhearted tone so he'd know that I meant it. Whatever Dre was going through, he needed to work out without me, and I wasn't wavering from that belief.

I tried days ago to figure out what it could be on my own, but the only thing that came to mind was that he was spending too much time with Sade and felt guilty about not having his son with him. Maybe spending time with our daughter caused him to miss his son, Andre Jr., and sent him to spiral into depression over it. I don't know, but I reminded my daddy why I asked him to come over in the first place.

"No, Daddy. Dre needs to talk with a man. That's why I called you. I'm not about to let him cry on my shoulder. I'm not carrying no nigga's tears for him. Oh, and when y'all talk, please let him know that the weak shit he's doing is pushing me away rapidly, and he needs to bathe. I can't take any more of his funk. Here is twenty dollars to get his ass some deodorant and some extra strength mouthwash!"

"I know I raised you better than this, Savannah!"

"Um, no, you didn't! I love you, and thanks again."

I was in my car backing out of the driveway before my daddy could say anything else. I wasn't about to sit and debate with him today. I needed to stick to my schedule.

Next on my schedule was to call Stephanie and come up with a lie to keep her from calling me or popping up at my house over the next 24 hours. I couldn't tell her I just needed to get away because she would invite me to stay with her. The words came to me as soon as she answered the phone.

"Hey, Stephanie, I told Dre and my family that I would be staying with you until tomorrow afternoon so that they wouldn't worry about me. The truth is, my mother asked if I could come and stay with her and try to work things out. I don't know why I agreed to it, but I did. Please don't tell anyone."

I took a deep breath like the words that came out of my mouth killed me to say it. I even started crying and sniffling.

"I got you, Savannah. Stay strong, Mommy, and if you need to get away from her, you are more than welcomed to come here. I'll be praying for you."

Stephanie needed to be praying I find some good dick and not waste a good prayer on me and Trisha's relationship. I reminded her not to call the house looking for me, and if she should run into anyone, to say that I was at her house.

"Of course, you know I got you, but why wouldn't you tell Dre?"

"Dre isn't my best friend. I only have two of those, you and Will, and y'all both know it. I'll tell Dre when the time is right, and right now, it isn't. I haven't decided if I want a mother or not yet. It's too complicated and confusing to bring other people's opinions into it."

I wrapped up the phone call and pulled into my new favorite spot in Seattle, Washington, the hotel. I checked into my room, showered, and got dressed to impress.

I loved the way my ass looked in jeans, so I threw on a pair of stone-washed jeans with designs stitched into the pockets to draw attention to my butt.

Since the weather had started changing from summer to fall, it was a little chilly out, so I put on a white, sheer blouse and a bloodred satin bra with heels to match the bloodred designs on my back pockets.

I sprayed a thin layer of perfume in between my breasts to give a sweet green apple smell to my body and left the top two buttons open for a peek at my twin girls. For added affect, I pinned my hair up with strands of curls falling from my updo and threw on a pair of reading glasses to give off a sexy teacher look. I was now ready to attack my prey.

There were men galore when I walked into the steak house. I doubled-checked the door just to make sure it didn't say men's night.

I was offered to be seated at a table, but I requested the bar. Not even ten minutes had passed before I was being hit on. I knew I shouldn't be picky, but with all the men in here tonight, why not? I had turned down two men, and they took the news pretty well, but the next man was persistent.

"Suga, your marital status doesn't mean much to me. I think I care more about flies on cow shit than who you claim to belong to. Whether you're single, taken, or confused are your problems, not mine. I'm a man who gets what he wants, by whatever it takes to get it. I'm comfortable with using force when required."

He was an overweight Texan with a heavy drawl. I didn't mind a fat man; some chunky niggas were well kept, but not this one. He had steak sauce all over his face and a two-sizes-too-small shirt. His cowboy boots were leaning to the side like his feet were too wide to fit in them, and I could see his stomach sitting on his lap covering his pants zipper completely. The irony in it was there wasn't any doubt in my mind that he was filthy rich, but I couldn't get past the fact that he was filthy and probably beat a few rape cases in his day thanks to his money.

I tried everything to get his fat ass up. I told him I was saving the seat for someone; he said in a voice that resembled snoring and being out of breath, "I'll move when that special someone that you didn't give a title to arrives."

"It's my husband." I told him to remind him of the lie I told him about being happily married again, and he said, "I don't care that you're married. I didn't care when you first made the announcement, nor do I care this time around. I did give it a quick thought, but the thought didn't linger long enough for me to care. I don't believe I've ever called your husband a friend or relative and, hell, if I did, I'd just give him a few dollars to temporarily divorce you until I've done my business with you and my britches are back on my waist."

"Your britches can't fit around your waist, you cocky fat piece of shit, and you need to move!" I protested, and he just looked at me, smiled, and ordered his next drink.

"Let me get another adios motherfucker and get this doll next to me whatever it is that she'd like to drink. Make it strong."

Just when I started feeling hopeless, a tap on my shoulder saved the day. I turned around and was greeted by Royce's words.

"Well, look who we have here."

I jumped out of the chair and hugged Royce and whispered in his ear, "Please get me away from this porker. He doesn't understand the words 'I'm not interested.'"

He grabbed my hand while looking at the Texan and said, "Our table is ready now, baby. Tell your friend good night."

My farewell was one word long. "Bye." Then I joined Royce at a table in the back of the restaurant until I watched Big and Sloppy leave.

"Thank you, Royce. I was dying over there. Well, I guess I'll be going. I don't want to hold up any more of your time."

Surprisingly, Royce said, "You're not holding up my time, Savannah. Why don't you stay and have a meal with me? My treat."

I didn't plan on eating at the steak house; I hadn't included food on my schedule. I took Royce up on his offer to feed me and all three of the drinks he ordered me after we were done eating. I was honestly enjoying being in his company. His conversation was interesting, and his sense of humor was to my liking. If he didn't have me laughing, I was relaxing with a smile on my face.

Royce told me during our conversation that he had been staying at one of the hotels in the area that offered extended stays because he couldn't muscle up the courage to sleep in his house after his ex-wife had moved out.

"It feels empty in there since the love is gone. It almost feels like I'm sleeping in a morgue, and I refuse to be the lifeless undertaker. Once everything is final, I'm going to sell it and get a condo."

"Why a condo?"

"It's suitable for a lawyer, and it's my lifestyle now. I'm done chasing that big house, wife, and kids dream someone brainwashed us into thinking we want. All I want now is peace."

We kept the conversation flowing, and he mentioned that he was a regular at every restaurant and bar in the area and that the building at the end of the road was where he practices law. I deduced from our lengthy chat that Royce hadn't left this street in months besides heading downtown for court.

"So, that's your definition of peace?" I asked.

"No, it's not my definition, but it's the only option I have right now to get it."

For some odd reason, I couldn't see Royce as weak. He had his shit together unlike Dre; he just wanted a new beginning free of ties and memories of his ex. I admired him for his strength which made him a lot sexier to me than my first opinion of him.

"What are you doing once you leave here? You look nice, which I'm sure you always do, but you look like you're headed to a night on the town," he said.

I had no clue what I'd do once we went our separate ways. He had thrown me off course, and now, I wanted my next move to include him.

"I did want to get out, but that feeling didn't last long," I said with a giggle. "I don't know what I'll get into now. I guess I'll head back to my hotel and drink a little more before falling asleep. Would you like to join me?"

His response was not what I expected or wanted to hear.

"That's very tempting, but I think I'm going to pass up on that offer. Maybe the next time the wind blows you my way I'll be up for a visit." He pulled a pen out of his pocket, wrote his room's telephone number down on a napkin, and handed it to me. "Give me a call once you get settled. I'll be up for a while watching *Martin* reruns."

Slightly upset, I accepted his number with no intention of calling him. I thanked him for the meal and then headed back to my car, which wouldn't start again. Dre told me he had the problem fixed, but apparently, it wasn't. I didn't feel like fighting with the car tonight. I'd call Dre tomorrow after lunch and tell him that it wouldn't crank up. I went back into the restaurant and requested to speak with management. The owner appeared, and I asked her if I could leave my car in their parking lot overnight until I could have it towed, and she said, yes.

The steak house was in walking distance to the hotel I was staying in, so I started walking in that direction. I knew if I had asked Royce for a ride, he would have given me one, but I wanted to enjoy the fresh air, and these thunder thighs I now owned needed the exercise.

Once I made it to the hotel, I passed the lobby and the elevators and headed straight to the bar.

"Let me guess, a Cranberry vodka with one piece of ice, right?" the bartender that Will attacked with his sexuality asked, and feeling slightly embarrassed, I nodded.

"That's the look of a lady who's embarrassed about her friend's actions. No worries, beautiful, I'm over it. I knew sooner or later I'd get hit with some gay shit looking this good. I just didn't think that I'd walk away with my freedom afterward. What's a pretty lady like yourself doing sitting at the bar alone?"

"Trying to have a drink in peace, but loser after loser keeps approaching me. They've been shooting these lousy pickup lines at me as if I were desperate. It's like, either they are stuck in the 1990s, or they are gay and haven't realized it yet. I wish my friend were here. He always knows exactly what to say to run the pests off. Did that answer your question?"

I paid for my drink although he insisted that it was on the house. My words were directed at him for thinking it would be okay to make a dry threat about losing his freedom behind Will flirting with him. Once he got the message that he had fucked up with any flirting session he planned on having with me, I sipped on my drink slowly and checked out the scenery. There was a lot of potential in the room; however, the urge to find a man for the night had been lost. All I wanted to do now was spend more time talking with Royce and getting to know him. He was great company. I knew this was breaking one of the rules I jotted down seeing that he lived in town, but what could a little friendly telephone conversation hurt?

I went up to my hotel room, showered, ordered a bottle of wine, and talked to Royce on the phone for a little over an hour. Our telephone conversation picked up right where our conversation at the steak house left off, except we were both tipsier. Before the next hour went by, Royce had made his way to my hotel room and was now sitting on the bed with me having a face-to-face conversation.

Thirty minutes after that, I was on my back with my legs suspended in the air being pleasured by Royce's deep strokes.

"Keep your hands right there," I demanded as he tightened his grip around my neck.

The transition from talk to strokes started surprisingly with a kiss. Kissing wasn't my claim to fame nor would it be the reason I'd earn a spot in anybody I've dated book of life. That sweet and simple form of affection has always been a no-no for me because kissing meant way more to me than sex. There was a connection to the soul that kissing caused which made it unbearable to follow up with just a meaningless fuck. It paved the way for lovemaking, and that's exactly what we had done. We made love without any true feelings to back it. It was my fault because I reached in to kiss him first, while he was talking. I could tell my kiss had caught him by surprise; yet, he welcomed it by kissing me back.

"I'll keep my hands where I want to keep them, you hear me?" he whispered the words in my ear and softly shook me before saying, "Let me handle this."

We kissed for five minutes, and when kissing was no longer enough, I gave Royce permission to do as he pleased. No matter what move he made, he kept his lips on me. The only change in his flow was the location he planted each kiss. Somehow, smoothly, he managed to keep his lips pressed against mine as he embarked on his mission of undressing me. We were lip-locked as he removed my blouse, bra, and cuffed my breasts. He was a breast man, and his dick poked me through our pants to acknowledge that fact. When it came time to remove my pants, he released the hold on my lips and dragged the kiss down my chin, jaw, neck, and continued down to my left shoulder blade. He lingered in the area quite awhile, and the kisses he planted softened until they went unnoticeable. The sound of his lips clasping together quickly only to release and repeat the movement is what made me aware that he hadn't terminated his kiss. I took a peek to see if I could find the motivating factor that brought on the change in speed as his kisses reached my breasts.

"Yes!"

I moaned adding sound to our noiseless encounter, and there went my jeans down to my ankles. He pulled them down in the same soft manner in which he kissed each of my hardened nipples. He had been standing, but that too changed at the sound of my moan. He released my neck.

"Say it again."

"Yes, Royce, yes!"

He made his way to his knees again, dragging his lips in the same direction. Now that he was on bended knee, my navel and stomach became the new recipient of his kisses and not wanting to seem inactive, I stepped out of my jeans.

It was becoming a sex scene you'd find in the pages of a romance novel, but when he approached my thong, it seemed like he was having second thoughts.

"Damn," Royce said, putting his hands on both sides of my hips with his fingertips under the lace of my thong and froze. He stayed in that stance frozen for about a minute, with his head resting on my lower stomach as I rubbed his head.

"What's wrong? I'm ready for you to listen to my moans."

He kissed me across the rim of my thong and then pulled them down in one quick motion without answering me. I leaned forward, and we started kissing again. As we kissed, he removed his clothes and whispered to me, "Savannah, please tell me you have protection, baby."

Before I answered, I grabbed his rock-hard penis and measured it with my hands. It took three squeezes to make it down his shaft to the base. Without a ruler, I would say he had eight inches to give. I glanced up at the ceiling to say, "Thank you, Jesus" and nodded my head to answer his question. I got up to hand him the condoms out of my purse and made my way back to the bed.

"You know once I open and apply this condom, there's no turning back, and I'm going to want to open plenty more with you, right?"

"Right, and I'm going to want you to open plenty more," I lied in fear that telling him I have a one-fuck rule would make him want to preserve it for a later date.

"I'm serious. I know you heard my friend say some not-so-good things about my sex life, but I promise you, it's by choice. I'm not trying to brag, but I win in court and the bedroom. You're going to want more."

I laughed and then said, "Good. That means we will have the same problem." I lay back and spread my legs so that he could get a good look at her. Holding the hood of my shaved meat that sat over my clit to ensure I set his sight on me, I asked, "Isn't she breathtaking?"

"I don't know, but I'll let you know shortly."

We found pleasure in each other until the wee hours of the morning and then fell asleep, entangled in each other's limbs.

At 6:00 a.m., he was up dressing to head back to his hotel to prepare for church. He asked me to join him, but, of course, I declined.

"I'm getting myself together one step at a time. I'm not saying I'll never join you; I'm just saying not today."

"I understand. I'll pray for you anyway."

"Please do. Lord knows I'll need it if Dre ever finds out that I'm fucking you," I mumbled.

"I'm sorry, sweetheart, I couldn't hear you," he said, taking a step closer.

"I said, please do, Pray to the Lord every day."

"I will, every day."

He hugged me, and then we kissed like he was leaving for war. Holding hands, I went with him down to the lobby to say our goodbyes again and then headed to the free fitness center to work out. Royce sent a text before I could get on the treadmill.

"Yes, she's breathtaking, but so are you."

I did a sixty-minute workout, showered, dressed, and then checked out of the hotel around ten o'clock. When I walked back to the steak house to check on my car, I could see there was something under my windshield wiper. If it was a ticket, I was going to be pissed. I snatched the folded piece of paper off my window and read it. It was a handwritten letter from Trisha.

Hey, Savannah,

You must be staying in the neighborhood too. I noticed your car stayed parked here overnight. I just wanted to give you a chance to reconsider giving our relationship a new start. I'm planning my departure and need to know ASAP, because money

is becoming an issue for me, and as you said, you're in a position to give. Give me a call. My number is (253) 555-1113.
    Love,
    Trisha

I ripped the letter up and jumped in the car, which started without a jump. I didn't know what was wrong with the car, but I knew Dre's mechanics didn't know what they were doing, so I decided I take it to the dealership to be looked at myself as soon as I had some extra time.

On my way home, I kept wondering what Trisha meant in her letter by saying she needed to know ASAP because money was becoming an issue for her. What would my decision do to help her money situation? I changed my mind. I didn't owe her shit and wasn't going to give her a dime. If anything, she owed Memphis and me back child support and should be dishing out the dough. Something wasn't right about her, and my gut feeling confirmed it. I wish I wouldn't have torn the letter up or I would be calling to tell her my decision was made, and I didn't want her in my life.

When I made it to the house, Dre wasn't home. The house was clean and smelled fresh. The dent he had made in the couch from lying across it all day and night was now gone, and the pillows had been fluffed back out to their original shape. The glass coffee table was cleared from all of Dre's junk except for his ziplock bag of weed, box of rolling papers, and ashtray. Since his weed was left out like a candy bowl on the table for guests, I rolled up a blunt to smoke while I thawed out some meat to cook for dinner. I smoked half the blunt and then placed it in the ashtray. I stared at my hands for at least five minutes for no reason. Dre didn't smoke loud. He smoked dummy because that's exactly how I felt.

I was high, a little too high and too fast. I knew Dre only smoked the good shit, but, damn, he went all out with this sack. I started hearing my heart beating and drawers slamming in our bedroom. I yelled "Who's there?" but didn't receive an answer. Feeling paranoid now, I kept thinking about Keisha and her friends breaking out of jail to come and kill me for what I had done to them. I hadn't heard from any of them directly since the event. Will was providing any updates he got on them, and as far as I knew, there hadn't been any recently. I pictured Keisha in my bedroom searching for clues that would help her plan to kill me flow smoothly. Out of everyone I wronged, she always held a starring role in my nightmare because she not only beat me unconscious, she had shot me. My mind would never believe that she sat uncomfortably behind bars serving her attempted murder and arson charge, and the weed made it worse. Not only did my imagination give me three ideas on how she was able to break out of prison, but it had also placed her in my bedroom only a few feet away from me. I yelled another warning to the intruder to let them know I was aware of their presence.

"I know you're here, Keisha, or whoever you are, and I'm calling the police. That's if I decide not to shoot you first!"

"Ouch!"

I thought I heard a male voice speak, but I was high. I was sure my mind had made it up. There was silence for ten minutes, so I turned on the TV and tried to watch a movie to take my mind off it, but the thoughts kept resurfacing. I felt like I was being watched. I felt like the trespasser was awaiting the police to arrive, and if they didn't see them come soon, they would continue their attack on me. Not to alert the prowler or prowlers that I was aware they were still watching me, I turned the volume up on the television and then walked over to the refrigerator to open the freezer door. I grabbed the cordless phone from the charger and called Dre's cell with my head deep in the coldness.

"Where are you?" I whispered into the phone.

The fear in my voice caught Dre's attention, and I could hear him telling Sade to go with the Jeffersons.

"I just got out of church with Sade and the family. What's wrong, baby? Why are you whispering?"

The concern in his voice made me scared. It made me feel like there *was* something out there that he was protecting me from, and he wasn't telling me what it was.

"Please come home, Dre! I keep hearing stuff. Something isn't right; someone's here."

He said he was on his way and told me not to hang up the phone with him until he made it. Within fifteen minutes, he was at the house, gun in hand, and searching each room for any signs of trouble. I felt like I temporarily went crazy when Dre said the house was clear.

As Dre came close to me, so did the smell of fresh linen, soap, and mint-flavored mouthwash. His dreads had been twisted, and he was freshly shaved. He had on a dark gray suit with black button nose shoes that looked expensive and a black shirt under his suit jacket to match. He wasn't wearing a tie, and that was fine because the way he was looking, the tie would have been an added distraction from his beauty. He placed his gun back in its holster that rested on his hip and leaned in to kiss me on my cheek.

"Are you okay, baby?"

I didn't answer him. Instead, I went back into the living room, reached for the other half of the already rolled blunt, and then lit it up. After I took three long hits, I passed it to Dre's sexy ass. I wasn't worried about paranoia coming back; I knew the thought of having sex with Dre would put it on the back burner.

I made Dre take a seat next to me on the couch. When it was my turn to smoke again, I only hit it once and then reached for the button on his suit pants as I passed him the blunt again. Dre laughed and said, "What are you doing, baby?"

I had his pants unbuttoned and halfway unzipped when I looked up at him to answer.

"About to give my man some head."

He smiled and said, "First, you get me to rush home, ready to kill a nigga, and now look at you. You know what you're doing, Savannah?"

With my hand in the hole of his boxers, fighting to squeeze his hardened manhood through it, I said, "You tell me," and then pulled it out with a tug.

"I can't properly judge until the job is done, but, um, you don't have to prove yourself right now. I'm just glad I didn't have to catch a body in here. I'm starting to like this house."

Dre gave a slight chuckle and seemed like he was unsure if he wanted to accept the attention my mouth was about to give him, but his uncertainty got thrown out the window after my first attempt to swallow him whole. It must have been my tonsils that convinced him that he wanted it because as soon as the tip of his head touched them, he snatched himself out of my mouth, pushed his meat back through the hole in his boxers, and then pulled his pants and boxers down to his knees. I guess he wanted to get more comfortable. I resumed my position in the fight and let his head and shaft put a beating on my throat.

"Let me fuck up that throat!" he said, thrusting his meat in my mouth, and I took each deep plunge like a pro with no gaging or squinting of my eyes. I knew I was the champ in this fight because Dre was wearing his loss on his sleeve, better yet, his face.

"OK, come up on it, baby, suck on the head."

He was looking into my eyes, moaning and begging me to take it easy because it had been a long time since he had experienced this feeling. With every plea in Dre's eyes and from his mouth, I wanted to put on my best performance. I pulled my shirt over my head and popped the snaps on my bra. While stroking his penis with my hands, I licked the space in between my breasts until it was filled with my saliva. Then I placed his manhood in the now wet and warm space in between my breasts and moved them up and down his shaft. Dre caught on quickly and began stroking in and out of my breasts as if he was stroking the warmth in between my legs. Once I saw him close his eyes, I caught his stroke with my mouth and continued to squeeze my breasts around him. I let my mouth fill with saliva and then let it drop all over him and my breasts. Dre moaned something that almost sounded painful, and his eyes opened wider than I had ever seen them. Not even a second later, he shot his hot pleasure serum from my chin down my breasts with a beastlike roar. I smiled at him, knowing he was satisfied with my performance. I wiped the evidence of his satisfaction with my shirt, thanked him for rushing home as I got off my knees, and headed to the bathroom to take another shower.

My shower lasted about forty-five minutes which was enough time to let my high come down. Once I was dressed, I exited the bedroom to meet Dre back in the living room, but he wasn't there. Dre was in the kitchen cooking dinner with a satisfied smile on his face. As I approached the kitchen, he said, "You see how you got me, Savannah? Cooking for you and shit. That mouth of yours is something terrible, girl. It will bring the strongest man to his knees. Got me ready to bake yo' ass a cake or something."

He followed his words with a shake of his head as if he remembered the pleasure my mouth had given him. I didn't know what to say after that, so I hit him with a question. "Is that right?" I didn't want to toot my own horn, but I didn't mind letting him do it.

"Hell yeah, that's right!"

Dre was handy with the knife. I watched him dice and slice the onions and bell peppers as if he were on Food Network in a cooking competition. All those hours he had put in at the restaurant was showing. Now that Dre was back to his old self, I wonder if he had planned to go back to work. I didn't want to come out and ask like I wanted him gone, but I was talking to Dre, and he would detect bullshit if I allowed it to come out of my mouth, so I just asked.

"How was your talk with my daddy? I see and smell that you are doing a lot better." I laughed, but Dre didn't seem to find it funny.

He put the knife down and looked up at me sitting on the bar stool at the island in our kitchen. "Savannah, I ain't never felt that low in my life. The talk with your daddy only made shit worse for me. After he left, I smoked three blunts back-to-back and killed a bottle of Rémy trying to get shit off my mind, but it wasn't working."

I wasn't trying to be rude, not purposely this time, but I had to ask him what was wrong with him. That question seemed to make him get even more serious.

"You really don't know what was wrong with me, Savannah? Your daddy said you were blind to my feelings, but I thought he was wrong. Damn, baby, you can't see how you affect me? That damn cologne you were wearing, the stay-out-all-night shit with Will without calling home, and your past all attacked me at once. I love you, baby, but the baggage you come with is a lot to handle, and I was convinced that I could, but apparently, I was wrong."

Dre should have known I wasn't going to be able to sit here and let him attack me like that without saying shit back.

"What do you mean, 'apparently you were wrong'? I didn't ask you to follow me all over Las Vegas and Los Angeles, Dre. Nor did I ask you to come back and be by my side and try to start a family with me. All of that was your decision, and I promise it ain't too late for you to get your shit and walk out that door. I love you too, but we can't have shit without trust, and you don't seem to trust me at all."

I stopped myself right there because Dre had every right not to trust me. Just last night, I was up under Royce being made love to, and I knew I had all intentions on being under or on top of Royce again. I had decided this while I was in the shower. Dre would be my main thing, and I would keep Royce on the side until Dre and I had built something that would turn into marriage or send us in separate ways. I got lost in my thoughts for a second, but Dre was able to get me to snap out of it by saying, "Hell no, I don't trust you. I jumped in my truck and drove over to Stephanie's house around 11:00 last night. Your car wasn't there, so I parked and stared at the house debating on knocking to see if you were there. After about an hour or so, I started peeping through every window and blind she left open and didn't see you in there."

Did this fool just say he was peeping through her windows? Before I could snap about how crazy that was, Dre continued talking.

"I know it sounds crazy, but I had reached my lowest point, and knew I needed to deal with it right then and there. I finally saw Stephanie on her living room floor polishing her toenails and watching a movie, so I went and rang the doorbell. She answered and said you left to grab something to eat, and she would have you call me when you made it back. I pushed past her and sat on the couch and demanded to wait."

I had to interrupt, "Dre, you just don't do shit like that. You don't involve outsiders in house issues. You did it by asking Trisha to come back, and there isn't anything trustworthy about that, and now with Stephanie . . . You should have gone home and waited to talk to me about it. I'm sure she was scared to death."

Dre nodded his head in agreement and said, "Stephanie was scared shitless. I was fucked up last night. I went over there in a beater and some jeans with my gun in the holster. She kept her eyes on my gun the entire time. After an hour had passed, when I questioned her on your whereabouts again, she broke down and made me promise not to tell you she told me."

This is exactly why I didn't want to tell her bigmouthed ass shit. I knew a little pressure from Dre's ass would have her telling it all, I thought.

He continued talking.

"I made the meaningless promise to her because my loyalty lies with you, and that's when she told me you had been spending a lot of time with your mama at her hotel trying to figure y'all shit out."

Thank goodness for the lie I planted in her head. It would be smooth sailing from here because this wasn't a hard lie to keep up with, especially when I had just decided that I wasn't going to let Trisha back into my life. I now had to act like Stephanie violated the trust I had in our friendship, and then I could change the subject.

"I told her not to tell anyone, Dre! I can't believe she betrayed me like that for you. I thought she was trust-worthy. Guess she's just like every other bitch I know. Well, now that you know what I've been doing, let's just leave it alone. I'm not in the mood to discuss the drama Trisha keeps up."

I grabbed a bowl out of the dishwasher and began placing the chopped onions and bell peppers Dre had cut into it and then changed the subject. "So, when did you get your hair done? It looks good."

Dre started fumbling through the cabinets looking for seasonings like he was guilty of something. He quickly answered, "Stephanie did it while I was over there." I repeated his last sentence to him so he could confirm what I heard was correct, and he did. "Before you get upset and start thinking crazy shit, I was too drunk to drive home, and it was already in the wee hours of the morning. I had planned on going to church and couldn't walk into church looking the way I've been looking, so I just asked if she could retwist them. As soon as my hair was washed and twisted, I bounced and came home to shower, shave, clean up the house, and get ready for church. That's it, Savannah."

Dre could have saved that shit for somebody stupid. I'm not a big churchgoer, but I do know that you can "come as you are"! Immediately, visions of Dre sitting in between Stephanie's thighs with the warmth of her womanhood bouncing off the back of his head and neck played jealously in my head. I had to shake my head to get the visions to stop and to bring myself back to the reality that they would never cross those lines.

"You said that like I don't trust you. I know you wouldn't sleep with my best friend, and even if you tried, she wouldn't sleep with you," I finished with a giggle.

"I wouldn't try, and you're right. Stephanie loves your dirty drawers. I'm surprised she didn't text you to tell you I was there," he chuckled.

"Yeah, me too."

I can't believe I felt jealous about Dre getting his hair done by Stephanie. I knew they both were too loyal to me to betray my trust, but I guess I wouldn't be human or a woman if the thought didn't cross my mind. You can say you trust your man all you want, but you're dumb as hell if you think you can trust a female lingering around him all the time. Whether she's a friend or foe, there ain't no bitch on this earth that I'm going to trust around mine, especially not for long periods of time. Men think with their dicks, and our thoughts flow off our emotions. We tend to take nice words and compliments for more than what they really are, so leaving a female around my nice, sweet, and caring man is out of the picture. I don't need a bitch catching feelings for mine just because he showed her a little respect. Nope, I'll pass.

I knew deep inside that they hadn't slept together; it was just the guilt of making love to Royce last night kicking in. The shit always worked like that when you're guilty of cheating. Your guilt makes you think your mate is doing the same as you. I assured Dre I believed him and trusted Stephanie wholeheartedly.

When dinner was ready, we ate and talked about Sade and the thoughts of Dre and Stephanie possibly doing more than hair disappeared.

Chapter Six

The Transfer

Maybe I was spending too much time with Royce, and that's why I felt like Dre and Stephanie were fooling around behind my back. Whatever Dre and Stephanie talked about the night he invaded her space seemed to have made them a hell of a lot closer. These two went from barely saying hi and bye to best friends in a matter of days.

Stephanie had become Dre's official beautician and hang out buddy. On nights when I was out with Royce, Dre and Stephanie had been together. They even went as far as eating at the Jeffersons' family restaurant together every Wednesday and Sunday after Bible study and church.

Stephanie didn't even speak to me at work unless it was mandatory, nor did she volunteer to pick up the extra work I might've been slacking on like she usually did. Something about her had changed, and before I could discover what it was, she volunteered a portion of it.

"Hey, Savannah, do you have a minute?"

Stephanie was wearing the biggest smile I had ever seen on her face. My first thought was she closed a huge deal that would force my partners and me to make her one, or she had gotten some good dick and wanted to brag about it.

"Sure, love, meet me in my office in ten minutes. I need to run to my car really fast."

There wasn't a true need to run to my car, but since she hadn't said shit to me in weeks, I wanted her to know she wasn't a priority. Besides, I was the marionettist in our dying friendship, and she was the fool on the strings. I controlled her moves; it would never be the other way around. Making her wait gave me an opportunity to check on my car. I still hadn't taken it to be looked at and wanted to see if it would start on its own. It was almost time for lunch, and Royce needed to eat. I was enjoying being the meal he wanted and had to make sure I could deliver it.

Like magic, the car cranked without a hitch. I had my radio on the slow jams station on my ride to work, and when the engine cranked, one of my jams had just come on. I didn't know the lyrics nor the artist's name, but his moans entwined in his singing made my panties wet. That reason alone made it one of my favorite songs.

I hummed along to the beat more than I kept up with the lyrics until the commercials came on. There was one for a new weight loss drug, some old-school concert, and another for a free psychic reading. I punched in the number for the reading the second time the woman's voice made the announcement and put it on speakerphone. I had never called in to one before, but I needed to buy myself time, and if the call lasted longer than the ten minutes I gave Stephanie, it was fine by me.

"Thank you for calling Washington's premier psychic line, and welcome, Savannah, to our network of over 100 psychic friends."

At the sound of my name, I almost pressed the red button on my phone to end the call out of fear of hearing my name before I ever told it, but quickly, I remembered that although the first call was free, I still was asked for my credit card and billing information if I made future calls.

"Um, thank you," I said in a shaky voice.

"Are you calling to find out what lies in your future for love, money, and happiness?"

"Well, I would think anyone who picked up the phone and called would be calling in for that information. You don't have to be psychic to know that."

"Yes, you are right, but you do have to be psychic to know that you love Andre and hate yourself."

"Excuse me?" I nervously laughed, "I don't hate myself. Honestly, I love myself way more than anyone on this earth."

"That is true, including the child you birthed and refused to mother because of your own relationship with your mother, but this man Andre is not on earth. He has a special place in your heart, and because he does, it makes you uncomfortable."

"OK, who is this?" I asked, laughing. "Did I call you by accident, Will? Your woman's voice is pretty good, boy. For a second there, you had me fooled."

"Will, oh yes, Will. He's the man you call a friend, but only because you've found a way to benefit off of him. He speaks the truth to you, and at times, you see it as an attack of harsh words. That's why you assumed that I was him. No, my name is Carol, and I am your new psychic friend."

I stopped myself from asking how she knew so much about me and decided to play the game. I'm guessing my credit card information links me to the people I've used it with or for. It was my turn to control the call.

"Okay, Carol, since you seem to be able to read my future without getting to know me, what do you see in my future monetarily?"

She was silent, but I could hear cards being shuffled, then pressed against something solid, and then she spoke.

"Eight of cups."

"Eight of cups? What does that mean?"

"The eight of cups represent a possibility that a decision will have to be made between love, money, and or security."

"OK, so that didn't answer my question. That was general as fuck! Can you give me a little more if I give you a more detailed question?"

"Yes, of course."

"Good, my next question is by the end of the year, what will my money look like?" I chuckled as the next card was flipped onto the table.

"Nine of swords."

"Now, that sounds better. Will I be stabbing a bitch with my wealth that's multiplied by nine?"

"No, you will battle terrible anguish over your finances . . . or lack thereof."

"Bitch, please, I have bread already stacked. You don't know what the hell you're talking about, but this is what I get for calling the devil for answers in my life anyway. Bye."

I heard another card flip, and two more followed that one. As my finger reached the button on the screen, she screamed, *"You can find happiness in the death card!"*

She had to be employed by the devil to say happiness and death in the same sentence. I got out of the car laughing that I had been bored enough to make that call.

"That was a long ten minutes," Stephanie said, sitting in a chair at my desk as I walked in.

"I'm sorry. I forgot that I had agreed to meet with you. So many other important things to do, but what's up? You got my attention now."

The smile she was wearing earlier was now a frown, but after crossing her legs and leaning back in the chair, it quickly returned.

"So, as you know, your man popped up acting all crazy over your missing whereabouts—"

"I know, and I truly apologize. I don't know why Dre would involve—" I cut her off, and she returned the favor.

"No, it's okay. We were best friends, and I understood why he'd come to me first, but that's not what this meeting is about."

"Then spill it."

I really wasn't interested in anything she had to say next because she had confirmed my suspicions when she said, "were" about our friendship.

"Well, remember when you told me you had been spending all that extra time with your mom or whatever?"

"Yes."

"I told Dre that's where you were that night, but I had done so, already knowing that it was a lie."

"Excuse me, are you trying to say that I lied about being with my mother?" I questioned.

"No, I'm saying you *did* lie. In fact, you hadn't spent one Saturday or Wednesday with her because when you left the office Friday evening, she was in the parking lot waiting for me."

"Why would that mean she wasn't meeting up with me because she wanted to meet with you? Furthermore, I don't appreciate you—"

Stephanie held her hand in the air like we were in class and her foolery caused me to lose my train of thought.

"If you would allow me to finish, I'll tell you what I had been told. Peaches said she needed to speak with you before leaving town, and I assured her that you had all intentions on meeting with her again. She was shocked and didn't have a clue of what I was talking about. You asked me not to tell anyone, but I was sure it would be okay to discuss what was going on with the horse, but the horse said that it was all a lie. She said y'all would talk by phone when you were on bed rest, but you were only using her for entertainment. There was no rekindling, nor were the two of you building a mother-and-daughter relationship. Sad part is, she offered to play me the recordings of your call when you asked her to act like a friend, which is funny because you had me. I've always been a phone call away, and I've always put your needs before my own. Anyway, she had no idea of why you'd make up fake meetings with her and lie to your best friend about having them. She made me reevaluate our friendship, and it damn near broke my heart to realize we've never had one. I was your slave, personally and professionally, and I didn't mind it because the way you fucked me made me think that I really meant something to you. Your game is tight, and I'm done being played with by you. Don't worry, as I said before, I fed Dre the lie, but I wanted to take a minute to sit down and tell you how much I appreciate you and thank you for the opportunity."

I was too busy racking my brain for a lie to tell that would trump whatever Trisha had put in her head, but from what I was hearing, it wasn't necessary. If I heard correctly, it sounded like Stephanie was going to conclude her talk with a resignation letter. I didn't want to say anything that would make her change her mind.

"You thank and appreciate me for *what* opportunity?" I asked through the growing smile on my face.

"The opportunity to make a true lifelong friend. Dre is so amazing, and our friendship means the world to me. I'd never betray my loyalty to you by telling him the truth behind your lies, but I want you to know that I value his friendship and thank you for allowing us to spend so much time together as we grow it. From this point on, we are nothing more than coworkers, so keep all that ho shit and lies to yourself, or it might get back to Dre. That's all I wanted with you."

She left my office before I could say anything since I was busy picking my jaw up off the floor.

Something had definitely gotten into her, and I was sure that something was Dre. She was on Dre's side from the beginning, like everybody else when it came to the shit I pulled on him, and I knew this. However, I never imagined that she would cut off our friendship to pursue one with him. You would think they knew each other for years how they both were acting lately, and that *I* was the third wheel in their friendship. I understood that good dick could do this to a woman, but what I couldn't understand is why she would think it would be okay for it to be *my* good dick.

Stephanie and I had been friends for almost eight years and lovers for almost as long, but that wasn't an okay for her to chase Dre. I wasn't about to share him with her; this wasn't going to be a group event, but if it were more than friendship and they were truly creeping behind my back, it would have been nice to have at least been invited to join.

I made sure to keep my love affair with Royce under lock, so there was no way she knew about it. Stephanie wasn't spending time with Dre because she knew I lied about spending time with my mama, was cheating on him, and she felt bad about it; she was spending time with Dre because she enjoyed his company. I don't have proof of their betrayal to me besides Stephanie's actions, but I was determined to get to the bottom of it, one way or another.

It had been over a month since the first night Royce and I slept together, and we had made it a twice-a-week fling. Wednesday and Saturday nights had become my favorite days of the week because those were the nights I dedicated to spending time with Royce. I knew I would have to cancel on one of those nights to find out what was going on between Dre and Stephanie. I wouldn't stop believing that she was still somewhat loyal to me and without having facts as to where I was spending my mysterious days of the week, I was certain she wouldn't tell Dre a half-truth. I wasn't as good at this detective shit as Dre, but I was willing to try.

I waited until Friday night when we were lying in bed to ask Dre what his plans for the weekend were, and just as I predicted, they involved that bitch, Stephanie, in some kind of way. He said, "Nothing really, baby. I'm supposed to get my hair retwisted Saturday night, then head to church Sunday with the family and have dinner afterward. Why? What's up?"

"I was hoping we could hang out Saturday night. Maybe go to a restaurant, catch a movie, or go out to check out the city. I still don't know what's available for us to do here, but if you want, we can stay in the house and relax together. I don't mind retwisting your dreads, and then we can head to church together Sunday morning. We can even let Sade spend the night and maybe have a slumber party in our room since she likes sleeping in bed with us."

Dre had the nerve to look at me and laugh before saying, "You do some manual labor and sit through church and dinner with Sade? What's *really* going on, Savannah?"

I knew he could read my bullshit, so I joined in with his laughter too. There was no way in hell I was going to retwist all them long-ass dreads, and I'm glad he knew it, so I just said what was on my mind.

"You've been spending so much time with Stephanie lately, I guess I'm starting to get jealous. She doesn't even speak to me at work anymore because of y'all's new friendship. I just said that shit to be saying it; ain't no way in hell I'm doing your hair. I don't even do mines."

I continued to laugh but realized I was laughing alone now. Dre had a look of disgust on his face, and the words that came out of his mouth mirrored his look.

"You're jealous of what, Savannah? Stephanie is a family friend and auntie to Sade, so that makes her a sister to us. You do know she spends more time with your daughter than *you* do, right? It kills her to have to give Sade a lie on why you're not coming around. She's trying to show our daughter love on behalf of yo' missing-in-action ass. Your daddy is right. You're doing Sade exactly the way your mama did you; yet, you got it in that thick-ass head of yours that what you're doing is different. Everybody sees how your neglect Sade, and no one likes that shit. Instead of Stephanie checking you about it, she plays auntie of the year to her."

"I didn't ask her to do shit for Sade," I yelled, and he continued like I hadn't cut him off.

"Have you even taken the time out to think that maybe she doesn't speak to you at work anymore because you keep her in the middle of your bullshit all the time? How do you expect her to keep being in your corner when everything you do is shady?"

Dre snapped on me like he was a female. It took a second for me to remember he was my man and not my bitch as he continued his rant.

"Her name was all over that California shit because of you, and you keep using her in shit now. You don't respect her as a friend or coworker. She's not bred to be a full-bloodied bitch like you. That girl loves the Lord, but riding for your ass keeps her living in sin."

The tone of his voice let me know he wasn't speaking as an outsider on her behalf but expressing concerns she had expressed to him about me behind my back. Where in the fuck was Dre's loyalty to me? He let this bitch talk to him about me like I was the snake forcing Eve to give Adam the apple in Eden.

"Aye," Dre said, snapping his fingers in my face to bring me back to his world of shit talking before he finished making his point. "The reason we don't spend time together, Savannah, is because you don't have time to spend with me. You're with your mother every Wednesday and Saturday night; then you act too tired to meet me at the restaurant any other day of the week. I try to get you to make love to me, but you seem to settle for giving me head like you don't want me inside you or something. I know I should be asking you who *you* are fucking, but I don't because I pretend to be able to account for your time away from home. Have you noticed that I've stopped trying to get you to bond with our daughter because all you do is talk about how she drains you with all them damn questions she asks? Sade loves the hell out of you, and what breaks my heart the most is, she tells everybody that she wants to be just like you when she grows up. The shit brings me to tears to know my daughter wants to grow up to be a heartless, self-centered bitch just like her mother."

I couldn't get the words I was thinking to come out of my mouth. Dre has always had a way to put me on mute and keep me there. His girl talk with Stephanie had pissed me off, and, instead of forcing myself to speak, my words flew out of my hand as I reached across to Dre's side of the bed and slapped him across his face like the bitch he was acting like.

I closed my eyes as soon as my hand made contact with his skin. At that point, I quickly remembered that Dre was far from being anybody's bitch, including mine, and I had just assaulted a man with a criminal record. Expecting to feel his retaliation, I kept my eyes shut.

After a minute or so without feeling anything, I opened them and watched Dre as he dressed and grabbed his keys from the nightstand to leave the house. I should have known he wouldn't strike me back. Dre was a real man, and he knew how to treat a woman, even when the woman didn't know how to treat him.

Everything that happened tonight was all Stephanie's fault. I wasn't about to take the blame for it. She caused me to feel the way I did by changing on me. Dre wouldn't have felt the need to defend her or call me a bitch if she hadn't played the victim role to him. I wouldn't have slapped him, and he wouldn't have left me all alone in this house in the middle of the night.

That victim role she was trying to play was getting old. Stephanie was a grown woman with her own mind. I didn't force her into doing anything that she didn't want to be a part of. If the bitch couldn't handle what I asked of her, or if she had a problem with it, she should have brought the shit to me—not my man.

Pissed off all over again, I showered, dressed, and then followed Dre's example by leaving the house to head over to Royce for some comforting. I wasn't staying there overnight by myself, especially not after thinking I heard some rumbling through my drawers a few weeks back. I know Dre didn't find anyone in the house, nor was anything missing, but the feeling of being watched was too strong for it just to be the weed creating paranoia.

I made sure to drive the long way to Royce's hotel so I could drive past Stephanie's house to see if Dre's truck was there, but it wasn't, nor was Stephanie's car. That bitch must have called herself running to him in his time of need and meeting him wherever he went. If she did, I'd make sure she regretted it.

I made it to Royce's hotel in fifteen minutes flat. I had been there so many times that the overnight front desk attendant knew me by name. As he spoke my name in greeting, "Hi, Ms. James," I asked, "Can you please print me a new room key? I've misplaced mine," and then I greeted him in return, "Hello, Mr. Wang," reading his name badge on his shirt. I dropped the Lee, which was his first name and added Mr. to show respect. The 50-something-year-old Asian gentleman printed my key card without hesitation. I knew Royce would be shocked when he woke up with my face in his lap, pleasuring him with my mouth. I had never done it to him before, but, tonight, I was in the mood to. I hadn't given Royce head because I felt like that was just for Dre. I wanted to keep something special for him since I had been giving away his pussy, but after Dre's words an hour ago, I didn't feel like Dre deserved shit.

When I made it up to room 304, I silently slid the key in the door and watched the lighted locking pattern turn from red to green to allow me entrance. I could hear jazz music playing softly in his bedroom as I tiptoed past the kitchenette in his suite. Once I made it to the living room area, I took off all of my clothes except for the green, lace thong and bra set I had put on since green was his favorite color. I made my way to his bedroom door. My heart began beating fast as I opened the door and took a few steps toward his bed. I had never popped up on anyone unannounced; that was dead wrong in my book, and I would die if someone were to pop up on me. I froze in place and thought about putting my clothes back on and calling him from my car for permission to visit, but it was already too late. *Why leave when I've already come so far?* I thought.

Before I could take my next couple of steps, I was stopped by a pile of clothes that, at first glance, looked like a blanket because there were so many. At first, I thought Royce might have sorted a pile of laundry on his floor . . . until I reached down to remove whatever it was that had wrapped around my heels. It was a bra, a *big* bra at that. It must have been a 46 double-D with extra padding in the cups that felt damp; I dropped the bra in disgust. I was trying to adjust my eyes in the dark to focus on the bed so I could make sure what I thought I was seeing was right. If my eyes weren't playing tricks on me, it looked like Royce was on the bottom of a 69-position with what looked like an ape in the dark. His toes were extended wide, spread apart and wiggling like he was in pleasure. From the looks of it, the ape had a mouth full of Royce's manhood, jerking its head up and down, which looked like it would cause more pain than pleasure in the dark. I reached for the bedside light switch for a better view. When the lights came on, I wish I had left this scene in the dark. Royce's face was covered in juices from what looked to be a nine-month pregnant woman and, like I saw in the dark, her mouth was full of him. Even with the lights on, she kept bobbing her head up and down without noticing me standing there. That was because her eyes were closed so tightly you would think he was forcing her to do something she didn't want to do. She didn't know how to suck dick, and it made me want to slap her for trying. She didn't stop until Royce said my name while moving her off of him quickly, yet cautiously because of her present physical state.

"Savannah, what are you doing here?" he managed to say before I made it out of his room and back to the living room to get dressed. I was almost in my pants when he came out of the room naked; closing the door behind him to silence the yells of the woman he had abandoned to follow me. "Savannah, that's not what it looks like. She came here to talk; then one thing led to another—"

I cut him off by placing my index finger in front of my mouth to nonverbally tell him to shut up and then said, "It's my fault for popping up; I'm wrong. I wanted to make love to you, but I should have called first. I assumed we were exclusive to each other. This is my fault, and it will *never* happen again." Then I grabbed my purse and headed out the door. I was pissed off, and my feelings were hurt, but what more could I say? I got too comfortable with thinking Royce wasn't ready to date after his divorce and that what happened between us was special. He wasn't my man, to begin with. My man was reaching out to my secretary to get the affection he wasn't getting from me while I chased after another. When I stepped on the elevator, I gave one last look back at Royce's room. He was halfway down the hallway dressed in his birthday suit, with his hands covering his piece, begging me to stay.

I hoped the front desk agent got a look at his naked ass on the surveillance camera as I laughed on my way down. When I passed the man sitting at the desk, the guilty smile he wore confirmed he had seen Royce naked. I bid the attendant good night and exited the hotel, vowing never to return.

"Did he introduce you to his wife? I know she's pregnant, but I can tell that bitch is naturally big and as ugly as a tadpole. You were in and out of there pretty fast. Did y'all have a falling out?"

Trisha was sitting in her car blocking mine so that I couldn't pull off. I ignored her as I unlocked my door. "Would you like me to move?"

"No, I'd prefer you to stay right there until the police arrive."

I dialed 911 on my cell phone and placed the call on speaker.

"911, what's your emergency?" the emergency operaotor asked.

"So I take it you've decided to pass up my offer to have a mother, then, huh? Well, I'm throwing in the towel. Write me a check for $20,000, and I'll be out your life for good."

"Bitch, you get 20,000 fuck-yous," I said, sliding my hand on the mute button without her noticing. "Now, leave me alone and take your ass back to wherever you came from."

"This is your last chance, Savannah. Do what's right for the first time in your life. Walk away from your problems in defeat. Losing a battle from time to time doesn't mean you lost the war, sweetie. What are you going to do?"

"911, are you there?"

I unmuted my phone and locked eyes with her.

"Yes, I'm here."

"There's a car blocking me in at—" she drove off before I could give my location.

There was no reason for me to head back home, so I drove up the street to my favorite hotel and got a room for the night. It was time to drink and come up with some consequences for everybody's crimes against me.

Everyone knows I'm presidential when it comes to this revenge shit. They must've been relying on me learning a lesson from the California shit I pulled, and I did learn a lesson, which was Karma is a bitch. I learned that I needed to stop looking at Karma as uncontrollable, but like the bitch she was. If you give a bitch what she wants, then she's happy. That's why if you dish out good, Karma lets you get it back. When you don't dish out good like she wants you to, then the bitch gives you hell. Hell, that's worse than what you dished out, or so it feels that way since you have now become the recipient. I knew I needed to cater to Karma this time. I would get my revenge, not as heavy as before, but just enough to make my point and then live right.

Yes, I said it. I would live right, and it's not the alcohol talking, even though I had almost drunk everything in the minibar. I knew exactly what I was saying. Dre needed a strong woman like me as his wife, Sade needed her biological mother, and I needed the new start that I had planned to get before my mother popped back into my life.

I'll attend church and get some therapy; I might even sign up for parenting classes. My change won't happen overnight, but I'll make positive steps in that direction. I'm tired of living in a soap opera. It's time to try something new. If the shit doesn't work, I can always go back to being me. But, first things first; I needed to break up this little bond Stephanie and Dre call themselves having. Then I'll deal with Trisha and save Royce for last since he means the least to me.

I sat up all night trying to come up with a plan for Stephanie's ass. If I hadn't been drunk, it wouldn't have taken so long. When I checked out of the hotel the next day, I went home, and Dre still wasn't there. That would have pissed me off, but by that time, I knew he was leaving church, headed to the restaurant for Sunday dinner with the family. Since I had just showered at the hotel, I changed clothes and then headed to meet him.

When I walked into the door at the restaurant, I saw my entire family sitting at the table. My daddy, Memphis, the Jeffersons, and Sade, who was seated in between Dre and Stephanie. I thought to myself, *This bitch really thinks they are a family*. I devilishly laughed aloud as I approached the table. Everyone looked at me as if they saw a ghost with their jaws dropped, leaving their mouths wide open. I assumed Dre must have told them what happened between us last night, and that's why

I received all the funny looks. That was fine; I would change everyone's opinion of me once I execute my plan.

I swear, if it weren't for my daddy greeting me, I don't think anyone else would have. Once again, everyone was on Dre's side, without hearing mine.

"Hey, Savannah, baby, let me pull you up a chair right here next to Dre and me," my daddy said, once his shock was lifted.

I was on a mission, so I shook my head no to decline his offer and then kissed Dre on his cheek. I whispered, "I'm so sorry, baby; I'll never raise a hand to you again. I heard everything you said to me, and you were right. It's time for a change because I don't want to lose you." Standing upright I turned to face my daddy and said, "No, Daddy, I think I want to sit next to Sade. We got some catching to do, don't we?"

Sade excitedly responded, "Yes, Mama; sit next to Auntie Stephanie and me." Shock was now back on everyone's faces since I volunteered to spend time with my daughter except for Stephanie. She had a "Bitch, please" or "Yeah, right" look on her face, which made me want to sit next to her even more.

Sade and I must have talked about everything over dinner, and, as always, her thousands of questions irritated the shit out of me, but it kept a smile on Dre's face and a frown on Stephanie's, which I loved. After dinner, I took Sade to the restroom to wash her hands and face. That's when listening to Sade talk her pretty little head off paid off.

"Mama, guess what?"

Sade had said that for the hundredth time that day alone. Since we were alone now, I thought I'd give her a quick rule on all this "guess what-ing" she was doing. Since my goal is to be a part of her life, we needed to get an understanding.

"You don't have to say guess what about everything you want to say to me, Sade. We both know I can't guess what it is you have to say, so how about you just tell me from now on. Okay, baby?"

She looked a little disappointed that I wasn't planning to guess but began to tell me anyway. "Okay, Mama. Auntie Stephanie asked me and Daddy to spend the night at her house Saturday, so we can go to the circus and see the animals put on a show. She said if I'm a good girl, I can have popcorn and cotton candy too. You should come too, Mama. It's going to be fun!"

Why would Stephanie invite Sade and Dre to spend the night at her house when we stay less than twenty miles from each other? Before attempting to answer my question, Sade answered it for me.

"It's Auntie Stephanie's birthday on Saturday, and she doesn't want to spend it alone, so we are going to the circus and out to dinner; then Auntie said I would have to go to sleep because her and Daddy are going to have a drink to celebrate."

Did Stephanie think she could get him drunk, and then they "accidentally" have birthday sex? Bitch, please, who in this day still falls for that old-school trick? Not only was she planning to get some of my dick, but she was also planning to get it while my daughter slept comfortably in the other room. *That disrespectful bitch! I don't even have sex when Sade is present; what gives her more rights than me?* Sade cut my thoughts off and brought me back from the bitches and hoes I was now calling Stephanie in my head when she asked me out of pure curiosity, "Mama, why can't I have drinks to celebrate with them?"

I explained it to her the best way I could, but I knew I wasn't the right person for the job. I'd have Mrs. Jefferson break it down to her better later. I then headed out of the contact while he did it. Something wasn't right with his fuck session. He never wanted to receive head over five minutes, and I soon found out what the problem was.

"Aye, you know why I'm letting you suck on Savannah's dick like this, bitch? It's because I feel sorry for your ass. You ain't got shit on Savannah, and you know it. I see you trying to walk and talk like her, but the shit ain't getting you nowhere. You're a second-string bitch with some second-rate pussy and head to match. Yep, you ain't got shit on Savannah, and you just confirmed it. I'll make sure to tell her that when I get home."

Dre pulled his penis out of her grasp and then grabbed the towel from behind the couch.

"Fuck you, Dre," Stephanie said, with tears in her eyes. "Your bitch has some second-rate pussy; just ask every nigga in Nashville, Atlanta, and Los Angeles. I'm sure a few niggas here know it by now too. Her ass is lying about spending time with her mother every Wednesday and Saturday, and I'm sure of it because that's a pattern, and that bitch don't do them. Commitment isn't in her vocabulary. She's a ho and will always be a ho," Stephanie laughed, as Dre waved her off like she was nothing. "Go ahead, Dre, and try to make your ho a housewife. She has slept with everybody, including me. She ate this pussy, and I've stuck everything in arm's reach inside of hers as I ate hers, and the bitch was too loose to feel it. She ain't got nothing left special to give to you that I ain't already had. I tried to let you see what a real woman was like and show you that you can do better than Savannah; that's why I've been hanging around with you, but you're too stupid to see it."

Dre zipped up his pants and started to get his things together. He didn't even try to defend me from all the hoes Stephanie had been calling me. I knew he didn't defend me because he agreed with her. I even had to bathroom to start part one of Stephanie's consequence for trying to sneak behind me and get my man. I waited until we were all about to call it a night and Sade had been taken off by Dre to get her toys out of his car to make my announcement.

"Hey, everybody, Saturday night, I would like all of you here for dinner around seven. It's a very important night for me. I'm planning to take the initiative and propose to Dre. I've put him through hell the past five years, but I know there is no one else in this world that I want to spend forever with but him."

There were silence and stares of disbelief at the table, so I thought I'd pour it on real thick.

"Last night, Dre tried to tell me the truth in love, and I turned it into an exchange of hurtful words, which resulted in me getting physical and him leaving me. When he left, I never felt so alone in my life, so I went and got a room at a hotel to reflect on my life and all the hurt I caused people."

I then turned to my daddy and said, "Your words stuck to me from the talk we had in my room, and I don't want to die without knowing what love is. I don't want just to receive it; I want to give it back too, and there is no other man I'd want to give it and myself to but Dre. Is Saturday fine with everyone, and if you don't want to be there, I understand?"

I ended my announcement with tears flowing from my eyes. The whole table agreed excitedly, and Mrs. Jefferson offered to cook all of his favorite foods and desserts for the event. My daddy rushed over to me with tears in his eyes and hugged me tightly.

"That's right, baby. Forever is a long time to be alone. Love that man, and you'll never be by yourself again. I'm so proud of you. Do you hear that, Memphis? Your sister will be a married woman soon!"

"That's if Dre says yes," Stephanie mumbled under her breath, making sure I was the only one to hear her, and I pretended I didn't. I turned to look at her, knowing she would have some type of response because she didn't agree to be here, nor did she disagree. After hearing her mumble that dumb shit underneath her breath, it was time to pick at her.

"Stephanie, you're right about what you said to me in my office. You're not my best friend; you are my sister. Is Saturday at seven good with you? I'll need you to bring Dre here for me." She hesitated, gave me a fake smile, and said, "I wouldn't miss it for the world, sis." I died laughing on the inside.

Monday at work, Stephanie continued to keep her distance from me. We passed each other in the hallway after lunch, and she gave me the same fake smile she wore at the restaurant. I hadn't really looked at her lately, but when I did, I noticed something familiar about her look. It was "Savannah James" familiar. Stephanie was dressed and wearing her hair the way I did before my hospitalization. Come to think about it, she was even wearing the same perfume as me. That's why I could smell it so loudly whenever I was in her presence. This bitch was trying to become me, and that was fine because when I made it to work that morning, I had already put in motion the final stage of my revenge against her. I hadn't come up with this plan until late last night. It was evil and coldhearted, but how else could you serve revenge?

I spoke with my partners from the firm back in Atlanta and requested to transfer Stephanie back to our home office in Atlanta to handle a new, large account. Now she can go be me on the other side of the country because there wasn't enough room for two Savannahs in Washington—or in Dre's life.

It wasn't a problem getting Mr. Williams and Mr. Williamson to agree since Stephanie was our best senior accountant and had been trained by me. Of course, Mr. Williams wanted to know why I would be willing to give her up so easily. He knew Stephanie and I had a bond from back when she was first hired as my secretary, and he knew she acted as my secretary now even though she had been promoted to senior accountant. With all the sincerity in my voice I could muster, I said, "Yes, I will miss Stephanie working directly with me, but as a team player, I am willing to make sacrifices to ensure our company's growth. I know we need her managing this deal for us; it's in the company's best interest that someone with her skill and love for the job takes over this account."

There was no arguing with the truth, and Mr. Williams let it go. I was only asked one more question, and it came from Mr. Williamson.

"Do you mind breaking the news to her?"

It would be my pleasure is the way I wanted to answer; instead, I said, "Yes, give me a few days, and I'll let her know. It's best that she hears it from me, anyway."

Stephanie and I went through the whole week without saying a word to each other until Friday, an hour before her shift ended.

"Hey, Savannah, your doctor's office called Dre's phone for you while we were at lunch and—"

"While y'all were at lunch?" I asked with a laugh and quickly got out of my feelings so I could put her in hers. "Did Dre give you a message to pass on to me?"

"No, I answered his phone. Well, he kind of made it my job to answer it since he was busy cooking for me. Anyway, the doctor wants you to make a follow-up appointment. It's been well over six weeks, and you missed your checkup. I'm only guessing, but I think they wanted to check your lady parts before you started back having sex. If I know you, I'm sure they are more than a little late, but, hey, I understand they still have a job to do," she laughed, and I joined in.

"Yes, a lot lately. Dre could barely wait until those six weeks were up. I almost made an appointment to confirm he hadn't knocked nothing out of place the way he put it on me. Boy, did he miss me. Anyway, before you leave for the day, I need you to stop by my office for a quick meeting. I have some news that came in from the bosses that I must share with you." I hung up in her face, and five minutes later, she was outside of my door.

"Yes, Savannah," she said, after knocking on my door and receiving permission to enter. Stephanie looked like a picture I might have taken of myself two years ago, minus the breasts I own and adding more butt. Irritation was plastered on her face at my summons.

"Have a seat, Stephanie." I made sure to say this in my business voice and to remain professional in this conversation. "We were just given a new, extremely large account in Atlanta, and all the partners are in agreement that you are the best accountant to take over the account. They want you to move back to the home office to handle it properly." The look of anger and shock on Stephanie's face was priceless.

"Savannah, I don't *want* to move back down South. Can't you pull some strings for me and send a senior accountant from our California office there instead? I'm building a life here."

I wanted to laugh in her face as she pleaded with me, but I didn't. I waited until she was finished to continue throwing salt into her open wound.

"I'm sorry, Stephanie, but you are the best we have, and we need you to handle this account, not the next best to you." I threw in a lie to make it sound even better. "With successful numbers, this account can land you a partnership with us. Isn't that your goal?"

She didn't open her mouth; she just nodded her head. I asked her if she had any questions, and she said, "Yes, when will this all take place?" I almost choked on my saliva trying not to laugh at her. I looked over my desk at her like she was a piece of gum stuck to the bottom of my chair.

"You will need to clean out your office tonight. As of Monday, your badge will no longer allow you entrance to this building. Your first day to report to work is not until the following Monday, which gives you a little over a week to pack your belongings to be shipped, which the company is willing to pay for. We have also arranged for your vehicle to be shipped, but it will not arrive until two weeks after you, so we are also providing a rental until it arrives. I informed my partners that you own a two-bedroom house in Atlanta, so we will not be paying for you to find a place. It would be in your best interest to let your sister know you will be returning to your home. While you arrange for her to move out or make room for you, we are willing to get you a one-month stay at an extended stay hotel of your choice. Just let one of us know once you have selected a place. Your flight leaves a week from tomorrow, and I think that's about it. Do you have any other questions?"

Stephanie wasn't dumb after all. She had been working with me for almost eight years and knew my style. Her next remark was more of a personal question than a business one.

"What in the hell did I do to you? This transfer shit reeks of you. You're not a snake; you're a slug, and you leave a trace on everything you touch. I know this was all of your doing."

There was no more holding shit in. I laughed hysterically and had to catch my breath to respond. "This was a business decision, Stephanie. We haven't truly spoken in over a month, and you haven't acted as my secretary for about the same length of time. I thought I needed you here with me, but I guess I don't. I'm sorry."

She stood up and started heading to the door. "Dre said you had become jealous of our friendship, but I didn't think you'd go this far. I'll make sure he is at the dinner at seven Saturday; then I'll remove myself from your personal life completely."

She waited for my response, and you know I had one. With the biggest smile of satisfaction on my face, I said, "Thank you and happy early birthday. Make sure to enjoy yourself at the circus after you drop my man and Sade off to me. By the way, I love your new look because it once belonged to me. You can try to look like me all you want, but you will *never* be me."

Stephanie rolled her eyes and said, "Thank God for that!" and then exited my office, closing my door with force but not slamming it. Now *that's* how you make a bitch disappear.

Chapter Seven

The Big Payback

I ran around Saturday morning like a chicken with its head cut off trying to get everything ready for Saturday night. It hadn't hit me what I was actually preparing for until I looked at my things-to-do list, and the last task on it was to buy Dre's engagement ring. Was I *really* ready to settle down and become one man's woman? Or was I letting this spur-of-the-moment revelation direct me down the wrong path? After going over the pros and cons a thousand times, I decided that it was a green light, and I'd go through with it. Just because we were about to be officially engaged didn't mean we would have to rush a wedding date. I've heard of people being engaged for years. I would add our names to that waiting list. Karma had been kicking my ass all my life; it was time to play by her rules, and I was determined to make myself ready.

"What kind of ring are you looking for or the price range?" the jeweler asked, and not wanting to sound prejudiced, but he was foreign and up in age. Everything about him matched the stereotypes listed for good jewelers.

"Price doesn't matter, and I'm not sure. If I tell you about him, do you think you could help me? He doesn't wear any jewelry, so I'm completely clueless on where to start."

"But of course, let's start with something simple. I'm sorry, how rude of me. My name is Stuart, and you are?"

"Savannah, Savannah James."

"That is a beautiful name and fitting. Savannah is a very beautiful place to visit year-round. I take my wife there once a year. What is the occasion that has you ring shopping with us today?" he asked, offering me a seat across from his desk.

"It's for our engagement."

"How wonderful!" he cheered and clapped his hands. "Let me see the style he has gotten you. It's an old jeweler's trick, and I will share it with you. The man leaves a trace of his taste in the ring he purchases for his bride. Now, you don't have to get him an engagement ring in return, but it is a beautiful gesture." He held out his hand to receive mine. "May I take a look at yours?"

"That's the thing; he hasn't gotten me a ring yet. I'm actually proposing to him."

Stuart's eyebrows raised and a mixture of shock and confusion took over the muscles in his face.

"Why would a beautiful woman like yourself feel the need to break tradition and propose? Call me old-fashioned, and I am aware that it often happens nowadays, but in Scotland, it's only appropriate for a woman to propose on the 29th of February. Which only occurs every four years. What's your reason for not allowing him time to ask for your hand at his will?"

I didn't want to answer his question, nor did I feel a need to, but I was proud of my decision. Why not?

"Honestly, he would have proposed to me years ago, but he knew that I wasn't ready. Now that I am, I want to show him by asking for his hand in marriage."

"And you couldn't simply write him a note updating him of your change of heart?"

"No," I retorted, "This is the way I want to do it, so this is the way it will be done!"

"Oh, I understand. It all evolves around you." He leaned back in his chair, crossed his legs at the knee, and wrapped his arms around his body before continuing. "You are privy to this man's innermost thoughts? Have you've been given access to his fears, personal goals, and dreams? You love him, but do you know his secrets and shortcomings?"

"No, and I'm not saying I do, but I know he loves me, and that's what marriage is about."

There was a roar of laughter that came from the back of the store. I couldn't see anyone but could identify that the voice belonged to a lady.

"I'm sorry about that, Savannah. That's my wife."

"If your wife finds my words that funny, how about asking her to join us? If I'm wrong, I'd like to be proved of it."

"It's not our place to steer you away from doing what you wish in love. Again, I apologize. Let's continue shopping for this engagement ring. What is your future husband's name?"

"His name is Andre, but everyone knows him by Dre, and I'm curious to know what your wife found funny. If it takes more than love for marriage to work, I want to know what else is needed."

"Love is the main rope in marriage because it ties the two of you to God, but that is not why I laughed." The woman was still out of sight, but I could hear her voice moving closer as she spoke. "I laughed because you said, 'I know he loves me and that's what marriage is about.'"

"And what's wrong with me saying that? Dre does love me and goes out of his way to show me. He puts his life on the line for me all the time and has never turned his back on me from the beginning. He is even great with our daughter. On nights when she's scared to sleep alone, he climbs in bed with her. He even combs her hair, reads to her, and takes her to church every Sunday."

"And what about you?"

I could have screamed at the sight before me. There was a little person, no more than four-foot-something standing next to me with visible chemical burn marks on her face. The reason I hadn't jumped was through the damage on her face, her beauty shined brightly. If it weren't for the burns, she might have been the most beautiful woman I'd ever laid eyes on; short in height but absolutely gorgeous.

"Savannah, this is my wife, Hilda." She nodded at the introduction and repeated her question.

"What about you, Savannah? You spoke on his love for you, the sacrifices he makes, and his love for your daughter, but what are *you* feeling?"

"I'm sorry, but I don't understand the question."

"Do you love him? Do you love Andre?"

"I wouldn't be here if I didn't," I giggled, feeling that her question was dumb.

"Then why have you not said it one time since you walked in here? You mentioned him attending church and doing your daughter's hair, but where are you during this time?"

"That's easy; I'm at work. I have a real job that doesn't let me have as much free time as his, so he handles our family time with her," I concluded with a smile, and Hilda frowned.

"Well wishes, Savannah," she said with the original warmth she had in her voice absent before speaking to her husband in a language I'd never heard before. He was Scottish, and I could tell she wasn't, but I had no clue what her nationality was. Stuart replied in the same language; then she disappeared behind the tall jewelry display counters. I would have thought she returned to the back of the store until I saw her arms go up, and she was holding a ziplock bag full of men's rings.

"My wife thinks it is best that you buy a temporary ring for the proposal, then bring him back to pick out yours and upgrade his. This way, you both get what you want and deserve."

I purchased his engagement ring which tickled the shit out of me. I kept picturing myself on one knee, proposing to him. The roles were completely reversed in my head. I decided since the proposal wasn't traditional, I could cut out the on-one-knee thing and make it more surprising. Since I was technically the one who was supposed to wear the engagement ring like the jeweler explained, I picked one out for myself and agreed with his wife about getting what I really wanted. I asked for it to be held until Monday because I'd be returning with Dre to purchase it.

I made it to the restaurant at six to make sure everything was perfect. I had requested that the band only play love songs during the hour of 6:30 to 7:30 to help set the mood. Mrs. Jefferson was putting the final touches on the food when I went into the kitchen. She had cooked a five-course meal that would be served to us as if we were in a five-star restaurant.

There was rosemary and garlic roasted chicken, a medley of steamed vegetables with her homemade tomato sauce that she created to complement the seasonings the vegetables were steamed in. She handcrafted loaded mashed potatoes on saucers in spiral shapes, and all of her dishes had different garnishes on them. Her use of bright colors made each meal look like artwork that was too pretty to eat. I had no clue that she was that talented. Dre and Stephanie weren't due to arrive until seven, so I headed to the restroom to freshen up and practice my proposal. Every time I started it, my eyes would water. I wasn't sure if they were tears of joy or pain, but either way, I was sure they were connected to some real emotion, which would be enough to let Dre know I was serious with my request to spend forever with him.

It was now 6:50 p.m., and everyone was seated at the table eating bread and sipping wine awaiting Dre's arrival. Thirty minutes passed, and we were still waiting on Dre and Stephanie to show up. Memphis volunteered to call Stephanie on her cell phone to see what the delay was, but he was forwarded to voicemail. My daddy attempted to call Dre, but he received the same forwarding message as Memphis. We waited until 8:30 p.m. before we all decided to split up and drive around looking for them. Mr. Jefferson and my daddy rode together, Memphis jumped in the car with me, and Sade and Mrs. Jefferson stayed at the restaurant just in case they were to show up.

I went by my house, Stephanie's house, and even drove through the parking lot at the circus to find one of their cars but had no luck. It was now 10:00 p.m., and I was ready to give up when Mrs. Jefferson called my cell phone.

"Savannah, I was getting ready to take Sade home when she asked me why everybody was mad at her daddy for taking Stephanie to eat at a different restaurant and not here with us. When I asked what she was talking about, Sade said that Stephanie had told her this morning that the circus was canceled, and that she and Dre would be going out for dinner and dancing instead."

"That sneaky bitch," I yelled into the phone. Before I could apologize to Mrs. Jefferson for the use of words that I chose, she said, "That's exactly what I was thinking, Savannah. She and Dre have been getting real close over the last few weeks, and I told my husband I didn't like it, nor did I trust her. Go get your man, baby!" I thanked her and then hung up the phone.

I must have checked every club's parking lot in Seattle and couldn't find either one of their cars. I decided to take Memphis home around midnight. He hadn't said a word to me, and even his presence at the dinner seemed like my daddy had forced it. I never asked him how he felt about me proposing, but it was obvious that he didn't like it. As I waited for him to get inside the house, I got a text message from Trisha.

If you are looking for your man, go back to Stephanie's house and check her pussy.

I didn't have time to figure out how she knew what was going on, but I needed to take the tip that she provided. When I made it to her house, both of their vehicles were parked in her driveway, so I parked my car on the street but made sure it blocked their vehicles in just in case they tried to leave. Before getting out of my car, I kicked off my heels for a quieter approach and put my hair back in a ponytail so the long curls wouldn't distract me. My blood was boiling over, and I saw red. I made my way up the pathway that led to the door and then changed my mind. I wanted to catch them in the act. I started walking on the grass which would lead me to the side of the house and her living room window.

Thank goodness this bitch was cheap because, with the lights on in her living room, I could see straight through her cheap-ass curtains, and she wouldn't be able to see out. Dre was sitting on the couch smoking a blunt and drinking out of a plastic champagne glass. Stephanie wasn't in the living room at first, so I was going to look in the other windows. Then this bitch entered the room, wrapped in a towel, with a bottle of lotion in her hand. I was glad that not only could I see in the room, but I could also hear the conversation.

"Dre, this was the best birthday ever. Thank you so much for spending it with me. I still can't believe Savannah declined my offer to join us. I don't understand why she hates me all of a sudden."

He didn't seem to mind being in her presence while she wore nothing but a towel. He didn't even seem shocked that she walked in like this.

"You're welcome, Steph; I'm glad you enjoyed yourself, even though I got two left feet. Look, I know it's been bothering you, but it's your birthday. Don't even think about Savannah tonight."

"You're right, and you do have two left feet."

They laughed, and then she handed Dre the lotion. Like it was routine, he handed her the blunt in return and stood on his feet as she sat in his place. He opened up the lotion, poured some in his hands, and began rubbing it on her back and shoulders and wherever else the towel didn't cover. Stephanie tilted her head back to look up at him.

"That feels so good, Dre. I've been so stressed about this move back to Atlanta; it's had me tense." She put her head back down and pointed to the left middle portion of her back. "Can you please work that knot out for me? It's killing me." As if Dre were hypnotized, he did as he was told.

"Yeah, Stephanie, I can feel it; you real tense, girl. Stop looking at the bad side of it. You might make partner handling this deal, and once you get the account under control, you can always move back here if you want."

She wasn't listening to Dre's words; she was enjoying his hands on her back. She hit the blunt one more time and then passed it back to Dre and handed him his drink.

"Drink up, Dre. This is a celebration. We celebrated my birthday, now let's celebrate my promotion." Dre didn't see her because her back was to him, but I watched the bitch bite her bottom lip.

"That's better, Steph; hell yeah, this a celebration. You want me to dance again?"

"No, please don't dance. My eyes have already seen enough. All I want us to do now is smoke, drink, and chill. It was a beautiful night."

She motioned for Dre to sit down next to her as she started to rub lotion on her legs.

"Sounds like you're ready for me to spark up another blunt," he said, sitting down and pulling out another one from his pocket.

"You know I am. I keep telling you I can hang with you, and tonight, I'm going to prove it."

Dre sparked up the blunt and inhaled deeply, which caused ashes to fall on his pants.

"Oh shit, I'm fucking up."

As he started dusting his pants off, Stephanie reached over to his lap to help dust him off, which caused her breast to fall out of her towel. Immediately, Dre looked at her breast and then turned his head.

"I'm sorry, I didn't mean to look." Stephanie didn't say a word. She kept rubbing her hand across his zipper pretending to continue to dust him off. Dre looked down at his lap, and the ashes were all gone. He turned his head to the side to face Stephanie to thank her for her help and was now face-to-face with her breast. His dick must have jumped in his pants because Stephanie confirmed she felt it.

"Dre, you said you didn't mean to look, but your dick just said you're lying," she said now, rubbing on his hardened penis through his jeans.

I was at the window ready to break through it. Dre wasn't stopping her or objecting to her findings. I would have stopped them right then and there, but I wanted to see how far they would really go. It would help me decide if I was making the right decision when it came to Dre.

She was still rubbing on his manhood, and Dre still hadn't moved her hands off his lap. He just hit the blunt again. Stephanie snatched the blunt out of his mouth and straddled his lap like she was riding a horse. She placed the blunt in her mouth, and her breast was in Dre's face, less than an inch away from his mouth. Dre made eye contact with her breast again as if her nipple was leading a conversation with him. Next thing I know, he was going from left to right, sucking on her breasts, and then he grabbed her big-ass booty with both of his hands and began bouncing her up and down on his lap. My heart started aching, but I continued to watch. Karma wanted me to see that what goes around comes back around, and I couldn't move if I wanted to. I was frozen in my Peeping Tom position at the window.

Stephanie removed the towel completely and tossed it behind her couch. She stood on her feet and turned around in a complete circle to show Dre her entire body. With her ass now in Dre's face, she said, "Spank it, Dre. Spank all that ass!"

Dre spanked the right cheek, then kissed it. He repeated the actions with the left cheek. He rubbed her booty again, then said, "You been wanting this dick for a while now, huh?"

Stephanie said, "Yes, boo," in a moan that almost sounded like a purr. Stephanie turned back around and leaned in to kiss Dre, but he turned his face away.

"Savannah must have fucked up and told you this dick was good, didn't she? She told you how I tear her little pussy up, didn't she?" Dre didn't sound like Dre anymore. He had his freaky bedroom voice and conversation going on. It made me remember the first time we had sex. It was the same voice he asked me to be his woman. I felt the warm tears fall down my face as Stephanie responded.

"Yes, boo, she told me that dick was big as fuck, and you knew exactly what you were doing with it."

Dre smiled and pushed his dreads back, taking a mouthful of Stephanie's breast as he did it. She began to moan loudly. Dre reached down and felt his lap that was now covered in her juices.

"Damn, I got that pussy wet, didn't I?" She was still shaking from her orgasm and nodded her head yes.

"The last time I was this wet, Dre, was when your bitch was eating my pussy back in Atlanta. I can't stand her ass now, but Savannah's tongue used to leave this pussy weak."

I had never told Dre about my sexual relationship with Stephanie, or women. Period. He looked shocked but didn't comment.

"Suck my dick, then, bitch, and show me how bad you want this big motherfucka. I want to feel your throat. Suck that dick nasty for me."

It was now Stephanie's turn to follow directions. She fell on her knees, then unbuttoned and unzipped Dre's pants. She started with slow licks all over it, then took it into her mouth.

"Yeah, bitch, that feels good, but it ain't better than Savannah's. Is that all you got for me? You're supposed to be making me forget about her. Suck on the head or something. Drool on it."

She must have felt like she was in a competition because she started bobbing her head in overtime. Dre rested his head on the back of the couch with his face turned up to the ceiling, enjoying the pleasure Stephanie's mouth was giving him. More tears poured out of my eyes as I watched him wrap his fingers around a patch of her hair in the back of her head and bob her head up and down on his penis. Two minutes into it, he slid a finger inside of her cave of love and then removed it with juices dripping from it. I noticed he wiped his finger on the couch. With me, Dre would lick his finger clean, making sure to give me eye contact while he did it. Something wasn't right with his fuck session. He never wanted to receive head over five minutes, and I soon found out what the problem was.

"Aye, you know why I'm letting you suck on Savannah's dick like this, bitch? It's because I feel sorry for your ass. You ain't got shit on Savannah, and you know it. I see you trying to walk and talk like her, but the shit ain't getting you nowhere. You're a second-string bitch with some second-rate pussy and head to match. Yep, you ain't got shit on Savannah, and you just confirmed it. I'll make sure to tell her that when I get home."

Dre pulled his penis out of her grasp and then grabbed the towel from behind the couch.

"Fuck you, Dre," Stephanie said, with tears in her eyes. "Your bitch has some second-rate pussy; just ask every nigga in Nashville, Atlanta, and Los Angeles. I'm sure a few niggas here know it by now too. Her ass is lying about spending time with her mother every Wednesday and Saturday, and I'm sure of it because that's a pattern, and that bitch don't do them. Commitment isn't in her vocabulary. She's a ho and will always be a ho," Stephanie laughed, as Dre waved her off like she was nothing. "Go ahead, Dre, and try to make your ho a housewife. She has slept with everybody, including me. She ate this pussy, and I've stuck everything in arm's reach inside of hers as I ate hers, and the bitch was too loose to feel it. She ain't got nothing left special to give to you that I ain't already had. I tried to let you see what a real woman was like and show you that you can do better than Savannah; that's why I've been hanging around with you, but you're too stupid to see it."

Dre zipped up his pants and started to get his things together. He didn't even try to defend me from all the hoes Stephanie had been calling me. I knew he didn't defend me because he agreed with her. I even had to agree with her. My secret was out, and there was no way for me to defend my love for sex with multiple people. Since Dre had made no comments at all, I took his silence as my clue to make my way to my car, but not before I heard him say, "Who said I'm still going to fuck with Savannah?"

I drove away doing 70 mph on residential streets to beat Dre to the house. Once I made it there, I sat on the couch and rolled up a blunt, replaying Dre's last words, *"Who said I'm still going to fuck with Savannah?"* If I had any say-so, it would be me saying he was. Dre was crazy if he thought I would let him walk away after I finally convinced myself that I wanted him. I would prove it to him tonight and not just in my words, but in my actions as well.

Dre walked in the house and went straight to the shower. I followed closely behind him, with the blunt in my hand. I wasn't mad that he had cheated on me. I just wanted confirmation he was mine and wouldn't do it again.

"Want to hit it?"

He reached for the blunt but didn't answer. I sat on the toilet as he smoked, removed his clothes, and entered the running water. I took three hits of the blunt and then stuck it in the back of the shower so Dre could hit it. I knew his hands would be wet, so I held it to his mouth. Three minutes into his shower and after the blunt was too small to hold up against his lips, he finally spoke.

"When I get out of the shower, we need to talk; you were right about that bitch, Stephanie. She ain't your friend."

I pleaded for him to spark up the conversation then, but he wouldn't. I wanted to see if Dre would be honest and tell the story the way it happened, including all the sexual events that occurred. While he finished his shower, I went and poured myself a glass of his liquor mixed with soda so that I could kill it. I wasn't in the mood to sip. When I made it back to the bedroom, Dre was out of the shower with his towel around his waist, lighting up half a blunt he had in his pocket and passing it to me.

I was already buzzed, but the more, the merrier, and, by the looks of it, Dre had been thinking the same thing. I sat on the bed and waited for him to talk.

"You know it was Stephanie's birthday, so we went to eat and out to a club. We were supposed to go to the circus and spend time with Sade, but Stephanie said Sade didn't want to go anymore."

Damn, this bitch lied on my daughter, I thought. What child would turn down going to the circus? Dre should have known she was lying then. I should have asked him why he felt the need to be there for her on her birthday, but I let it go. Continuing to tell his story, he had finally gotten to the part that I witnessed with my own eyes. I was glad the weed and liquor had kicked in before he started; otherwise, I would be crying as I had done outside the window. He was honest, a little too honest, as he said verbatim what he had said to Stephanie while she sucked on him.

When he was done telling his story, he just stared at me, waiting for my reaction. His brutal honesty had turned me on in a weird way. I climbed on his lap like Stephanie had done earlier, the same way he had just finished describing. I retold the story to him by acting it out in its entirety. Pretending as if I had forgotten bits and pieces of it, I made Dre walk me through it. I put my breasts in his face when he said she did it and even turned around naked as he said she had done.

Dre seemed unsure about me acting out the scene, but I asked him to go with the flow. I told him it would help the pain I felt from his words go away. He looked as though he wanted to defend his betrayal but decided to follow my directions instead. As he began to suck on my breast from left to right like he had done Stephanie's, I could tell the reenactment was turning him on. Dre had purposely left out the part where he stuck his finger inside of her as he told his story, but he still slid his finger in me. I noticed he licked it clean and didn't wipe it off.

"So, Dre, if it would have been me naked on you like this, what would you have done differently?"

He didn't say another word, and he couldn't because he had flipped me over and buried his face in between my legs. When he was done feeding his face, we made love like we had done the first time five years ago. Dre was still the best lover I ever had, and I knew I didn't want to let him go. I made sure to scream out "I love you, Dre" with every deep stroke he gave me. Dre didn't respond to any of my displays of affection and only seemed to moan "Damn" or "Oh shit, girl." My mind made me think he was now pretending to be fucking Stephanie, but the feel of his touch convinced me otherwise. After he had exploded for the third time inside of me, I asked him to join me in the shower. I fell to my knees with the water hitting me all over the back of my head to continue pleasing him and his body. Once I looked up and saw his eyes closed, I slid the ring off my thumb that I had grabbed out of my purse on the way to the shower and placed it on his finger. He looked down at me, and with a mouth full of him, I asked, "Do you still want to give me your last name?" He fixed the ring on his finger and then placed the hand with the ring on it on the back of my head and started pushing himself in and out of my mouth. I tried to make it the best head I had ever given him since he had yet to answer my question.

There was still silence; then he finally said, "Prove to me that you want and can earn my last name, and it's yours, baby." I twisted my tongue making him shoot his pleasure serum down my throat, and I swallowed it.

"That sounds like a yes to me because I want it and will show you I can earn it," I said and got off my knees to clean my body.

As we dried off, I told him about the engagement dinner and Stephanie's part in it. He apologized a thousand times, saying he didn't know, and I believed him. Stephanie had no intention of bringing Dre to the restaurant, so I'm sure she never mentioned taking him there, either. I wouldn't pick at Dre tonight, but he didn't seem sure about wanting to marry me anymore, but he hadn't said no. He accepted his ring and even adjusted it on his finger, which meant there was hope. We headed back to the bed to pick up where we had left off, and I knew we would be going at it all night, which was perfectly fine with me. Guess I ended up proposing on bended knees after all. Ain't that some shit?

Chapter Eight

Mama's Words

It felt good walking around with my engagement ring on. I was showing it off every chance I'd get. I flashed it at the miserable bitches at work and the single but slutty-lookers at my gym. Every time I glanced down at my hand, it made me want to scream excitedly. I couldn't believe a small piece of metal with a rock on it could change me the way it did.

I called my best friend, Will, to tell him about my change of heart, but he was so negative I was ready to end the call.

"You can't have a change of heart; the devil doesn't have a heart. Bitch, you don't even have a piece of coal in your chest. That space is just as empty as the one in your head," he declared.

Since his relationship with his man, Alvin, was completely over with, now, of course, he was miserable and being his best friend, he wanted me to be miserable too. I kept talking, and when I told him I couldn't wait to change my last name to Burns, he said, "You just want Dre's ass now because you know he really don't want you. Now the shoe is on the other foot, and it doesn't feel good, do it? You get to feel what Dre went through chasing you down. He isn't going to marry you, sweetie; he's just getting his payback."

"Whatever, Will!"

"You don't get to 'whatever' me, ever again. Do you know why?"

"Because you're miserable your man cheated on you, and you're trying your best to keep me from being happy, is that it?" I clapped back.

"Oh no, bitch, not even close. You don't get to 'whatever' me because your little demonic ways have finally landed on my desk. While you're chasing down a man that you don't know shit about, I'm facing an inquiry at work over the shit you pulled in California."

"You don't have shit to do with my problems in California!"

"Yes, I do, and you know it. You used me, my house, and my basketball trip to hide out after the shit you pulled hit the fan. All the while I'm thinking we're building something special, you were using me as security."

"That's not true!" I screamed into the phone, hoping to sound believable. I did use him for protection, but there wasn't any proof he could find saying that. It was a coincidence. That was my fable, and I would stick to it when asked to tell it.

"Whether or not it's true, that's how it looks. While Keisha and the rest of them are in jail hiring the best lawyers their food stamp cases can buy, they all are retracing your steps and that plane ticket, the cell phone tower you answered your father's call from, and your incoming and outgoing calls to me looks like I might have been using my pull at the sheriff's office to help you out."

"I'm so sorry, Will. I never meant for anything to fall on you."

"I know you are, and I know you didn't mean to. Don't lose any sleep over it because nothing can be proved, but it's real hard to prove that we were best friends before you went on your little revenge binge. You are so poisonous, vampire, and that's why what you have with Dre will never work. Karma is coming for you, and if Dre's smart, he'd get the fuck away from you before he becomes a victim of your Karma too."

I wasn't about to keep miserable company and lied about another call coming in to get off the phone. Will was right to be upset with me about the inquiry at his job. That was his livelihood, but he was wrong if he thought that the only reason I wanted Dre was because he no longer wanted me. At first, that was the reason I proposed to him, but after spending so much time with him lately and really getting to know him, it made me want him.

I didn't care what Will thought, or anybody else, for that matter. I knew Dre was done chasing me and at the point of giving up. I didn't need anybody else to remind me that if I didn't get my shit together, I'd be losing him for good. Dre made sure to remind me of this himself, every chance he could.

The first time he said it was when he took me back to the jewelry store two weeks ago to buy my ring. He made it clear we wouldn't be getting married anytime soon by saying, "You know there's more to that ring than just wearing it, right?" as I held my hand in front of me, watching my diamond sparkle in the sunlight.

"Yes, Dre, I know, and I told you I would prove to you that I'm ready."

He grabbed my hand and pulled me into him for a long kiss as we stood in the parking lot behind the jewelry store. Once the kiss had ended, he said, "Good, I'm glad you know you will have to prove it to me first. So don't start getting wedding fever and planning shit. We ain't getting married any time soon."

At first, it bothered me that he kept reminding me we weren't ready to be married . . . until I remembered that I had known we weren't ready before I had even purchased his ring. Knowing Dre was ready to move on without me hurt, but if I knew I wasn't ready this time, I'd let him leave.

I can't lie, seeing him come that close to sleeping with Stephanie had me ready to hit fast-forward on all of my plans for us. Rushing the wedding would lock him down and legally make him mine. It was wrong for me to think like that, but I still tried. I went to church and Bible study with him for the past two weeks, joined the family for dinner whenever it was possible, and even requested for Sade to spend the night with us while I did all the entertaining. At work, in between projects, I would chat and comment on blog posts that I found while searching for "How to be a better parent" on the internet. I would take the advice given to me there and use it when dealing with Sade.

My small, positive steps toward changing had become giant leaps, and I was feeling good about it. That's when reality kicked back in. I had never cut Trisha out of my life, nor completely terminated communication with Royce, and everything was moving so fast around me that I forgot to make time to think about how I shitted on Stephanie and the possible repercussions that I could face from it. Stephanie was back in Atlanta, an office away from my partners, and that wasn't a good place for her to be. Focusing on fucking her over put her in the best position to fuck me in ways that I might not recover from.

She knew every bad move and horrible action I've made, both business and personal, and I had given her the gas that could fuel her into telling it all.

"Hey, I just wanted you to know that I've gotten my place packed and getting ready to head to the airport to catch this flight. I'm sure you are aware of what I'm about to say, but I would rather make shit clear than for you to have to assume. I'm coming for you, Savannah, and everything you own because we both know that everything you have is mine. It was me working overtime while you chased your next nut, and now that I'm not glued to your side, it will show. In other words, bitch, it's *my* turn to seek revenge!"

I laughed at the message she left on my answering machine, but I knew she meant what she said. Stephanie knew who I was and all the rotten shit I can do because my dumbass made her my secret keeper. I let her execute a lot of bullshit on my behalf after I realized it excited her, and if she were as smart as I thought she was, she'd execute her own plans better seeing that she learned from all my mistakes.

I fucked up and sent my new enemy to undergo training to become just as powerful as me, and she wasn't going to stop until she got her hunger for revenge satisfied. I was sure of it because I trained her that way.

I had to prioritize my problems and knock them out by severity, so I tried to find Trisha but didn't know where to start looking. I had thrown away the number she had given me, and my only hope was that she'd return to the bar in the hotel we had our drinks at. I left my telephone number with the waitress who had served us that night and asked her to give it to Trisha if she came back.

With Royce, forwarding him to voicemail and not listening to his message was the way I decided to handle him,

and that wasn't working at all. It started out with three
calls a week to now three times a day, which included calls
to my office. I knew I would have to talk to him eventually
and planned to listen to his messages whenever Dre wasn't
around, and I had a free moment.

From some of the articles that I read online and from
chatting with different therapists, they all recommended
that I get closure with Trisha before opening any new
doors in my life. They felt that Sade would benefit from
me facing my past and making peace with it, and I agreed.

You know the old saying, "Don't go looking for trouble,
or it will find you"? Well, that saying is true, and I have
proof of it. Just when I went looking for Trisha, she came
looking for me. It was Friday, and I left work early to pick
Sade up for the weekend from her school. Picking her up
on Fridays was starting to become my weekly routine.
Something was wrong when I picked her up this time; I
could feel it. Sade wasn't talking as much as she usually
did, nor would she look at me when I talked to her. I
didn't want to bring her home, and Dre assume I did
something to make her upset, so I attempted to kiss her
ass and take her to a fast-food restaurant so that we could
eat and talk. I got that idea online too.

Some 36-year-old woman from Phoenix, Arizona, said
in the chat room, *"When I need to find out what is going
on with my 7-year-old daughter, I take her to places
she enjoys eating and order all her favorite foods. The
atmosphere seems to make her comfortable enough
to open up and talk to me. I even allow her to run the
conversation at her pace and only ask questions that
will lead to concrete answers."*

If it worked for her, I thought I'd try it. I got her some
chicken nuggets, fries, chocolate milk, and her meal

came with a small toy. We sat in a booth away from everyone else in the back of the burger joint so we could talk in private. The bright yellow swivel seats at our booth seemed to have her attention as she moved side to side on the one she was seated on. I joined in swinging my seat too until she noticed and smiled at me. That's when I decided to talk.

"How was your day, Sade?" I asked, as I normally did, but still swiveling in my chair.

"Good," she responded, with her head down, staring at her feet.

"That's it? Only good? What could have made it great?" She always answered that question with "great." She hesitated and then shrugged her shoulders. I noticed she started moving her chair slower, so I changed my approach.

"Well, what happened today that didn't make your day great?" She looked up at me, stopped moving completely, and said, "You're sick again, Mama, and I want you to be better; that would make my day great."

Her words had completely caught me off guard. Still moving in my chair, I said, "Sade, baby, I'm not sick anymore; I'm all better." She shook her head.

"No, you're not, Mama. Your nurse came to my school today and gave me her telephone number to give to you. She said you need to call her, or something bad was going to happen to you. She said that she didn't want to see me sad, but if you didn't call her, she couldn't stop it from happening. She told me not to tell anybody but you."

I was lost and wasn't sure if Sade knew exactly what she was talking about. It took me a moment to say, "Nurse?" out loud for me to fully comprehend it.

"Yes, Mama, your nurse from the hospital. The pretty one." Sade dug in her pocket and handed me a folded-up piece of paper. Once I saw the writing on it, I knew it was Trisha.

"Put your food back into the bag, Sade. You can eat it at home with your daddy."

I snatched Sade and her food up and then zoomed out of the restaurant so fast that when I took a look back to make sure I didn't leave anything at our table, I could see the swivel chair swaying side to side as if I still occupied it. That bitch must have lost her mind thinking there wasn't going to be any backlash for approaching my baby with her bullshit. I don't care if she did feel like Sade was her granddaughter; there is a proper way to handle things. You don't go through anybody's kids to handle adult issues, nor do you put kids in the middle of them, and she had the nerve to have my child pass on a threat for her.

I wondered what she meant by saying something "bad was going to happen" if I didn't contact her. Because the shit wasn't making any sense to me. She asked for $20,000, but what would the bitch do if I didn't give it to her, and if she was out to get me, why did she send the tip that helped me find Dre?

When we made it to the house, I told Dre what had happened and that I was going to call and meet up with her to get this shit resolved. Dre was just as much upset as I was and even madder at the preschool Sade attended for allowing the stranger to interact with our baby. Before I stormed out the door, Dre said he would question Sade some more and then head up to the school to "check sum folks." That was the first time I heard Dre's Southern accent in years. It turned me on slightly, but I knew it wasn't the time to tell him that. I pecked him on the lips instead and then headed out the door.

Hi, you've reached Peaches, and as you can see, I can't get to my phone right now, but if you leave a message including your name, and the time and date on which you called, I'll be sure to return your call at my earliest convenience. Thank you for calling and have a beautiful and blessed day. Beep

Trisha's phone went straight to voicemail both times I called, so I left a message.

"I got your message, Trisha, and we need to talk. It's Friday at 3:30 p.m. I need you to meet me at the steak house you saw my car parked at by the airport at 5:00 p.m. Not a minute later, and I'm sure you know who this is!"

I'm sure she could hear the anger in my voice, and I wanted to say more, but I didn't want her afraid to show up. I called Dre, updated him, and then headed to my daddy's house to tell him what was going on. As I started telling him the story, he took a seat on the arm of his couch and lit a cigarette. When I was done, he said, "Well, now I know where your brother is. He's been in and out all week with no conversation for me, just evil looks. This morning, he packed his things and said he was moving out and that it was time for him to be a man." My daddy ended his words with a dry laugh.

"What's funny, Daddy?" I asked, with irritation in my voice.

"He said it was time for him to be a man but made sure he grabbed his video games and cartoon collection before he left. That boy even took the box of fruity cereal he begs me to buy every time I go grocery shopping."

Maybe laughter was the way my daddy was choosing to deal with it, but I wasn't.

"Do you want to go with me to meet her at five? She might have won over Memphis, but she didn't get me, and I'm going to make sure she understands this, even if I have to get a restraining order."

Looking up in to my daddy's face, reading his expression which said, "I'm tired," I knew his answer was no. He didn't have to say it. After years of putting up with her shit and parenting Memphis alone, even after he turned into an adult, he deserved a break. I picked up my purse and hugged him. Before walking out of the door, I said, "I love you, Daddy, and I thank you for protecting me from her as long as you did. I'll call you tomorrow."

"Wait, Savannah, before you go, there's something I think you should hear. Hold on while I go get it."

"Sure, Daddy."

His face held so much pain in it that I couldn't remind him that I had somewhere that I needed to be. He went in his room, and I could hear him slamming boxes around. It was almost six minutes before he returned.

"I apologize for keeping you this long, but I wanted you to know everything before you go duke it out with her. Do you still have time to listen? I don't want to lie to you and say this will be quick."

"For you, Daddy, I have all the time in the world."

He stood in front of me before he spoke again. "I've been holding on to this for all these years, and I'm ready to let it go." He had a letter in his shaking hands and was fanning it in the air as if it held great powers. "Bear with me, baby, I don't know where I put my reading glasses."

"Here, you can give it to me, and I'll read it," I said with my hand out, but he shook his head in disagreement.

Clearing his throat, he started reading. *"Dear Dwight, I've asked you to please stop trying to hunt me down. You're causing me and my man problems. We already said our goodbyes, remember? Remember when you told me I couldn't be in our kids' lives, and if I tried, you'd put me in jail with you? There was nothing more we need to say to each other, and I've forgiven you for it. You were right. My life is too busy to be trying to drag around two kids with me while I try to force myself to believe that a part of me loves them . . ."*

"Daddy, you can stop. I know she doesn't love us, and that she never has. When I'm around her, I don't feel anything for her either. She's no more than a stranger to me," I said, feeling like cutting him off would spare him from reliving the pain.

"No, Savannah, I need this. Please let me finish, baby."

I fell silent, and after a few seconds, he started where he left off.

"Loving anyone other than myself and you is asking too much from me. Yes, Dwight, I was in love with you, which is still hard for me to believe, but you had to go and get me pregnant. You rushed me into marriage and threw me into a life I never wanted. I hate kids, and I hate what they did to my mind and body even more. Look at my shape. Those stretch marks and the elastic in the pocketbook between my legs has been stretched. I only asked to take them with me because it felt like the right thing to do. Kids should be with their mama is what I've always been told. If they had been with me, I could have used them as my excuse for not wanting more with my next man, and he would be forced to help me raise them. I know it sounds dumb, but all I ever wanted was you, and you fucked that up by adding two more to us. Sorry, Dwight, but your math is off. Take those brats and move on. There's a woman out there that wants to be the Clair in your sitcom. I'm dying a Golden Girl."

He fell silent again, and I thought he might have been crying.

"Daddy?"

"Yes, baby, I'm fine." He came and sat next to me on the couch and put his arm behind my shoulder. With his free hand, he placed that letter on the table and pulled out another from his back pocket. "This is my response to her letter. I never sent it to her, but I never threw it away either. I want you to know who your daddy was so you can understand who I am. I'm not proud of any of this."

"You don't have to read it to me. Tear it up. She never deserved a response or to be loved by you."

"You're right; she didn't. I know that now, but I didn't back then." I heard the envelope being torn open, him ruffling out the paper because something felt like I shouldn't look at him, and then he started reading. *"Trisha, I don't know what that man is putting in your head, but nothing you said to me is true. You love our kids and me. You can't look at any of us without smiling, especially our princess. The way you hold Savannah for hours pisses me off because you never held Memphis that way. You don't give her time to cry because you're constantly singing to her and rocking her in your arms. You treated her like a baby doll, and you want me to believe you don't love her when I saw you love her? You've just been gone away from us too long, and dammit, it's time for you to come home. You've had your fun and made your money, but it's time to let it go. You said you hate kids, which might be the truth if I were judging you from how you treat our son, but that's a bold-faced lie when it comes to Savannah. Come on home, Trisha. Please, baby, come home. I love you, and I'm going crazy without you—"*

My daddy stopped reading and looked me in my eyes. He stared deep into them for thirty or so seconds, and my eyes began to water. I don't know why, but they were. He squeezed my shoulder and then continued.

"I haven't bathed, eaten, or left the house. I'm the walking dead without you, girl. You're my strength, and I need you. Do you hear me, Trisha? I need you, so you need to come on home. I'd do anything to get you back. I'll even give up our kids—"

"Daddy, let me have a cigarette," I demanded, and he handed me one and his lighter.

As I lit it and took a puff, he said, "That's where I stopped writing because writing those words made me realize how weak I was over that woman. The truth is, I meant it when I wrote it, but writing it helped me see the truth, and it was a sad one. When I saw Dre sitting on that couch with his soul gone, I saw me. Hell, I saw me when you described what he had been doing by phone. I didn't come talk to Dre for you or his sake. I did it for therapy for me. When you said your mother was back—"

"—You were happy; you thought she came back to work things out with you, and after thirty-plus years, your Trisha came home." I finished his sentence as I let the smoke out of my lungs.

"Yes, and that's when I realized I had never moved on. I've been waiting for her all these years, and when she came back, it wasn't for me. It was for the kids she claimed to hate.

"Savannah," he yelled, "what are you doing?"

I had both letters at the tip of the cigarette as I puffed away until they both owned their own flames. I let the letters get a good fire going, then placed them in his ashtray before answering. "Helping you get over your past so you can move on. You're not that man anymore, Daddy. You never dated anyone after her because you felt guilty about your thoughts of giving us up, and guess what? You never left our side, and you're a damn good grandfather to Sade."

He wrapped his arms around me and what I thought were cries was really laughter.

"Savannah, you're a lot like your mother, and I hate it, but everything you don't have in common with her is what makes you special to Dre and me. It's in your blood, baby, and if you don't want it in there, you have to fight it."

"I know, and I want to fight it."

"Well, this is what you don't know. If your mother has Memphis with her, she's using him. She hated your brother from the moment they told her his mind would develop slower than kids his age. He instantly became her 'flaws in the flesh.' She thought she was perfect, smart, and the prettiest woman to grace the streets of Los Angeles, and then she gave birth to a child with developmental delays. She blamed his lack of smarts on my family and me. Be careful, because your brother has always questioned me about her. He has been waiting for her to return all his life, and he is not going to pass up the chance to have her in his life. He will do anything to keep her, and if she's been around him this long, she already has a plan in place on how she'll use him before she throws him away."

I kissed him on his cheek and felt all the anger I had built up from everything I blamed her for surge through my body.

"Thanks, Daddy, but that old ho better be careful of me. She's hurt everyone that I love, and if she doesn't disappear, I'm going to make sure that I hurt her!"

***

I made it to the steak house at a quarter to five and sat on the empty side of the bar. It didn't surprise me to see Trisha stroll in at 5:30 casually as if she were on time. What did surprise me was that she walked in with Memphis, color-coordinated. They both had on blue jeans and black tops. Memphis's five foot eleven ass was her twin, minus the hair. He had her slanted eyes, her skin tone, and maybe it was the anger of seeing them together, but it looked like he even had her dimples. Trisha must have been using money to win Memphis over because he had a fresh, low haircut, new shoes, and a thick gold chain around his neck. In all the years I've known Memphis, I've never seen him in jewelry; yet, today, he's sporting two bright red earlobes from the new piercings in his ears with princess cut diamond earrings and a chain that looks like he borrowed it from a rap video. It was the best he had ever looked, and by the looks on the women's faces who sat around the bar, they agreed with me. Before I could say anything to them, Memphis opened his mouth and, like fire from a dragon, words flew out.

"Why didn't you tell me Mama came back? You and Daddy, I mean, Dwight, always on some secretive shit. I hate you. You're a dumb-ass bitch!"

Trisha smiled at me with the same winning smile she gave me at the bar that night, then turned to Memphis and said, "Hush, boy, I told you she couldn't help but do what your father wanted her to do. He has her brainwashed. Now, go sit on the other end of the bar until I'm done talking with your sister; then we will go get that football game you want."

There was a stutter in his step, but Memphis obeyed her command. At 33 years old, this fool of a brother of mine still needed parental guidance. I would have felt sorry for him if I hadn't watched him mouth the word "bitch" at me as he walked away. It seems like *bitch* was becoming my new nickname, but that didn't bother me because I know it's not what you're called that matters, but what you answer to that counts. I wasn't going to let being called a bitch by a grown-ass child affect me.

"So, Savannah, you got me up here, so what did you want to talk about?" Trisha asked and then shrugged her shoulders like she had no clue why we were meeting.

"Don't play stupid, Trisha, you know why we're here. You had the nerve to go up to my daughter's school to have her summon me for you. Bitch, don't you *ever* approach my child again! She isn't related to you, just like I'm not. I don't want nor need you in my life, so take your ho ass back down South and make sure you take dumb-ass Memphis with you."

"You need to be really careful with what you say to me and how you fix your mouth to say it. I'm not going to keep reminding you that you don't know me."

"I don't have to know, because I already know enough. You're a stretched out, pussy-slagging prostitute that I could have died without meeting. You hate kids. Isn't that what you wrote in your letter to my daddy? I know there ain't shit about you motherly, and there will never be. My daddy told me the truth about you, ho. Get out of my face, you raggedy bitch!"

Trisha reached across the two bar stools separating us and popped me in my mouth. I wasn't a fighter, but my reflexes kicked in and caused me to pop her ass back. Before I knew it, we were in a full-fledged bar fight, girl style, of course, with nothing but slapping, scratching, and pulling hair after both of our initial blows. I tried to claw my fingers into her face, but she was protecting it, leaving me with no choice but to dig my nails into her neck while she attempted to choke me. Her hands gripping my neck felt weak after being choked multiple times by grown, strong-handed men as I took dick. That made it easy to get some space between us to slap fire from her face. My slap caused her to release my neck and lock on my hair. She began trying to control my movements, and my cheekbone hit the edge of the bar. Memphis and the bartender attempted to separate us, but our roles had changed. I had my fingers locked in her hair, and she had her nails clawed into my neck. Through all the yells and screams from the bartender and the owner ordering us to leave with threats to call the police, I could hear Trisha talking shit to me.

"I told you to respect me like we were strangers on the street, you little bitch."

I was full of tears and crying loudly, but it wasn't from her words or the blows she gave me. After longing for a mother all my life, I received a tramp woman who reeked of the streets—*that's* what was heartbreaking. I had always seen myself slapping or hitting her if she returned, but I never truly meant it. This was my mother, the woman who gave birth to me, and, regardless of whether I wanted her in my life, I shouldn't have struck her back. I should have grabbed my things and walked away or just accepted the hit as I had done with my father's, but she pushed me to do it. I lost control, and I know why I did. Nothing in me saw Trisha as my mother, so the respect that should have been there wasn't. The therapist was right. I needed this closure.

With every second that passed and the more it sank in that Trisha and I just went toe to toe, the more I felt distant from her. I didn't need my mother for me to be a good mother to Sade. Dre was wrong when he thought that. Trisha had just shown me what *not* to do to your children, and now, I will dedicate myself to being different with my own child. As of today, Trisha was officially dead to me. I would leave here knowing my mother died when she left me before I turned 2. I balled my fist and punched her in her eye. It sent her stumbling out of my reach.

"All I wanted to do was reunite with you, and look how it's turned out. You need therapy, Savannah. Please seek help, baby," Trisha said, as she was now in Memphis's arms, being escorted out of the building. What a great actress Trisha was. She wanted to make Memphis think she was the victim in all of this, and at the moment, I didn't care what he thought.

"You stay here!"

The owner suggested I waited until they had pulled off before I left. The entire room was staring at me, but the only eyes I could feel looking at me full of pain yet searching my wounded face for some type of understanding about what had just taken place was Royce. He was seated at a table not too far from the exit doors with a clear view to the bar. Alone with nothing but a newspaper on the opposite side of the table and his plate of food which he had yet to touch. I take it that the fight at the bar prevented him from enjoying his meal.

I could endure the stares of strangers, but not the one from Royce. When the license plate on Trisha's Benz was no longer legible, I darted out of the restaurant, heading to my car.

"Savannah, Savannah, please, hold on a second."

There wasn't a need to look back. I knew Royce's voice, and I had the feeling he would be following me out of the restaurant too.

"Royce, I don't have time for this. I'll call you later this week; I need to get home."

My words did nothing to stop him from continuing to follow me. I sped up my walk and made it to my car, hoping to have the engine started and backed away before he reached me, but that plan was soiled when I went to reach for my purse, and it no longer rested on my shoulder. I must have dropped it during the fight, which meant it was somewhere in the restaurant on the floor. I was wrong again! Royce was gripping my purse in his hands.

"I'm sure you can't leave without your car keys, which I bet are in your purse."

I was trapped, with no choice but to give in so I could get my purse. Turning to face him with my arms out reaching for my purse, I said, "Okay, Royce, you win. What is it that you want? And please make it quick; I need to attend to my wounds."

When he placed the purse in my hands, Royce went to reach for my face. I turned my head as soon as I realized what his hands' destination would be.

"What happened in there? Who was the lady you were tousling with? Let me take a look at your cuts," he said, with concern in his voice.

If I hadn't caught him in an oral double Dutch, I would have believed he cared, but the hurt and anger of catching him came toppling back. I remained silent as if his words had no sound to them.

"Look, Savannah, I'm not out here to discuss us or the incident that happened in my room. I'm here to make sure you are all right, and by the looks of your scratches, you might want to see a doctor and have them properly cleaned," he said while looking at the red streaks around my neck that were burning in the night's air.

"I don't need a doctor, and thank you for your concern, but what happened in there is none of your business. I'll grab some things from over the counter and clean my wounds when I get home."

I couldn't go home. Not with Sade there, looking like this. Nor could I go to my father. I refused to let him stress any more over this.

"There's a 24-hour pharmacy right there on the corner. At least, let me grab you a few things while you wait in my room so you can clean them, then leave. All I want to do is be a friend."

With no alternate place to go, I agreed. I took his room keys, and he headed to the pharmacy. There was a huge bottle of rum on his kitchen counter. I took the liberty of pouring myself two shots. As the liquor touched my lips, a burning sensation shot through my body, letting me know my lip was busted. After I swallowed the second shot, I went to the mirror to look at the damage.

My hair was all over my head, but a brush and a rubber band could fix that in less than a minute. I wish I could say that about everything else. My face was untouched except for my bottom lip being busted at the far-left corner. That must have been the result of her initial blow. Tears came falling down my face when I thought of the force that was used to cause this injury, so I took another shot of the rum. My neck had claw marks on it, four on each side. I would have to wear turtlenecks to cover them until they healed. Good thing it was the middle of fall; getting away with turtlenecks would be easy, and if we had any more rain like we have been getting, I could get away with scarves too.

I went ahead and had one more shot to try to numb the aches and pains I was having in my back and legs from rolling around the hard floor with Trisha, and that was all she wrote. By the time Royce had made it back, I was on my sixth shot and wearing it proudly.

"So, Royce I'm ready to talk about the other night. I have a few questions I want answered like, who was that pregnant bitch I caught you sharing a meal with?" I asked, snatching the bag out of his hand and going back to the bathroom mirror.

"What are you talking about, Savannah? I haven't shared a meal with anyone," he said, confused. My mind told me to shut up, but I couldn't turn my mouth off. The rum was in control.

"Don't play stupid, motherfucka; you know damn well what I'm talking about. Whose thighs did you have your face buried in between? You were licking that pussy. It made me want to put mine in your face for you to lick on too."

He took the alcohol swabs away from me and began cleaning my neck with them. It was obvious I was drunk and needed help.

"Savannah, we'll talk about it at another time. You had a rough day, and I don't want—"

"No, we are going to talk about this now. Who was she? And don't lie. I could see your face in the dark. You were licking that pussy like it was your favorite flavor of ice cream. You knew that bitch real good, and it wasn't a random fuck."

He must have felt like he was in a losing battle. As he placed the Neosporin on my neck, he began spilling his guts.

"It wasn't my favorite flavor of ice cream, but it used to be."

"That was Mrs. Reed? Are you serious?" My laughter was out of control.

He confirmed it was his ex-wife, Mrs. Tiffany Reed like Trisha had told me, and she had come to organize their final paperwork. She started complaining about her new husband, the unwanted pregnancy, and how if she could go back in time, she would make different choices, blah blah blah! To sum up the violin music, one thing led to another, and I ended up walking in on their

69. I had to be drunk because the next words that came out of my mouth even shocked me.

"I can't believe that you were married to a woman who couldn't even suck your dick right."

"*Savannah!*" Royce yelled, clearly shocked at my words. He was so shocked, he dropped the gauze he was wrapping around my neck and then fumbled with it when he went to pick it up.

"Don't look shocked, Royce, you know I'm speaking the truth. There weren't any signs of pleasure in her face while she did it. As a matter of fact, she had her eyes closed tightly the whole time. Did you bathe first? Maybe she was sucking a salty dick."

"You need to stop. You're drunk and don't know what you're saying," he said, as he continued to cover my wounds.

"I know *exactly* what I'm saying. So, which one was it? Were you salty, or has her head always been lousy?"

Royce was done doctoring me. He remained silent as he packed up the store bag with the items I needed to use over the next week. He finally opened his mouth to give directions.

"You need to apply ice to your lip until some of the swelling goes down, and try to keep your cuts dry and clean."

I paid his instructions no attention. I wanted to keep talking about the head I saw him receive. I knew he wouldn't join the conversation, so that's when I decided to make him confess. I fell on my knees and started unzipping his pants.

"Savannah, get up. What are you doing?" he said in a boyish tone.

"I'm about to show you what real oral pleasure is like, like I . . . I planned to do the . . . the night I caught you."

My words were slurring, but I'm sure he understood them.

"Savannah, you're drunk, and this isn't right. You can show me another time."

"No, Royce . . . I can s . . . s-show you now, or you can answer the fucking question. Can you-u . . . ur ex-wife blow pipe or not?"

He hesitated a few seconds and then confessed, "No, Savannah, she can't 'blow pipe,' as you call it. She doesn't like to do it; it's mentally degrading to her. She wanted to do it to show me how bad she felt about the way things went down between us. Now, please, please, get up."

Royce said all the right words, but he never moved my hands from his crotch or zipped up his pants. I kept going until I had his hardened manhood in both of my hands with my fingers wrapped tightly around. Royce's next words scared the shit out of me.

"Is that an engagement ring on your finger?"

My buzz was gone, and his manhood shrunk like a grape in the sun. I got off my knees, grabbed my bag, and then made my way to the door.

"You're right, Royce, I'm drunk. I'll call you later this week."

It was history repeating itself, but this time, Royce was fully dressed. He stood in the hallway, begging me to stay. I jumped on the elevator and made my way past the front desk attendant without glancing his way. I knew I was too drunk to drive, so I parked my car at my favorite home away from home and jumped in one of the taxis that had been dropping people off at the hotel from the airport.

Once the driver had my address and turned on the meter, I called Dre and told him all that had happened except the part that included Royce. Instead of mentioning Royce, I told Dre I got a room to clean myself up and then sat at the bar to stomach everything that happened. I told him my car was parked, and he would have to bring me to pick it up in the morning. He sounded as if he believed me, and I knew when he saw my bandages and lip, all doubt would disappear. There had to be something in my voice whenever I lied to him that gave him a signal because he seemed always to detect when I was bullshitting.

"Nineteen dollars and thirty cents," the taxi driver said when we reached my house. I handed him a twenty-dollar bill and told him to keep the change. As I stepped out of the taxi, a car started up a house away from mine. I didn't pay it any attention until the driver rolled down her window and stopped in the middle of the street.

"Had to make a dick, I mean, quick stop before you made it home, I see." It was Trisha, in her car alone, and laughing hysterically at her use of words. Her eye was swollen almost shut.

I didn't respond, nor did I have time to. Dre must have heard me pull up because the porch light came on, and he was unlocking the door, preparing to open it. I looked at him, and then at her, hoping she wouldn't repeat her statement in front of Dre, and she must have read my mind.

"Don't worry, Savannah, your secrets are safe with me . . . for now, that is." She put her index finger over her lips.

Dre saw that it was Trisha and rushed out to meet me in the driveway. He could see the troubled look on my face to go along with the patched-up wounds.

"Are you okay, baby?" He gripped my chin to inspect my cuts, and Trisha laughed again before I could answer, so I nodded my head instead. She was enjoying the show, so I tugged on Dre's arm so we could go into the house. Dre had all his attention focused on Trisha like he was trying to read her like he normally did me.

"What do you want, Peaches?" he said, with more base in his voice than I had ever heard before.

"I just wanted to come by and say congratulations on the engagement, that's all. Maybe we should all get together and chat sometime. You know, we will be officially family soon."

Dre took a few steps in the direction of the house and then yelled over his shoulder, "Yeah, maybe."

Before we made it to the door, Trisha clapped her hands and laughed excitedly as if she had won the lottery, then said, "I believe we will, Dre. I do believe we will." Then she drove off laughing loudly down the road until she was out of view. Something about Trisha's laugh let me know that this was just the beginning.

The beginning of *what* was the question.

Chapter Nine

The Interrogation

"Tell me what happened after you left the steak house again."

This was Dre's third time this week asking me to explain what happened after my fight with Trisha, and I was tired of answering.

"I've told you at least ten times already, Dre. I drove to the 24-hour pharmacy on the corner, and the pharmacist got what I needed to clean these wounds. After that, I got a room at the hotel to clean myself up because I knew Sade was here. After that, I went down to the bar and crawled in a bottle of rum before coming home."

I walked past him to go to our bathroom so I could take a shower before getting some sleep for work in the morning. Dre followed closely behind, still shooting off questions.

"And you said Peaches didn't follow you here; she was already parked when you pulled up at the house, right? You said you think Memphis told her where we lived at?"

"Yes, Dre, that's exactly what I told you."

I pulled the shower curtain closed and turned the water on high, hoping to drown him out, but more questions came.

"And the hotel you parked your car at the other night, you said that the only time you've been there was to meet Peaches and that's why you went there instead of any other hotels on the street because you were familiar with it?"

"Yes, Dre, that's where Trisha asked us to meet every Wednesday and Saturday. I had never been there before until she invited me there. And stop calling her Peaches. Only her close friends can call her that, or that's the lie she told me."

Finally, the questions stopped, and I was sure Dre had left the bathroom. I finished my shower in peace, making sure to stay in the water until it turned cold. When I pulled the powder-blue shower curtain back, Dre was sitting on the toilet with my dry towel in his hand with a mixture of hurt and anger on his face.

"What's wrong with you, Dre?" I said, snatching the towel out of his hand.

"Shit just ain't adding up. I took a trip to the steak house and was told the fight happened between two women. One came in with a younger man, and the other had already been seated at the bar alone. I asked to see the footage of the parking lot, but they said the cameras didn't work. They had them up for appearance only. I wanted to make sure she or no one else had followed you. From there, I went to the pharmacy. The pharmacist that was there that night wasn't due to come for a few hours, so I left and came back. I questioned him, but he doesn't remember helping a wounded woman last Friday, but he recalled helping one of his regulars grab some over-the-counter items for the lacerations I described. He took my number and said he'd have him call me on his next visit."

Oh shit, I thought to myself. I didn't think Dre would take it that far and go back to the pharmacy to retrace my steps. He really didn't trust me! My heart started beating hard behind my breasts, and instead of drying off with the beach towel, I fumbled with it from my right hand to my left as if it were covered in baby oil, too slippery to grasp.

You just need to stay calm for a second and come up with your next lie, I told myself. While I stood there cooking up my next words, Dre started back up.

"Then, I've asked you all week was Trisha the only person you've been to this hotel with, and you said yes, every single time, which I know is a lie. Like I told you at the barbecue, I asked Will to come and get you out of bed for me. I paid for his flight and booked his room at that hotel. Either you lied to me about staying the night with him, or you're lying now. Which one is it, Savannah?"

Dre was now towering over me, waiting on an answer, and I was ready to give it. I wrapped the towel around my body and put on some of Hollywood's finest acting.

"I forgot all about Will's visit. I told you we don't talk anymore, so it slipped my mind. Look through your records for his room number, if you don't believe me. I don't remember the room number, but we were on the fifth floor toward the end of the hallway. If you booked the room, you should be able to confirm the floor and location of it."

That part was true, which meant I didn't have to think about it. The next part was fictional, but I made sure to memorize it like the lyrics of my favorite song as I sang the lying words to his listening ears.

"I never once told you that I had personally spoken with the pharmacist. I told you the pharmacist got what I needed to clean my wounds. I sat in the car, too embarrassed to be seen out in public all beaten up, so I

parked by the entrance and asked the first person I saw
if they would speak with the pharmacist for me. I handed
him cash to buy the items, and he brought them out to
me with my change. I didn't know the guy; I just asked a
stranger for some help and got it. If you think I'm wrong
for not wanting to be stared at or whispered about, then
that's on you."

I walked out of the bathroom, leaving Dre standing
there alone. I oiled my body in my bedroom, threw on a
pink baby doll nightgown, and got in the bed. Minutes
later, Dre joined me, making sure to stay on his side of
the bed with his back to me. I wasn't going to accept his
distance tonight, so I rolled over, tugged on his arm until
he lay on his back, and then lay my head on his chest.
After a few minutes of debating with his thoughts, he
placed his arm around me to help me get comfortable.
I smiled in the darkness, feeling like I had won. A little
over five minutes later, I was back in the loser's seat
when my cell phone rang three times in a row, and it was
already 11:30 at night. I always remembered to put it on
silent when I came home and then to cut it off at 10:00,
but Dre's questioning had made me forget.

"You ain't gon' answer that?" Dre said, with a tone that
reminded me of sandpaper rubbing against wood.

"No, it must be the wrong number."

That worked for the first three calls, but when ten
minutes went by, and my phone rang two more times,
Dre lifted me off his chest and turned his back to me.

"You need to go handle that now! Let that nigga know
you're with your man now, and you can't answer his calls
after six." He fluffed his pillows and scooted all the way to
the edge of the bed on his side. If he made a wrong move
while he was asleep, he would end up falling off the bed
and land on the floor.

"What nigga, Dre? Stop playing with me like that. You are more than just my man; you're my fiancé," I said while flying out of bed before my phone rang again.

As soon as I had it in my hand, I hit silent before pretending to answer it. I read the caller ID and saw that it was Royce calling me.

"What, Stephanie?" I yelled into the unanswered phone, pretending as if it were she blowing me up. I waited about ten seconds like I was listening to her response and then said, "No, we can't be friends, bitch! You tried to fuck my man." I took that as the opportunity to power off my phone and crawled back into the bed, ready to fall straight asleep. However, Dre had to have the final word.

"If you wanted me to believe you were talking to somebody, you should have given them time to talk or put it on speakerphone."

"That was Stephanie. I knew what she wanted so—"

"Shut that shit up," he interrupted. "You powered that motherfucka off. Tell another motherfucking lie and watch me power that bitch back on and call that last number back. Take your lying ass to sleep."

I slid my phone into my pillowcase under my head and prayed that I was snoring before he changed his mind about giving me the pass.

When I woke up the next morning, I was in bed alone. I felt Dre get up around three in the morning but was too tired for a game of cat and mouse, especially since I had to get up in two hours.

It was another rainy day in Seattle, Washington, which meant I would need extra caffeine to make it through the day. I headed to the kitchen to put on the coffeemaker, and Dre was walking in the front door. I wanted to ask him where in the hell he was coming from at five in the morning, but he had the newspaper in his hand, which meant his answer would have been the driveway. I made us both a cup of coffee. When it was done brewing, we sat at the two-person breakfast nook, reading our preferred sections of the newspaper in silence. As I went to place my coffee mug in the stainless-steel dishwasher, Dre finally spoke up.

"What are you doing after work?"

He never questioned my moves before, and normally, I wasn't the person to answer when being questioned. However, I knew answering would show my progress with this change I'm working on.

"Coming straight home, just like I did today; why? What's up?"

"Just asking," he said and then turned the page of the Sports Section as I exited the room to get ready for work.

On the ride to work, I listened to Royce's begging and pleading messages. He was saying shit like, "Savannah, baby, please pick up. You know I can't stop thinking about you."

I laughed at those messages, and then there were the angrier, jealous-toned messages that said, "If that was an engagement ring on your finger, you could at least pick up the phone and tell me I'm barking up the wrong tree and that you belong to somebody else. That would be the decent and respectable thing to do."

But the majority of the messages left were like the Royce I knew, nice and sensible. They said things like, "Hello, Savannah, I was wondering if we could get together and discuss what exactly happened that night and see if the time we shared was worth holding on to or need to be treated like once-in-a-lifetime memory. When you have time, please return my call. I look forward to hearing from you."

It was his sensible messages that led me to decide to meet with him and tell him face-to-face about my engagement to Dre. I felt like I owed him that out of respect, and maybe, if I was lucky, we could have good-bye sex before I was completely devoted to Dre. As I said before, I was taking baby steps toward changing. If I give Royce a piece of me again, he would be the last man I slept with, and that's my word.

I called Royce's cell phone all day and was forwarded to voicemail, which was so full that I couldn't leave a message. When I called his office, his secretary said he was in court all day and would be back in the office around six. I'm sure after a long day in court and with me attempting to keep my word to Dre, today wasn't going to be a good day to have our farewell meeting. Instead, I'd meet him at his office at six to arrange a meet with him for some time tomorrow. It would be Saturday and a hell of a lot easier to get away from Dre. All I would have to say is I had a hair appointment and needed my nails done, and Dre would send me on my merry way.

"I don't know, Mama. The last time you sent me in there, she was home, and I could have gotten caught," Memphis voiced.

"She was high, baby. Those cancer medications don't mix well with street drugs. Weren't you able to get out without her making a move, and they're not home any-way? I told you, Dre is obsessed with your sister, and he follows her wherever she goes. All you have to do is grab that same box of papers you found, but this time, baby, bring them out with you."

"What are those paper for again?"

"They are the proof that Savannah has been getting money in my name for years illegally, and I need them so I can prove it. Why so many questions, son? I thought you were happy I came back to be in your life," Trisha said in a loving tone.

"I am, Mama, but something just don't feel right. Savannah has a real good job. Why would she steal your money, and if she did you wrong, why would you go to her first when you came back, and not me?"

"Oh, Memphis, I already answered this question at least a hundred times. I went to your sister to get my money from her the right way, and she wouldn't give it back. I told you how your father banned me from seeing y'all, and you didn't hesitate to believe. That's because you're smarter than your sister, and why would you trust and believe anything she says to you anyway? Didn't I play you the call when I asked her to tell you I was back? I gave you the date and time of it, and that was before she lied to you in the Jacuzzi, right?"

"Yeah," he answered, slightly upset.

"Why would she lie to you about something that important, especially after you shared your feelings with her about me? You know why. Because she's like your daddy. They want what's best for them, no matter who it hurts. The people you grew up with, almost all of your friends are in jail or fighting an incurable disease because your sister had a temper tantrum and had to have her way. I tried to meet with her like she asked, and she jumped on me because she was jealous that I was with you—"

"Is that what she said at the steak house?" Memphis asked quizzically.

"Yes, she said, 'Why are you spending time with his broke ass when I'm the rich, smart one? Memphis didn't turn out to be shit just like our daddy. I've been taking care of both of them for years, and don't forget poor, sweet Sade.' The things she's said to me about your niece is heartbreaking. I was forced to leave y'all alone. I would have never done it on my own."

"I know you wouldn't have, Mama."

"Then make Mama proud. Go in there the way I told you to and go save my life, so we can move far away from these devils and enjoy the time we lost."

"Okay, Mama, but you should have let me beat her ass for you. I hate that bitch, Savannah."

"Trust, son, once I get everything that's mine, it's going to hurt her more than any beating could."

I left the office at 5:30 p.m., thirty minutes before the end of my shift, so the stop to Royce's office would make my arrival home only a few minutes later than usual. Royce must have been running late because it was now 6:15, and he hadn't arrived. I couldn't wait any longer. Dre would be expecting me now, and my plan was to get home by 6:30. I walked into his office and left a note saying I would like to meet with him tomorrow afternoon and would be calling in the morning to arrange it. When I got into my car at 6:20, my car wouldn't crank up. I tried to let it sit for five minutes, but nothing seemed to be working.

"Just my fucking luck," I screamed at the dashboard as I tried again to start the car. It was 6:27, and Royce had finally pulled up. At that very same moment, my phone began to ring. Before Royce could address me, I hushed him with my finger and answered my phone.

"This is Savannah," I said into the receiver in my office voice, even though the contact was saved in my phone as My fiancé.

"Hey, baby, is everything all right? You said you'd be coming straight home from work. I was expecting you by now. What's the delay?"

Dre's background was silent, but not mine. Cars were moving about the street and the sounds of airplanes landing and taking off nearby. I shut the car door for a little more privacy and to prevent Dre from hearing some of the background noises, but it was already too late. Royce had stepped closer to my car door, and Dre had mentioned all the background noises.

"Everything is fine now. My meeting ran later than I thought it would for a Friday afternoon, and when I finally made it to my car, it wouldn't start," I said, maintaining a professional tone.

"Are you still at work? It sounds like a lot of cars in the background, like you're in a congested part of town," he said.

"As a matter of fact, right outside the door." I smiled at Royce once I said it to make him think I was talking to someone about him.

"Okay, baby, I'm going to grab the mechanic, and then I'm on my way; stay put. I love you."

"No," I yelled into the phone. This seemed to catch both Dre's and Royce's attention. I pulled myself back together, then said, "That won't be necessary. I'll be towed home shortly, and I'm safe. Please don't trouble yourself."

Royce wore a confused look on his face as if he was now having doubts that the person on the other end of the phone knew about him, and Dre's doubt was in his voice.

"You sure you don't want me to come? I don't like the idea of you riding in a tow truck alone."

I forced myself to giggle girlishly and then responded with, "I'm sure I'll be fine. I'm in good hands, daddy; I love you and will call you when the tow truck arrives."

I made sure to say "daddy" in a fatherly way, and the words "I love you" with no passion behind them before I hung up the phone on Dre and opened the car door.

"Sorry, that was my daddy. Ever since my little bar fight with my mother, he's been worried sick about me."

Dre knew when I was lying. He sure was good at detecting it. Good thing Royce's confused ass wasn't. I cast those few little lines at Royce, and he took the bait.

"That was your mom you were fighting? I thought maybe she was your older sister by the similarity in looks between you, her, and the gentleman she had with her. I assumed it was a sibling brawl."

I gave him a quick rundown of the situation between Trisha and me. He was like putty in my hands as I brought him up to date with current events.

"Why don't you just swing by my room tomorrow at three, and we can sit down and talk?" he said, trying to suppress the excitement he was feeling from me saying I would like to sit down and have a heart-to-heart with him.

I agreed and then asked if I could come in to call for a tow truck. When a heavy-breathing guy named Joe assured me that a tow truck was en route, we walked out of his office to my car. I couldn't confirm it, but it looked like Dre's tank had just passed by slowly and was now headed up the street. I had to be wrong because if that were him, he would have stopped, and there was no way he would have known where I was, anyway. If he stopped by the office and saw I wasn't there, his first thought would be that I was in the process of being towed, and he would have called me to confirm I was safe.

"Are you okay?" Royce asked, with a hand in the center of my back as if he thought I was going to topple over.

"Yes, I'm fine. It's been a really long week."

"Yes, it has. I've been in and out of court all week fighting a case that I know I can't win. If I could just get the guy to take a deal, it would be all over, but he insists on . . . blah blah blah."

I'm sure the word "blah" never came out of his mouth, but I didn't care about his week. I didn't care about his case or his hard time after his divorce. Hell, I didn't care about him. Royce was nothing but a sex replacement when Dre had cut me off. The only reason I was hurt about catching him with his ex-wife is that I felt second best. I like the feeling of being in first place and listening to Royce beg for another chance let me know I held that spot when it came to him. Otherwise, he wouldn't have wasted his energy after only knowing me for a short time. As he talked, he became more unattractive to me by the second. His looks went back to my first superficial judgment of him and that he was not my type. I would let him lay me down for one last time tomorrow, and when we were done, I'd break him into tiny pieces with my words. I was going to enjoy this.

My text message alert went off on my phone; it was Dre texting me. The text read, Have you tried to crank the car lately, or are you being towed?

I texted back to tell him I was still waiting on the tow truck to arrive and would try the car again. I excused myself from Royce's conversation that usually kept my attention but now didn't and walked over to my car. It started on the first try. I handed Royce the telephone number to the tow company out of the driver-side window and asked him to cancel it for me as I backed out of the parking space.

No matter what plans I made for tomorrow, nothing would come before having my car checked out. I grabbed my phone and called Dre to let him know I was on my way home and hungry.

"You've reached Dre, and I can't get to my phone. Go ahead and leave a message, and I'll get back with you shortly."

I heard that messages five times before I made it home, which was weird because I had never heard it before. It never crossed my mind that Dre would need to leave a personal greeting on his answering machine. I couldn't imagine anyone calling him besides myself, the Jeffersons, and his mother since she was raising his son. Who did he expect to receive a message from?

I parked my car next to his, still boggled by Dre's need for his voice to be on his answering machine and why he was forwarding my calls to it.

"What do you mean this isn't an emergency? I just told you my house had been broken into and because nothing noticeable is missing and there aren't any signs of forced entry, you will have someone come to take a report at their earliest convenience? That's some bullshit. Then you wonder why folks take the law into their own hands."

Dre was pacing the living room floor. One hand was holding his cell phone to his ear and the other, moving a cigar full of weed back and forth from his mouth. He had to be pissed and not thinking straight to be on the phone demanding the police to come out to our house while smoking weed. It's not like weed was legal.

I heard what he was saying to the police on the phone, but by the look of the living room, dining room, and kitchen, Dre was making a false report because the house hadn't been touched.

"Yes, I'll hold for the third time," he said into the phone. Dre looked at me over his shoulder with a guilty look, powered on the television, and turned the channel to three. He pressed the previous chapter on the DVD player and then hit play. I couldn't believe my eyes. I was now watching video surveillance of my own house. There was a shot of the backyard, pool, and then the camera jumped to the driveway and front of the house. Dre looked over his shoulder at me again and pressed fast-forward. The only movement on the camera was Dre getting in his truck and leaving, and then, thirty-five minutes later, coming back. I still didn't understand the need to have the police come out.

"That's a hell of a lot better. We will be here waiting," Dre finally said, then hung up his phone.

I didn't know what questions to ask first; why did he have cameras all over the outside of the house, or why did he assume the house had been broken into? The look on my face must have asked him both questions for me.

"This is the fucking reason I installed the cameras in the first damn place. When you said you felt like someone had been in here with you that Sunday, I could hear it in your voice you were being real, so I put them up to be safe. But like you just saw for yourself, the shit didn't work because someone *still* broke into our bedroom."

Dre continued to pace the living room floor, and I jetted to our bedroom to take a look for myself. Every one of the dressers had been ransacked. Clothes were dangling from every drawer and off their hangers in the closet. The boxes that used to be neatly stacked containing the clothes that were no longer in season were now on the floor.

I spun around the room to check for my electronics, and they were all there. The thief hadn't tried to take the television, my radio, or even the digital camera that was pocket size sitting on Dre's dresser. My jewelry was also untouched, and I'm sure if the thief would have made away with it, they would be at least $20,000 richer.

Who breaks into a house and walks off with nothing? I looked at the bedroom window. It sat on the windowsill in one piece. How did the burglar get in without breaking it? I took a few steps toward it, and Dre said, "It's unlocked; I already checked," startling me because I didn't hear him come down the hallway.

"I can't think of anything that's missing, can you?" I asked him.

He didn't open his mouth; he just nodded his head toward the bed, which led my eyes to it. Papers covered the bed from the foot to the headboard.

"I don't know, Savannah; I was hoping you would be able to tell me. Whoever broke in seemed to be concerned with your documents because nothing of mine or of value that I know of is missing."

The papers that covered the bed were all of my personal financial documents like old bank statements, previous year's tax documents, and receipts. There was no way to figure out what was missing without spending hours itemizing everything by date.

"Who would want to go through this stuff, Dre?"

He shrugged his shoulders and said, "I'm hoping you can tell me. The police are on their way to take a look and make a report. When they leave, we are going to play detective on our own."

He was pissed, but it seemed like some of his anger was with me. If I hadn't sensed his anger was directed at me, I would have replied with something smug about his request to play detective.

The police still took their time arriving and were no help at all. I was now pissed as the overweight black officer with no neck, bad breath, and the biggest eyes I had ever seen in my life handed me a copy of the report he made.

"You might want to get an alarm system on the house instead of the motion lights," he recommended.

"The surveillance cameras are set in good places, but I suggest putting some by the bedroom windows also. If you or Mr. Burns later find out what was stolen, call us with this report number, and we'll open an investigation, but this is all we can do for now. You all have a good night."

I slammed the door behind him and almost shitted my pants when I turned around to be face-to-face with Dre's chest.

"You ready to start the real investigation?" he said, seeing that his presence shocked me.

"I guess," I replied and then followed him to the couch.

There were two glasses of liquor already poured on the coffee table with a bottle of brandy and Coke next to them. I grabbed mine and took a sip. Dre rolled up another cigar of weed and passed it to me to smoke first.

"The only way this shit is going to work, or at least be helpful, is if you're truthful about everything, Savannah. I ain't trying to call you a liar, but I don't need you trying to hide shit so I won't get mad, or so you won't hurt my feelings. I need to know everything to protect us. It ain't just about you."

"Ask away then, Dre."

"It may not seem relevant to you, but trust me; everything is important. I need you to tell me everything that happened from the time we met to today's date. I know that's asking a lot, and you won't remember everything, but I'll ask questions as we move along."

I wasn't dumb. Dre just wanted to know more about me. He wanted to fill in the gaps and answer all the unanswered questions he had in his head. I'd play his little game with him, hoping that he maybe would uncover the answer to the break-in.

I started my story from the day after the police had raided my homes in Atlanta, Georgia, and Brentwood, Tennessee, looking for him, making sure I was giving detail after detail.

"That's real good, baby, but I need you to tell me how you knew I was the weed man. Who told you?"

"That dude in the Grand Prix with the gold in his mouth. He had a dollar sign on one of them. I don't remember his name. He was smoking a blunt, and I asked him where I could get an ounce. He told me to drive across the street, and you'd pull up on me."

"Cool, moving on. I know Sade is mine, but was there any other niggas in the picture that might have thought she could be theirs, or you thought she could have belonged to?"

Dre's shaky voice told on him. He was snooping. That wasn't one of the lifesaving questions he needed the answer to. He wanted to know who else was in the picture, and who I had let nut in me.

"Nope, you're the only one I let in me raw. When I found out I was pregnant, I knew she was yours. There was no one else who even came close to fucking me in that time frame."

He sparked another blunt and nodded his head in belief which didn't matter either way because he made sure to get a DNA test done and knew Sade was his blood.

"So, you got promoted, moved to Cali, and your ex-friends got word that you were back. Is that how it went down?"

"They were never my friends, and, no, I went looking for them."

"Why?" he asked, handing me the blunt.

"Why? Because I'm dumb, and a part of me was still childish. I wanted to show them bitches that I had made it out of the hood and was on top, but that wasn't enough. I had to get my revenge too."

The liquor had me running my mouth, and I knew it because I bragged about how easy it was to sleep with my three enemies' men without him asking the question.

Dre had a disgusted look on his face when I went into details about the sex party I threw for Tyrone and his boys with the prostitutes as the guests of honor. But he wanted this information, so I gave it to him.

"Stephanie wrote the diary without your approval and just left it lying around with all the shit you were doing in it inside?"

I was still giving the details of the sex party when he interrupted with his question. I guess he had heard enough about it.

"Yes, I'm sure after spending enough time with her to let her taste my dick that you figured out she was slow when it came to certain areas. She looked at it like it was a movie, and if for one second I would have known she was a damn screenplay writer, I would have destroyed the book myself."

"You're saying you knew of the book, but you didn't know it was that detailed."

"Exactly!"

"Now to the girl, Ericka. She was Keisha's little sister that you didn't remember, right?"

I let out an exaggerated breath and then agreed. "Yes, she was younger than the rest of us, and she never hung out with us, so I didn't put two and two together."

"Do you think Keisha sent her to work for you because she had a feeling you were plotting against her?"

I was shaking my head before he could finish.

"No, that shit was Kismet, and Karma did everything she could to warn me that I had a double agent in my midst."

"What do you mean by that?" he asked, reaching for the blunt. I was hogging it, but I needed it to relive the worst years of my life.

"My first trip back to the old neighborhood and almost everyone I spoke with mentioned her, but I thought nothing of it."

I shook my head and looked at Dre. He was already facedown shaking his head. He reached out to hand me the blunt.

"Until recently, do you think Stephanie has been A-1 with you?"

"Yes, she had my back, and I would have never thought she'd do me like she did. Stephanie didn't change on me until she realized she wanted you. I was mad at first, but why wouldn't she want you? You're a pain in my ass, but I wouldn't want to keep pushing through this life without you."

"This isn't the time to try to win points with me. Let's stick to answering all the questions, but for now, you can pick up telling the story from the morning of the day Keisha shot you." He followed his words with a wink.

"Let me ask you a question. Why did you make those moves on me in Cali?"

He laughed and shook his head before answering. "I wanted to leave an imprint on your mind, a memory that would fuck you up for the rest of your life, so you would always carry a piece of me with you. Yeah, Sade is a hell of a piece whether or not you were in her life, but why not make it a story you wouldn't forget. Does that answer your question?"

"Hell nah, it doesn't! You say this shit that doesn't mean anything to anybody but you, and you expect me to understand it like it makes sense. Dre, your ass is either weird or a government agent." I giggled, but he didn't join in on the laugh.

"I'll take that as a compliment, but a guilty mind can't get an understanding."

"What do you mean by that?"

"I mean, if you don't get your shit together and live right by our engagement, you're going to start thinking you see me everywhere, every time you do wrong. Now start from the morning you got shot, please."

I didn't stop talking until I made it to the part of the story where I woke up in the hospital.

"Why did you stop? Keep going."

Dre was trying to keep me talking at the same pace as I was, but I knew once I got to the part where I was released from the hospital is when I would have to remember all the lies I had told, so I slowed down. By nothing less than a miracle I made it to slamming the door behind the police officer tonight without forgetting every lie I had told him and repeating them verbatim.

"Did you ever borrow any money from anyone or promise to give anybody some money?" Dre asked, but, of course, my answer was no.

He asked a few more money questions that included if I gambled or had ever stolen any money from my clients, and the answer was no to those questions too. Then Dre asked me to repeat today's events. When I was finished, he asked me, "Where exactly did your car break down? I want street names."

I took my time to make sure I answered the question the same way I had earlier and then said, "My car broke down on Sixth Avenue, right in front of my office, and I sat outside and waited for the tow truck until you sent a message for me to try to crank it up."

I was nervous and waiting for him to prove that I was lying, but he didn't. He poured us both a drink, held his glass in the air like he was making a toast, and then swallowed all the contents of it.

"Baby, go ahead and start cleaning up the room while I go place a camera by these bedroom windows. I'll have an alarm put on the house tomorrow. You know daddy is going to keep you safe."

When Dre was finished setting up the cameras, he helped me clean up the room. I was in no mood to go to sleep, nor was he. We agreed to lie in bed and watch movies. Even with Dre lying next to me with his pistol on his nightstand, I knew I wasn't going to be able to sleep in this house again. Not until the thief was apprehended and identified. My house was no longer my safe haven; it was now a killing pond, and I was a duck awaiting its slaughter.

Chapter Ten

Connecting the Dots

Saturday came and showed its ugly face, but I had to admit, I was thankful that it wasn't raining. Dre was gone before I was finished brushing my teeth. He had mentioned something about getting a better surveillance system and meeting with me later for an early dinner. My brain was still asleep when he announced his departure so all I managed to say was, "All right, bye," when I should have been cussing his unthoughtful ass out.

I wasn't bothered by his early-morning venture. I was mad because he left me in the house alone after last night's break-in. The thinking pattern of men is completely opposite of ours. No matter how close women get to thinking we understand them, some shit that they do just doesn't make sense. Why would he leave me in this house by myself after I was the target for the break-in? It didn't matter that it was now morning, and the sun was out. Which I'm sure would have been his excuse for being absentminded. I expressed fear of being in the house even in his company, but that must have gone in one ear and out the other because he was gone.

I showered and dressed in record time, hoping the Cadillac dealership was open early. If it wasn't, then I'd have breakfast to kill time. I wouldn't dare wait at home, but, to my surprise, I wouldn't have to because it was open, and I was the first customer there.

The car lot was peaceful at its opening hour, meaning there wasn't the usual hustle, also known as bullshit, floating in the air. No overdressed car salesmen jacking up prices for a better commission. No window-shoppers were walking around asking questions about cars they knew they couldn't afford, nor were there potential buyers huddled up with finance officers going over terms.

When I drove inside the service area next to the main showroom, I could see a team of suited men and woman huddled up, planning today's attack and setting monthly goals. The group met in the center of the showroom's floors with the year's newest vehicles wrapped in over-sized ribbons and bows parked around them. I could tell by the look of comfort in the team members' faces that this was a normal routine. Everyone was sipping tea, coffee, hot chocolate, or some other heated beverage judging by the way they held their mugs by the handles or blew before taking a swallow. In the middle of the huddle and doing all the talking was my old friend and neighbor, Wayne Jacobs Jr., the happily married owner of the car lot whom I had to sleep with on three boring occasions just to get my fully equipped Cadillac DTS for $15,000 cheaper than the asking price. Wayne looked as if he had seen a ghost when our glances met, and he quickly dismissed his employees from the huddle.

"Ms. Jam-James," he stammered, as he approached me with his hand outreached for a shake. "What a surprise to see you here."

He wore the same shocked look on his face that he had when it was I that answered the door for him, his wife, and child when they knocked on the recently sold house in their subdivision to welcome their new neighbors to the community just two days after we had sex.

"Wayne, I need you to—"

"Why don't we take this conversation to somewhere more private, like my office?" He looked over his shoulder like we were being watched.

If it wasn't for the fear in his eyes, I would have thought he was attempting to try for another round of sex with me since all three encounters happened on the desk in his office. When we were securely behind closed doors, I picked up where I left off.

"Wayne, I need you to have your best mechanic check out my car. I've been having trouble getting it to start lately. Seems like it has to sit for a while after my first attempt to crank it up."

Wayne hadn't heard a word that I said. He was still searching his surroundings for whom or whatever he thought was watching.

"Hello . . . Wayne, did you hear me?"

"I didn't know you were married too. I would have never tried to contact you if I would have known." His voice was now shaky.

"What are you talking about?" I was lost completely.

"When I called you to apologize for not telling you I was married, your husband answered the phone and began questioning me. I lied at first and told him I was just a neighbor who sold you a car and wanted to make sure you were satisfied with your purchase."

"Well," I said, with a slight giggle, "that's not a lie, Wayne. That's the truth."

"Well, your husband seemed to think it was a lie because he showed up that following Saturday in your car demanding to speak with me only."

"Dre isn't my husband; he's my fiancé. I mean, when I met you I was single. We just got engaged, but that doesn't matter. I let you fuck me, and I didn't care if you were married or not, but what did Dre want when he talked with you?"

He finally sat down behind his desk, but the look of fear remained on his face. "He started off asking questions about the car, like if you had a car note or owed a balance. I told him no, that you paid cash for it. Next thing I know, he's asking me if I've ever cheated on my wife and how many of my customers have I slept with. I assumed you had told him about us, so I told him the truth."

"Why would any of that matter to him? We weren't together then." I was asking Wayne the question when I knew it was Dre who I needed to be questioning.

"I don't know why it mattered, but it did. He told me to stay away from you and never to contact you again. He reminded me that good, um . . . that good pussy was his good pussy in his words, and he'd kill before he shared it. He told me if he ever caught you on my lot, I'd have hell to pay, and that he always has someone watching what's his."

This shit really made no sense to me. Dre was out of his mind for threatening Wayne. I felt bad for Wayne and was about to apologize for Dre's behavior until he said his next words.

"I was nervous and didn't know what to do, so, with my apology, I tried to offer him a discount on a new vehicle or whatever he wanted to make the situation better. I was happy that he settled for a LoJack with an internet-tracking mechanism, and that's why I have to ask you to go. Leave now, please!"

I stood up and walked out. Now I knew what exactly was wrong with my car. Dre wasn't just using it to track me, but to keep my engine from cranking. The car lot I bought my 300 from in Nashville had a device that not only tracked the location of the car, but also could shut the engine down from the dealership when their customers were late on payments. The owner told me it saved them money on getting a tow truck for repossessions.

"Ms. James," Wayne said, as I backed out of the parking space, "did you still want us to look at your vehicle? Because if he comes, that's what I'm going to tell him was your reason for stopping by." I hit the gas like his words were inaudible to me. I had to get to Royce, but first, I needed to get to my office and park before Dre was done and could trace my whereabouts.

I can't recall a time this office or any of the other branches were ever completely empty . . . until today. There were no security guards, janitors, and there weren't any lingering account reps trying to get ahead of the workload of the upcoming week to impress me. All the company cars were signed out for the weekend, and the place looked like a ghost town. I had to use the light on my cell phone because the power in the building wouldn't come on. I made it to the receptionist desk and took a seat. My office was at the rear of the building, and after being shot at the California branch, I'd be a fool to travel to the back with nothing but the flashlight on my cell phone.

I used the office phone to call Seattle City Light to report the outage. As I held, the voicemail indicator light was flashing and gave a horror movie feel to the room.

"Thank you for calling Seattle City Light, Business Division. My name is Jonathan. How may I help you?"

"Good morning. My name is Savannah James, and I should be listed as the contact person over here at Williams and Williamson's. I'm calling to report a power outage."

Johnathan was typing away, and once he had the account opened, he asked me to verify a few things before continuing.

"Ms. James, we have a request to disconnect service as of yesterday at 6:00 p.m. with the final bill being forwarded to an Atlanta address."

"That's not possible because neither my partners nor I made that request."

"I'm sorry, ma'am, but the account was authenticated at the time of the request, and it says Savannah James made the request. Are you saying that someone used your identity?"

"That's *exactly* what I'm saying."

"If you don't mind, I'm going to place you on hold for a few minutes and get this worked out for you."

"Thank you!"

The hold music came on, and a vision of my hands wrapped around Stephanie's neck until her body fell lifeless played in my head. She knew that every Friday, the Atlanta and Los Angeles mail merged all of their files for the week over to us, and I was expected to get a forecast for the week every Tuesday morning. Sunday evening, our larger clients sent us focal points for the week, and payroll was automatically submitted to our processor Sunday evening. With the power being out, we'd lose more money on the days we are closed for business than when we were open, not to mention the staff would experience a delay in pay, which would mean I'd deal with a lot of attitudes while things were straightened out. Stephanie was trying to get me fired, but I wouldn't let her. She'd be the only bitch disappearing from this story.

"Ms. James, are you still there? I apologize for the wait."

"You're fine. How long will it take the power to come back on?"

"I spoke with my supervisor, and since you did confirm that you were a victim of an identity thief, we need you to come in Monday when our offices open with proof of your identity and relationship with the company. If you do so, we can have your power on no later than Tuesday night."

"No, I need it back on Monday. This is a place of business, and we can't afford the downtime!"

"Ms. James, when you come in, you can request rush services at a fee. Is there anything else I can do for you?"

I hung up in his ear and debated if I should call and make the partners aware now or come in Monday pretending to be clueless. I played the messages on speaker as I decided.

There were three messages from our high-speed provider, janitorial service, and the company that refills our coffee and vending machines, all confirming the cancellation of our accounts. I was shocked she hadn't requested the phone lines to be disconnected, but when the next message came, I learned why she hadn't.

Good morning, Seattle branch, and what a great morning it is. I'm hoping Eva runs across this message and plays it for you as a whole, but if she doesn't, Savannah has sent it to all of you through email. As you all know, I've been transferred back to the Atlanta branch to take on a very large account, and I'm excited for us all. This account can change everything for all of us, and I'm talking about a very good change. You know, the kind that shows up in our bank account. To celebrate, Savannah informed me that Mr. Williams and Mr. Williamson have decided that both the Seattle and Los Angeles branch will enjoy a five-day weekend with Monday through Wednesday off as paid work holidays. None of you will have to return until the open of business, Thursday morning.

Also, we are aware that this is last minute and many of you didn't have time to plan for a true vacation, so those of you with approved access to our onsite vehicles can use them as rental cars this weekend if you need them, and your gas cards will allow you up to $200 as I was told to expand the allotted monies. If you have *any questions, Savannah would like you to email her directly, seeing that I will be working hard because the Atlanta branch wasn't given the company holiday. Please enjoy yourself for me and make sure you thank Savannah for this. She spends so much time focusing on everyone else's life that it's amazing she still seems to manage hers. Thanks again for everything, Savannah, including this opportunity to make partner. It will be so nice to be on the same level in this company with you as best friends. Kiss Dre for me!*

I screamed the word "bitch" as loud as I could and listened to the word echo throughout the office. Stephanie's plot of revenge was on my level of the revenge scale, and a part of me felt like a proud parent. She had just given ninety-seven employees a three-day paid vacation, cut off every service that kept this office running, and I'm sure the same was done in California. The fucked-up part about it was she did it all in my name. Panic started consuming me, but it didn't last long because there was no way in hell I'd ever let her or any other bitch who comes for me get a chance to see me sweat. Instead of going through the company directory and calling each person and telling them that she lied and they had to come in, I decided that they did deserve the three-day vacation. It would give me time to get all the services back up and straighten out payroll. Now the delay could be blamed on the input of the vacation if there was any delay at all. The California branch wouldn't return until Thursday so there wouldn't be a need for the forecast. I'd have them resend the mail merge just to store in our records.

As far as Atlanta was concerned, "I'm so sorry to have disturbed you both with a Saturday conference call, but I've been so busy overworking our employees to ensure we triple our Q4 numbers from last year that I forgot to update you on the decisions I made."

"Savannah, we trust every decision you make," Mr. Williams chimed in after I explained the work holiday and the suspension of services to both locations to help cover it. "We see the number you have both offices bringing in weekly, and we are impressed."

"Actually," Mr. Williamson said, interrupting, "it's those numbers that got us this deal. We were hoping you'd move back and take it over, but sending Stephanie was a good replacement although she doesn't seem happy about returning. If you've done the numbers, and this work holiday will cut the end-of-the-year bonuses down by half, I'm all for it. Maybe next year it would be smart to schedule one day each quarter instead of three days consecutively."

"I agree. It will keep the office happy and us as partners ecstatic about not having to hear that two branches will be closed for three earning days," Mr. Williams said with a laugh. "Now what did you need us to get Stephanie to do?"

"Oh yes, when she comes in Monday, she will need to get Atlanta's forecast together for the week and have it ready to present to the client for Tuesday morning. Seeing that we have no power again until Wednesday, she will need to submit payroll for both offices for the work holiday manually, and she will also need to explain to the Atlanta branch why the holiday wasn't given to them. Make sure she explains that they will receive their full bonuses at the end of the year and the other branches will not.

"I also think it would be a good idea if she went ahead and composed an email for the branches with the holiday and advise them the paid holiday will be deducted out of their bonuses since she failed to mention that originally and make herself the contact person on handling any issues that may come from it. None of us should have to spend any time cleaning up her mistakes. Although I really like Stephanie, I'm noticing a change, and it's not for the good."

"Explain," Mr. Williamson demanded.

"She's all over the place when it comes to her personal life and professionally, which should be our only concern. She advised the employees that if this new account goes well, then, collectively, everyone will see a pay increase." There was a mixture of coughing and choking between the two men, and I didn't know which it was. "You may want to address this issue with her," I added.

"We will. That kind of thing gives off the wrong impression and is not a decision she can make on her own. Sounds like she's starting to think that she's you, and although we like her, she's not, nor does she have the same authority as you."

"Yes, Mr. Williams, I was thinking the same thing."

"Savannah, can you please give her a call and let her know we need to meet with her Monday morning, at 7:00. I want to get this handled before the office opens."

"Sure thing, Mr. Williamson. I'll call her now."

I didn't have Stephanie's number in my cell anymore. "Disappear" meant no traces of, so it was the first of her to be erased, but I knew who did have it. I scrolled through my contacts and got her cell phone number from our receptionist.

"Hello?" an irritated voice answered the phone, and it didn't belong to Stephanie.

"Who is this?"

"Bitch, *you* called here. Who do you think it is that you dialed?"

She was right, but she could have held on to that "bitch" word until I gave her a reason to drop it.

"Not the person I'm trying to reach, that's for damn sure. I thought this was my employee, Stephanie's number."

"Oh shit," the person on the other end began laughing. "I'm sorry. I forgot that my sister transferred her cell phone to my house phone."

"You mean transferred her cell phone to the phone you have service on in *her* house, don't you? How have you been doing, Tracey?"

"Who the fuck is this?"

"Savannah, that's who the fuck it is. Damn, your mouth is fucked up. What if this was her boss? Wait, this *is* her boss!"

Tracey and I have always gotten along even more so after she and a cleaning crew cleaned my place in Atlanta from top to bottom after the police raided it. I didn't know what her sister had told her nor where we stood now.

"Girl, you could have been the angel at the pearly gates calling, and you still would have gotten cussed the fuck out. How are you doing, beautiful? I've been asking my sister how you've been holding up after everything."

"That's water under the bridge. I beat cancer, and the bullet wasn't nothing more than an irritating flesh wound. You know nothing can or will ever have a strong hold on me," I said, followed by light laughter.

"I wasn't talking about that. I meant all the new stuff you got going. It seems like you're always in some shit."

The smart thing to do when in situations where you don't know what they know or if they are friend or foe is to play dumb. I got Academy Awards in this shit here.

"What new stuff? There's so much bullshit going on. As you said, I'm always in some shit."

"I know, but you're strong and will get through it. I couldn't believe that after all those years of working your ass off, those assholes you work for promoted my sister over you. I'm not saying that I'm not happy for her, but damn, she was your *secretary*. They could have at least offered to bring you back to Atlanta too. You dealing with this bullshit at work, and then Dre has the nerve to pull some shit too." She smacked her lips, then said, "A nigga is gon' be a nigga no matter how good we are to them, but I still don't believe he did you like that and you didn't find a way to get that nigga put back in jail. Isn't he still on probation? You better call and lie. If you say he hit you, that ass going back to jail."

I laughed, hummed my agreement, and then asked, "What part of Dre's bullshit don't you believe?"

"Hell, all of it. He gets out of jail, convinces you to let him move in, and then bans you from being around the baby because you gave her up so he could spend every moment he could trying to get with my sister. I called her one night to see how she was doing, and he answered the phone saying she was busy. Then he hung up in my face. I tried calling back, but he kept sending me to voicemail. I told Stephanie what he had done, and she told me that they were best friends. That 'best friend' shit he was feeding her was only so he could get in between her legs. I tried to warn her ass."

"Well, she didn't listen to you."

"I know, and now y'all friendship is on rocky terms. She'd probably be pissed with me for talking to you, but I don't care. You were like family to us, although y'all freaky bitches thought I couldn't tell that y'all be fucking from time to time," she laughed. "I hope you put that nigga out for trying to fuck my sister on her birthday. What real man tries to get a woman high to catch her slipping to fuck? Sounds like he might be used to doing that date rape stuff."

"Girl, I don't even know where to start when it comes to him, and no disrespect to you, but I'm tired of talking about it."

"I know you are. My bad."

"It's okay. You were concerned, and I appreciate it, but do you know how I can get a hold of Stephanie now? I really need to speak with her."

"That bitch is out being a slut. She's got her a little freaky-ass Jamaican dude named Ivan she's been staying with every night."

It took everything in me to hold in my laugh. Ivan was my ex-fuck toy Amir's roommate/cousin. That bitch Stephanie must have kept more than a notebook full of my revenge notes. She kept a list of my fucks and their affiliates too. "If you want me to, I'll hang up and not answer the phone, so you can leave a voicemail."

"Yes, that will be fine. Thanks, Tracey, and nice hearing from you again."

"You too, and if that nigga keeps bringing you problems, I know some niggas who can handle him for you."

I laughed, but she didn't.

"I'm serious. My sister is soft, but me, I'm not having it. I don't give out passes to nobody. I don't care if we've broken bread together. If you cross somebody I love, I'm coming for you!"

That was my warning. She didn't have to say it. I speak streets, and it was nice to know that she thought that I didn't. I was going to leave a "fuck you" but have a blessed day message; however, I found it best to only repeat the words of my partners, just in case her sister listened to my message first. I learned an important lesson from Keisha and her sister Ericka, and that is, never doubt, question, or sleep on the love between sisters. They can beat each other down, talk negatively about each other, and even profess hate for each other every day of their lives and *still* slit the next person's neck for one negative word against their blood.

There was only one more call I needed to make from the office phone.

"Royce, I know we were supposed to meet later on in the day, but do you mind if I come now?"

"I was still in bed, but come on over. I can—"

I hung up in his ear and headed out the door.

Chapter Eleven

Pay Me

I no longer wanted to have goodbye sex with Royce. I'd get to his room, tell him about Dre, and tell him to leave me the hell alone. Dre had me beat, and I wasn't as dumb as Will thought I was. I knew there was a thin line between love and hate and that Dre's heart was not the one to be played with. I had fucked him over once with his daughter; I wouldn't intentionally make it twice . . . or I might not live to tell it.

All of the detective work he was doing, I caused him to show up to the scene wearing his badge. I lied and played game after game, thinking I was smarter than him, but, apparently, I'm not. That high-tech GPS he had placed on my car was the straw that broke the camel's back. It was either do right by him or let him go, and I'm choosing to do right.

If I weren't so caught up in my thoughts when I pulled up at Royce's hotel, I would have paid more attention to the car that pulled in after me, but I didn't. Unplugging my car's battery was the only thing on my mind. I didn't know if it would really keep him from tracking me or using the kill switch to keep me stuck, but it didn't hurt to try. If I knew how to detach the alternator, I would have done it too for good measure.

The smartest move would have been to park my car somewhere else, but I had too much pride to do that.

What did I look like walking over to Royce to prevent getting caught if I was truly done with him? If Dre caught me and wanted an explanation, I'd lie and say I was seeking legal services on Trisha, and his office was closed on the weekend. If Dre needed proof, I'd introduce the niggas without feeling nothing more than lust of being in the room with two good dicks at the same time. And I didn't know enough about Royce to be able to judge how he was going to take the news that he'd never get me or this pussy again. I might need a quick getaway.

"Hello, Ms. James, I wasn't expecting to see you again," Mr. Wang said, and he went to make me a room key, but I stopped him.

"Hey, handsome, there's no need for the key this time. You won't see me here ever again after today; I can promise you that. If you don't mind, can you please inform Mr. Reed that I'm on my way up so he can welcome me in this time?"

He grinned, then said, "I see two is a crowd and you like your space. Look at you, simply breathtaking. I saw him go up with that ugly, pregnant mongoose and hoped you would pop up and catch him in the act. I apologize for not warning you, but I suffered the consequence when I had to see his little itty-bitty, tiny, microscopic—"

"I get your point," I said, interrupting and laughing. "It would have been nice to be warned that he had company, but I'm glad you didn't because I needed to see his naked ass with that ugly bitch too."

"Well, I didn't. His ass is so ashy I send lotion up by the housekeeper every day," he said, joining me in my laugh. He went to grab the phone off the cradle, and I noticed his pharmacy bag from down the street.

"Wait, before you call upstairs, I need to ask a favor of you."

"Anything for you. I owe you one for not warning of the mongoose."

"If anyone ever comes in here and asks you if you've seen me or my car here, I need you to say no. Even if they threaten you."

"Aww, shit, you enjoy playing the game too? You're a playa-playa, huh, girlfriend? I saw the ring when you first walked up, but the band is missing, so I thought you were on that independent woman trend that's going around." He leaned in closer before finishing. "Don't worry, your secret is safe with me, and I'm not scared of your husband. I know how to act like I don't speak good English, but what about your mother? She calls every Wednesday and Saturday to check if you've made it okay."

"My mother?"

"Yes. She's very pretty and looks just like you. I actually thought the two of you were sisters. Peaches checked out a week ago, and I was so sad because we would talk all night when she couldn't sleep. She said she had to go back home and that she was only in town to take care of you while you were sick and that you were her only daughter. That is so sweet of her. She really loves you a lot!"

I jetted to the elevator to ask Royce if Trisha had said anything to him and to wrap up everything I had going on with him, but not before I yelled, "That bitch doesn't love anything but peach cobbler. Go ahead and call Mr. Reed. Tell him that I'm on my way up!"

My request must have fallen on deaf ears because my knocks are what woke Royce up.

"Why are you banging on my door like that?"

"Move," I demanded as I brushed past him.

"How about 'Excuse me'? What's wrong with you, Savannah?" he questioned, and his morning breath almost knocked me out.

"Have you spoken to my mother?"

"Listen to what you're asking me. Why would I speak with your mother?" He must have gotten a whiff of his own breath because he asked that question into the palm of his hand.

"I didn't think you would, but I know she would try to talk to you if she's been talking to the guy at the front desk."

"Why would she be talking to him, and what do you think she'd want to discuss with me?"

"Cut the lawyer shit, OK? *I'm* asking all the questions. All I need from you are honest answers, like you've been sworn in."

"You need to take slow, deep breaths and calm down. I have never spoken to, nor have been spoken to, directly or indirectly, by your mother. The only time I can recall seeing her is tussling with you at the steak house. Does that answer your question?"

I took a deep breath, nodded my head in agreement, and then sat on his bed with my face in my hands. Trisha was driving me fucking crazy, and I didn't know why. I didn't want or need a mother in my life, and she didn't seem like a bitch who was ready to play Suzie Homemaker and bake cookies with warm glasses of milk to go with them. She snatched up my dumb-ass brother and made him look like one of those rappers with one too many members in their entourage. Memphis was rolling around Washington looking like his mama's side piece instead of her son.

Let's not forget the mention of money. I didn't know what money had to do with any of this. If Dre promised her anything for returning, he'd need to pay *his* debt. Their arrangement had nothing to do with me.

I wanted to cry and would have at the touch of Royce's hand rubbing my shoulder like my father had always done, but suddenly, there was a knock on his door.

"Who is it?" Royce bellowed from his bedroom where we sat on his bed. He was still in a pair of pin-striped boxers, no shirt, and white ankle socks.

"Housekeeping."

"Savannah, can you tell her I don't use their house-cleaning. I've tried to explain it to her thousands of times. She leaves a bottle of lotion at my door every day. She's driving me nuts."

We hadn't started talking yet about the true reason for my visit, but as soon as I ran off this pest of a housekeeper, I'd get the conversation going so I could leave.

"We don't need your services today, thank you!"

"What?" replied the housekeeper, like she couldn't hear me, so I said it again but louder.

"We don't need housekeeping. We will clean the room ourselves, thank you!"

"I'm sorry, ma'am, but I can't hear you. What did you say? Do you want me to leave the lotion by the door?"

Way past annoyed now, I removed the chain from the door, unlocked it, and swung it as wide as it would open. Before I had time to react, the knocker made her way past me and stood in the suite's kitchen. Looking around the room, she said, "What a nice extended stay hotel."

"Royce!" Not knowing what else to do, I screamed his name in horror. Royce entered the room, still in his socks and boxers, but quickly retreated to grab his clothes once he saw that we now had company.

"He didn't have to put on pants for me. I've seen men in their drawers before," she started with the same laugh I was beginning to hate.

"I'm sure you have, Trisha," I said, and once again, we rolled our eyes at each other at the same time, but our eyes were no longer identical sets. She was sporting a black eye on the left side that her funeral-style sunglasses didn't conceal. "What in the hell are you doing here?"

She pointed to the two chairs that sat under the small dining room table.

"Why don't we have a seat, Savannah? Seems we have some business to handle."

"We don't have shit to handle, Trisha. We handled what we needed to handle at the steak house's bar. Now, get the fuck out before I black that other eye."

My fear of her pop-up visit was now gone, and I was ready to talk shit or go another round, fist to fist. She was really moving farther away from my visions of her being my mother. As she made her way to sit in the chair, I had to stop myself from walking over to her and igniting the fight.

"I'm not going anywhere, Savannah. No, dear, not this time, and this business we need to handle has time restraints, so I recommend you sit your smart-ass down so we can get right to it. Don't let your lucky punch give you confidence in a losing battle."

I didn't understand her reference to the time, but I quickly learned what she meant by business. Trisha dug in her cheap black purse and pulled out the missing financial documents that had been stolen from my house during the break-in. Shocked and with the fear setting back in, I pulled out the chair next to hers and took a seat.

"I'd thought you'd see things my way, little girl."

Royce came into the room, fully dressed with his teeth brushed. I could smell the mint lingering on his breath.

"What is all this?" he asked, trying to figure out what was going on in his place of residence.

"Royce Reed, attorney at law. That's you, right? Have a seat; you have a great deal to do with all of this. We are going to need some of your legal advice."

I could tell Royce was ready to shoot off questions but remained silent so Trisha could explain herself.

"Well, Savannah, after coming across some of your information—"

"You mean *breaking* into my house and *stealing* it, don't you, Trisha?"

She placed her hand over her breast as if my words were causing her chest pains that would lead to her having a heart attack.

"How dare you accuse me of climbing over your neighbor's white picket fence, crawling through your bedroom window, and then finding something like your vanity's chair to stand on in your closet to reach these documents. I'm a little too old to commit this crime, don't you think?"

"Yeah, Trisha, you are too old to be climbing in and out of windows, but not Memphis. How did you convince my brother to do your dirty work?"

"I would never convince your brother to commit a burglary," she said with a grin on her face. "But I would like to confess, Royce, that I have full knowledge that my son committed this horrible crime. If Savannah would like to press charges on her brother, I am willing to write my confession. No one on this planet is worth an aiding and abetting charge, not even my lunatic son."

"You snake-in-the-grass-ass bitch!" I shouted at her, slightly standing on my feet.

"Oh, sit your dramatic ass back down, Savannah. I came to return your stolen property. Whether your brother faces jail time is your decision."

She glanced at her watch. "Now that we got that out of the way, let's get back to business." She dug into her purse and pulled out an envelope that was full of papers. Once she found the one she was looking for, she slid it to my side of the table. The paper had a routing and account number on it. The owner of the banking account was a LaTrisha Yancy of Kingston, Jamaica.

"What's this shit?" I asked.

"It's my going-away present from you. I hate that I have to leave your brother behind, but I just don't know how to tell my husband that I have another family here in the United States."

"I thought you said you lived in Louisiana and Hurricane Katrina brought you back to California. I'm confused."

Trisha shook her head, then said, "That slow gene you and your brother seem to have comes from your father's side, not mine." She said her next words as if she were talking to someone with a learning disability or a small child. "If the story I told you originally doesn't match what I'm saying now, Savannah, that means I lied to you, dear."

"I'm not slow, you lying-ass bitch, and the only going-away present I have for you is the beat down you're going to get if you don't leave now."

Trisha now turned her attention to Royce. She stared at him with a billion-dollar smile and then asked nonchalantly, "Royce, have you met Dre?"

Royce looked at us both confused and then said, "No, I don't know of any Dres here in Seattle. Is that Savannah's father?"

Trisha's laughed now filled the room.

"Although Dre is one of the many men my daughter has called daddy over the past ten years, he isn't her father. Dre is her fiancé and the father of her 4-year-old daughter. Didn't you notice the ring? It's really nice and very expensive. With all that drug money he has stashed, I wasn't surprised to see that he went all-out to propose to my daughter. It's a very expensive task to get a slut to agree to marriage."

Royce didn't respond to being asked if he noticed the ring. He just focused his look on me. I felt the need to speak up.

"Fuck you, Trisha!" I said, turning to face Royce before starting to back up. "That's what I came here to talk to you about. You said if I was engaged, the respectful thing to do was to tell you."

"You should have told me you were engaged from the beginning, Savannah! I clearly recall you telling me you were single and marriage wasn't for you. You never even mentioned to me that you had a child."

Trisha spoke up, "Oh yes, she does, and my granddaughter is absolutely beautiful. She's way too bright only to be 4 years old—"

"My daughter is no grandchild of yours—" I cut in to say before Trisha could say her next words.

"And that's the fucked-up attitude that got you in the situation you're in now, Savannah. I tried to come back and be a mother to you and a grandmother to Sade, and you rejected my offer every single time. You were going to be the first person I have ever gotten close to, the only person who I would honestly love and treat as family, but you fucked that up by holding on to anger that I thought you released in California. Now, I have no choice but to treat you like I treat everyone else."

"And how is that, Trisha? You gon' fuck me too?" I replied, referring to the fact that she's a ho, always has been, and always will be.

"Savannah, please don't confuse me with you. Your tongue strokes pussycats, not mine, baby girl. But I do have plans on treating you like I do my johns. Once they fuck me, they have to pay, and pay me good money."

She dug in her purse again, pulled out a cell phone, and handed it to me.

"Now this is what I need you to do. You're going to call your bank and do a wire transfer to mines for $150,000. No, let's make it $175,000 since I know Dre has money stashed away too. That should leave you with a little over $20,000 left in the bank which is more than enough to live off of with a good-paying career like yours—"

I had to interrupt. "What makes you think I'd give you the last of my life savings? The hospital bills and medi-

cine have almost cleaned it out. Why would you think I'd
be so willing to go broke for you?"

"I don't think you would; I *know* you will. See, I've
been watching you for a while now, like any good mother
would, and I've learned a lot about you. Let's just say
Memphis and your father aren't the only criminals in the
family."

I was speechless while I tried to figure out what crime
I had committed that she knew about. But not Royce, he
had a lot to say.

"I think you both need to leave. Savannah, I thought I
knew you, but I don't, and I don't want to be a witness to
blackmail. Thank you for coming and being honest, but
it's time for you to go." He started making his way to the
door.

"Hold on a second, Royce," Trisha said. "Savannah will
need your legal services, and I will need you to provide
them to her so I can get my going-away present. Please
let Savannah know that providing the police with false
information that turned a vehicular homicide into a
regular accident is a crime."

"You helped my father to lie to the police. You even fed
him the story that he needed to tell, Trisha, and you know
it!"

She laughed and said, "Prove it! I provided pain med-
ication to a patient in pain. Who's to say that the patient
didn't switch labels on the urine samples I left in the room
with him? After all these years, I still remember who the
other sample belonged to, and I'm sure that the 5-year-old
little girl in the room across the hall's chart says she was
asked for a urine sample twice. Your father will be behind
bars because the police took his statement, not mines."

I looked at Royce for help, but he had none to provide.
Seeing that he didn't have anything to say, Trisha continued.

"Don't you have a police report about your home being broken into? I have a recorded statement from my son on my answering machine confessing to the crime. He gave details on how he watched the neighbors leave, hopped the gate, crawled through your window, accidentally found your sex toys, and almost threw up. He even said he went as far as saying he only wanted papers with your Social Security Number on them and your four recent bank statements. Memphis gave a reason why he did it, which was because he hated you. I don't know what he planned on doing with it, but when he showed them to me, I collected them, and I'm here returning it. I didn't contact the police because I knew how to contact you directly. I knew the police wouldn't keep him in jail long if I would have reported it because you would drop the charges, but who's to say the DA's office wouldn't press charges since he admitted to trespassing to get on your property? The neighbors have a privacy fence up, and I'm sure they are fuming that someone destroyed their flower bed. There goes someone else you love behind bars."

Royce nodded his head in agreement that there was a possibility that Memphis could be arrested, and I knew Trisha was right.

"Did you know, Savannah, that hiring prostitutes is a crime in California? It's even worse when you intentionally have them sleep with men for revenge without protection, knowing they all were HIV positive."

"I didn't know they were HIV positive when I hired them!" I shot off instantly, realizing that I had just admitted, in front of an attorney, that I did hire the prostitutes.

"Wow, thanks for confessing to hiring them with a witness present who can't lie under oath, but I didn't need you to. Thanks to the little videos you made and a trip to the county jail to visit an inmate named Ericka Soto for the location of the diary you had your secretary write. Oh, and by the way, after the way you did Stephanie, I'm sure she wouldn't mind testifying against you or Dre to the courts. This forces me to think there would be a good case against you. With that almost professional basketball player trying to take his own life over, I'm sure the state of California would love to lock you up."

"Mama, you wouldn't." I regretted calling her mama as soon as I said it.

"I knew you would call me mama sooner or later. Too bad it's too late for that. I didn't go looking for you to blackmail you, Savannah. I went to clean up after the sloppy mess you made. You knew the diary was still floating around, but you didn't seek to find it. You left the videos just sitting on top of your trash can instead of destroying them. What were you thinking? If you gon' play the game, play it right! Doing a half-ass job left me no choice but to teach you this valuable lesson."

I was helpless, and she knew it. She didn't have a heart when it came to any of us. Her love was for money, and Trisha was willing to put her husband and two children in jail to get it. I tried to soften her up by saying, "What about Sade and Dre? They need me."

Her response was, "Sade needs you like she needs a bullet in her head, and you don't have legal custody of her because you did her the exact way that I did you. You hate my guts. Isn't that funny, but you're just like me, and as for Dre, I plan on him being back in jail before the sun goes down if you refuse my deal. He's my only real threat in all of this. You don't know the things that I know about him, and I won't tell you. That's the part of the game I'll let you learn on your own. Dre has been following you and Royce for weeks now, plotting on making Royce here disappear." She laughed like the shit was funny.

"Make me disappear? I had no idea Savannah was involved with anyone else. I'd love to talk to him, man-to-man, and apologize. I just lost my wife the same exact way. There's no way I'd let another feel what I felt."

Trisha didn't acknowledge Royce's shot at a plea; she just continued talking to me.

"That brings me back to the point of this meeting with you and Royce. You have a choice, Savannah; you can continue to reject my going-away gift and find everyone you love in jail, including yourself, or accept it by transferring the funds to my account. I'll leave all of you alone for good, and it will be like we never met, besides you having to rebuild your savings account, that is. I'm willing to give you the videos you made and the diary once the funds have cleared. I'll even fix this thing between you, Dre, and Royce by telling Dre that Royce is my lawyer, and we all have been meeting up for legal guidance to try to right all the wrongs in our past. I have enough documentation in this envelope to prove that's exactly what we've been doing all this time, but the decision is yours to make, Savannah."

There was a police officer-like knock on the door that made everyone look its way.

"You don't have that much time to decide because that's Dre on the other side of the door. More than likely so, he was hunting me down this time and saw your car parked next to mine. I pulled in after you and parked on the other side of the lot until you walked in, but just in case your security guard decided to come, I parked next to you so he would know that we were together."

If she thought having someone knock on the door to have me rush to transfer the funds was going to work, she had another think coming. I smiled as I walked to the door and then said, "Who is it?"

"You know who the fuck it is, Savannah. Open up the motherfucking door," Dre said, with too much base and anger in his voice.

I turned to face Royce and then to Trisha with a heavy heart and said, "Please, Mama, I'm sorry. I know you love me! My daddy told me how you sang with me and held me in your arms day and night. I promise I'll change my ways and give you a chance to mother me. I'll give you $25,000 to leave us all alone. You have to believe me when I say that I really do love that man."

I shifted my attention to the ceiling in hopes to speak with the Lord face-to-face.

"God, please help me. Please, Lord. You know my heart, and it's full of love for Dre. I'm sorry, I'm so sorry. If you give me one last chance, I swear I won't cheat on him again. Cross my heart and hope to die!"

I fell to my knees and continued my conversation with the Lord. Trisha stood up and made her way over to me. I thought she was extending her arm out to hug me or to help me back to my feet, but she wasn't. She placed her hand on the lock on the door, then nodded her head in the direction of her cell phone and account information that lay on the table.

"God and I heard your plea. And your prayer has been answered. $175,000 transferred to my banking account now will give you the change that you need in life. It will also give you a chance to start your life all over again with a clean slate. As for me, I'm sorry to have to tell you this, but I've never loved anyone besides myself except for your father, and in almost thirty-five years, I still don't know what he did to win over my heart that night at the hospital. Look at me."

I looked into her empty eyes, and she gave me the most beautiful smile I had ever seen.

Then she said, "How much are you willing to pay for peace in your life you've never known, Savannah?"

To be continued . . .